REAP & REDEEM

BOOK II OF THE REAPER SERIES

LISA MEDLEY

Reap & Redeem:
Book Two of the Reaper Series © 2015 Lisa Medley

ISBN: 978-0-9908856-5-8

Cover and formatting by Sweet 'N Spicy Designs
http://sweetnspicydesigns.com

First printing July 2014 by Harlequin E

This book is a work of fiction. While reference might be made to actual historical events or existing locations, the names, characters, places and incidents are either the product of the author's imagination or are used fictitiously, and any resemblance to actual persons, living or dead, business establishments, events, or locales is entirely coincidental.

Published in the United States of America

Lisa Medley

http://www.lisa-medley.com

To my first readers: Dawn Cosby and Allison Merritt.
You two girls make me better.

CHAPTER ONE

Kylen kicked the head across the floor of the dark shed with his steel-toed boot. Blood dripped into a pool on the floor from his scythe, which he still gripped tightly with one hand. He straightened to his full height and tilted his neck from side to side, listening to his spine crack and pop. Another demon down.

"You don't have to keep killing them yourself, you know," Deacon said, grimacing at the black ooze spilling out of the severed neck.

"Yeah, I do." Kylen turned and walked to the door, taking a quick survey of the cemetery. A dark, sticky trail marked his course.

"You have to admit, he's efficient." Nate picked up the head by the hair and dropped it into a black garbage bag.

"That's one way to look at it." Deacon pressed his hand, which was glowing with Reiki energy, to the center of the dead male's chest, directly over his heart chakra.

Kylen watched as light radiated from Deacon, encasing him and the body in a soft glow. The demon boiled forth from the dead human host in a thick black torrent of sulfurous haze. Spreading his arms wide, Deacon summoned the stream, which penetrated through his sternum. His body shuddered and the light around him sparked and cracked like the arc of a welder. The glow intensified to supernova status before winking out. Several smaller streams of gray light flowed forth from the ruined body, too, entering through Deacon's mouth.

"Well? Did you retrieve all the souls?" Nate lifted the feet and legs of the body onto the tarp he'd set beside it.

Deacon frowned. "Yes."

"How many?"

"Three." Deacon rose and grasped the body by the shoulders, helping Nate maneuver it. "And the demon."

"I really hate this shit." Nate said, pulling a spool of duct tape from his backpack.

They rolled the man tightly in the tarp, taping both ends so that none of the bodily fluids would discharge in transit.

"How many more demons do you think there are?" Nate walked toward the door.

"Grim thinks there are at least two dozen more," Deacon reminded him.

"Great. Slow and steady wins the race, yeah?"

"I'm not sure we have the luxury of slow and steady anymore. At this rate, we're never going to find them all. There's already way too much collateral damage. This many missing humans in town won't go unnoticed much longer. We need to find their exit portals and shut down the rest of the demons. Sooner would be better than later."

Kylen waited in the doorway, dividing his attention between the business in the shed and the cemetery grounds. Deacon was right of course. They needed to close the portals. Permanently. As it was, they were playing a game of supernatural Whac-A-Mole. Close one portal and another popped up. New entrance portals continued to open each week, which then had to be closed by Grim and Deacon. And while one batch of demons gathered their fill of souls before sliding down the small one-way shoots to Hell—the exit portals, the next batch waited for their chance. It had become a never-ending battle and the reapers needed to press on.

They didn't bother cleaning up the black ooze or the blood trail. The only way to make sure the scene was completely clean was fire, but arson would be sure to draw more attention to the mower garage by the edge of the cemetery than a few stains that could easily be oil or fuel. None of them were concerned about the law. There were far worse things for them to worry about.

They'd burn the body at home, and then bury the ashes and bits of bone. Just as they'd dealt with the other eleven. This host's disappearance would never be explained. Good thing, since the guy's head was detached.

* * *

Nate continued to insist they could at least *try* to save the hosts, but Kylen was adamant that it was in no one's best interest. After all, the hosts were only human. A demon's essence burned through a human body like dry tinder. If a host did manage to somehow survive the first twenty-four hours, their delicate psyche would be so damaged that there wouldn't be anything left to save. Without the demon to animate them, they would be nothing but a babbling husk.

Kylen knew a thing or two about possession.

He'd spent the past hundred years with a demon riding his body. Being a reaper had its perks as well as its challenges. One perk was that it was damn difficult to die. As long as a reaper fueled enough and kept his head, he was immortal, so Kylen's body could have withstood the demon's toxic venom indefinitely. The downside was that it was damn near impossible for a reaper to kill himself. The demon had always kept Kylen's body nourished enough to maintain the necessary energy flow, and though Kylen had occasionally been able to break through and wrest control from the demon, it had never been for long enough....

Kylen had possessed the will. Just not the means.

Then he had finally been freed, and somehow he had survived both the possession and the freeing.

Physically.

Most days, he wished he hadn't.

"Let's get out of here." Deacon hoisted the wrapped-up body over his shoulder and left the building, crossing the invisible barrier onto the consecrated soil of the dark cemetery. "Ready to go home, Kylen?" He placed his palm on the nearest headstone, and Nate followed suit.

"I can't wait." Kylen placed his hand on the stone as well, and the three men began to shimmer as they were drawn into the consecrated subway.

* * *

Ruth Scott sat drumming her fingers on top of her kitchen table, impatient for the men to return. Dinner had been ready for an hour. Stew simmered on the stove, and she fidgeted with the place settings for the ten thousandth time, rearranging glasses and realigning utensils. It was a useless task. One for which she was way overqualified.

Why they let Nate go on the hunts and not her was a real point of contention. He had way less experience than she did, and she'd proved herself plenty.

After all, she'd helped save both Deacon and Kylen. How quickly they had forgotten. Just because she was a newbie reaper didn't mean she couldn't do what needed to be done. Sure, she'd almost died a couple of times while coming to terms with her new reaper powers, but now they'd had plenty of time to work out the kinks.

Deacon was way too protective. Ever since the demons had been released in the early summer, he'd been on a mission to destroy them. As in a mission from God. She got that. For one thing, it was his job. For another, it was bad for any demons to be let loose on the world, let alone the three dozen that had been hunting the streets of Meridian. Very bad. But how was she ever going to be tough enough to face the danger that lurked at every corner unless she had more *experience?*

She wasn't afraid. She'd spent most of her life being afraid that people would discover her ability to see auras and use it against her. Back then she'd had no idea why she could do what she could do and what it all meant. Because of that fear, she hadn't really lived her life at all.

Until Deacon. Over the past few months, Deacon had trained her how to be a reaper. With a renewed sense of purpose and the encouragement of one fine man, she'd stopped thinking of her ability as a handicap and started appreciating it for the gift that it was.

But now she was sitting in her tiny rock-sided house, keeping the home fires burning while the men were off fighting the big bad demons. Well, that was going to end. Tonight. They were going to have to cowboy up and get over their ridiculous worries. She would be a prisoner in her own home no longer.

Besides, Nate couldn't even *see* auras, souls or demons for God's sake. Since returning from Hell, he could see the Reiki energy when one of them—or he himself—manifested it. Otherwise, he was useless as a reaper. Of course, he did have a nifty way of using his magic to trap the evil bastards from time to time. The demon trap burned into her living room floor was evidence of that. Also, he and Deacon were the only ones who could travel through the invisible reaper freeway without the aid of consecrated ground *and* he was an EMT, which had already come in handy way too many times for comfort. None of them were invincible. At least not completely.

She grumbled to herself over the injustice of it all as she pushed her dinner around her plate, and she was still fuming when they landed in the middle of the living room. With another body.

Perfect.

CHAPTER TWO

Kylen scowled as he landed in Ruth's living room. Home his ass. This was not his home. Not really. He knew he should feel all thankful and shit for what these people had done for him. For Ruth's sake, he dug deep and tried to keep his inner demons leashed—at least in her presence. After all, she'd done what his friend couldn't....

She had freed him.

And for that he owed her his gratitude. Even if it was impossible to muster at times.

"Finally!" Ruth jumped up from the table and rushed over to kiss Deacon on the cheek.

"Happy to see you too, babe," Deacon said, hoisting the body higher onto his shoulder. "We got another host."

"I can see that. Same drill as the other two?" Ruth frowned.

"Yes." Nate leveled a hard glare at Kylen. "Someone is a little too quick with the scythe. I'll take it from here." Retrieving the body from Deacon, he headed

10

to the basement without another word.

Kylen stalked, without comment, toward the back door to clean his weapon at the outside spigot. He felt no regret. The hosts could not be saved. Deacon knew it as well as Kylen did. Every reaper who'd ever killed a demon knew it. It was just one more example of Nate's naive humanity.

Kylen had been naive once. He had believed Deacon would fulfill his half of the pact that they'd made more than a century ago. The agreement had been crystal clear—neither would allow the other to continue to live in case of possession. What part of that had Deacon forgotten? Sure, he probably hadn't expected that his friend would *choose* to be possessed, but grief can make a guy reconsider his options. Kylen had counted on Deacon to end him when he'd opened himself to the demon. His act of submission had been more a matter of assisted suicide. Without Kara, he hadn't wanted to go on, anyway.

Deacon hadn't given him that choice.

And now? The one reason he was still here was that he had nowhere else to go. He'd spent the past hundred years at the mercy of a demon, and the home he'd once had was long gone. His one wish was to be reunited with Kara. Because of his history, there was zero chance of him ascending—the reaper equivalent of heavenly retirement—to do that. And Deacon had refused to return her to him. Instead, he was stuck here, in his own personal Hell on Earth. If it weren't for Ruth's hundred kindnesses toward him and his immense hatred for the demons that had been unleashed upon Meridian, he would already have checked out. Fallen out of sight and let himself flame out.

But Meridian had been ground zero for a demon invasion. The demons had entered through the now-closed release portal at St. Agnes Cathedral, and with each passing day, they grew more difficult to track, collecting soul after innocent soul before taking them straight to Hell. Even Deacon's new super-reaper abilities as a Powers hadn't developed enough to lead him to the few they'd already dispatched. Kylen had done that. His previous possession was the one advantage they had in this whole messy situation. He was still tuned in to the demon radio even though his channels were sometimes scrambled, and he was drawn to demons like a moth to flame—kin to kin. He'd tracked down the dozen they'd killed over the past four months of nightly hunts. Still, their progress was too slow. The city was big and Kylen hadn't fully recovered from his ordeal. Tonight had been the best night of hunting in weeks.

Even though his mission was to cut down every demon he could, Kylen's soul was black with the stain of his demon's sins, which he felt as keenly as if they were his own. The darkness sat in his chest like a gangrenous lump. No amount of Reiki reaper energy was going to cure that. Hell, Rashnu, the soul sorter of Purgatory, didn't even trust him to carry souls anymore. Kylen didn't blame him. He didn't trust himself. His proclivities and thoughts ran a little too dark even for Purgatory these days.

What fueled him through each torturous day was vengeance, pure and simple. Deacon might be a Powers, the newest guardian of the realms of Heaven, Hell and Purgatory, but Kylen was Heaven's self-proclaimed executioner.

He squatted in the darkness by the outdoor spigot on the side of the house, letting the water run over his hand and his blade. Pulling a soft cloth from his back pocket, he dipped it into the stream of water before turning off the spigot. He caressed it across the blade, removing the last traces of blood from his scythe, polishing it until the moonlight glinted off its deadly surface.

Satisfied, he crossed to the detached garage and pulled the whetstone down from the tool pegboard. He dragged a bucket outside the garage, overturned it and sat facing the woods. Reaching out with his senses, past the magical circle of protection that was vigilantly defended by Nate, he watched and listened.

There were things out there in the woods. Things that were drawn to him still; things that awaited his command.

He drew the whetstone across the curved blade of his scythe with a slow, easy pressure, stroking its length. He rocked his body forward and back with each rasp of the steel, enjoying the hypnotic rhythm of the work. Honing the scythe to perfection was a comforting task. Turning the blade, he sharpened the other side, careful to return its lethal edge. It was a supernatural weapon, given to each reaper upon his or her first reaping, so the task was unnecessary. Still, it was a ritual he'd performed for years, and it gave him peace in the darkness. A man needed to respect his weapon.

When he was finished, Kylen slashed it into the waist-high weeds before him, watching as they fell to the ground with a whisper. He stared off into the darkness again, resting the blade across his thighs. The night was soothing to him. At night he wasn't reminded that he could no longer see in color....

Ever since the demon had been torn from him, he saw the world in shades of gray, and he could no longer make out people's auras. He could see the light but only its intensity. The color had been stripped from him, which was handicapping him as a reaper. Every reaper worth his or her salt knew that the color gray represented dark thoughts and unclear intentions. Well, that pretty much summed up his inner world these days.

He hadn't bothered to mention this disturbing fact to any of his roommates.

He had thought it would be a temporary affliction. But now, months later, his color vision still hadn't returned. It was one more thing that had been stolen from him.

Damaged was an understatement... and he wanted revenge. If he had to, he would find each and every demon himself, making sure Deacon had ample opportunity to send them to their final deaths. Then he would find his own... death, that is.

He was more than ready for it.

* * *

Nate tossed the bag containing the head down the stairs in front of him so he could maneuver the body through the narrow passage to the root cellar. It landed on the dirt floor with a wet thud before rolling to a stop. A large wood-burning furnace sat on concrete blocks against the east wall. They'd had to reroute the ductwork so that the heat and smoke diverted outside...the sickening smell had almost suffocated them when they burned the first body.

He was thankful they lived in a remote enough area that the smell and smoke could dissipate outside without raising any alarms. Nate had moved into the house after it became clear that hanging out with reapers was potentially detrimental to his neighbors. No one wanted a herd of imps following him home. At least here, with a thousand square miles of National Forest patchworked around them, they were safe.

Getting rid of the hosts' bodies was a disgusting operation, and it didn't help that the heat was still a cloying thing in late September. Nate was in the business of saving lives and patching up bodies. In the past few months, this was the twelfth body he'd personally disposed of. It was a messed up deal all around. Nate continued to insist that they should at least try to save the hosts, but Kylen wouldn't have any of it. In an effort to contribute to the cause, Nate had volunteered for disposal duty. He was useless in tracking the demons. This he could do. Still, he was starting to regret his offer.

He should be the one down here cleaning up his mess.

Nate hadn't known Kylen before the possession, but he was a dark, scary bastard now.

Dude had seemed halfway tolerable after he and Ruth had healed him. As far as Nate could tell, Kylen had grown physically better, but mentally? Seemed like the guy was getting worse and worse since their return from Hell.

Part of the problem was that Kylen and Deacon kept getting into heated arguments over Kara, Kylen's long-dead reaper girlfriend.

After the last blowup a few weeks ago, Kylen stopped sleeping in the house with them. He'd used some of the reaper hazard-pay settlement Deacon had negotiated for him to purchase a used twenty-four-foot camping trailer. He'd dragged the eyesore home and parked it by the garage. God only knew where he'd found the thing. When he wasn't out hunting demons, he spent his time out there. Alone. Nate was pretty sure the guy would hunt 24/7 if Deacon didn't insist they sleep and eat on a regular basis. The guy was obsessed. The fact that they'd only killed a third of the demons so far weighed on them all, but Kylen seemed the most troubled.

Arranging his collection of kindling in a neat stack inside the furnace box, Nate lit it. He watched the flames lick and consume the smaller tinder, and then added some larger logs, waiting for them to catch. He was thankful the firebox was large enough for a body. He didn't think he could bear to dismember one, even if having the head off was more helpful than he'd anticipated. He wouldn't mention that to Kylen, though. The bastard didn't need any encouragement.

Hefting the body into the flaming box, he tossed the head in last before adding two more logs on top of the heap. This was going to be an all-night proposition. It had taken forever for the other bodies to dry enough to burn to ash, since the temperature didn't quite hit the sweet spot with wood alone. This arrangement was basically an indoor funeral pyre. They'd had to improvise.

He closed the door and adjusted the damper to keep the fire hot. His stomach growled as he headed upstairs for dinner. He hoped it wasn't barbecue.

CHAPTER THREE

Deacon, Nate and Ruth sat around the small kitchen table eating dinner. At last. It was after 3:00 a.m., but dinnertime was subjective these days, and she knew the men were famished. They'd learned not to wait for Kylen. He rarely seemed to eat these days, despite Deacon's insistence that he refuel. If he didn't show soon, Ruth would do what she always did—she'd leave a dish she'd prepared for him by the door of his trailer.

Deacon was still filled with the souls he'd collected from the demon. He needed to get them to Purgatory fast, but not before he refueled. Six souls was the max for most reapers, but with his promotion, Deacon could now carry an unlimited number of souls and now demons as well. Or so he'd been told by Grim. None of them were eager for him to test his limits.

If there was one vital lesson Ruth could take away from her first several months as a reaper, it was this: food equaled energy. It was true for humans but even more so for reapers. Besides decapitation, a fatal loss of energy was the only other way for a reaper to be felled.

Ignoring that all-important rule had landed her in a reaper coma before she'd officially even begun working as a reaper. Nate had saved her.

"This is great, Ruth." Deacon winked and shoveled in a heaping spoonful of stew.

"Ditto." Nate wiped the bottom of his bowl with a piece of bread.

"It would have been better an hour and a half ago." She smirked.

"You know we're not exactly on a schedule here." Deacon hesitated and shoved in another mouthful.

"I would know that better if I were out there with you."

"Ruth, we've talked about this. You've been doing a great job running the reaping circuit while we're out. Between you and Maeve, you've managed to keep things going so we can attend to our other problems."

"Right. I collected a paltry *two* souls today. Maeve collected a *dozen*. I'm pretty sure she left those two for me as a pity prize. She doesn't even need me," Ruth fumed.

Maeve was the replacement reaper, sent to attend to the daily collection of Meridian's most recent dearly departed while Deacon, Kylen and Nate hunted down the demons. She was nice enough, but she was also brusque. She had made it abundantly clear that Ruth was more of a hindrance than a help.

Deacon reached across the table and took her hand. "I need you, Ruth." He glanced over at Nate. "*We* need you. Here and safe."

Ruth shifted in her seat, uncomfortable with the attention, but she refused to back down. This was not how this conversation had gone in her head. She was tired of doing the grunt work. She wanted in on the real action.

"I don't want to be safe. I want to help. Besides. Won't I be safer with you?"

Deacon pulled his hand away. "You'll be a distraction."

"You are not the boss of me, Deacon Walker. I can travel the consecrated subway by myself now, you know. Or have you already forgotten the lengths Nate and I went to save Kylen? Not to mention your sorry ass?" Her heartbeat thumped in her ears as her anger rose.

"If you won't take me, I'll go off on my own. Maeve can handle things by herself. Is that what you want?"

Deacon closed his eyes, and she could almost hear his gears grind. "No. That is most assuredly *not* what I want. I want to protect you. I've failed before. More than once. Help me make sure that I don't fail again."

"You could undo one of your failures." Kylen stood in the back doorway, his eyes pinched at the corners.

Ruth shuddered. She hated it when they argued, and one thing was for sure—Kylen was raring for an argument.

Nate pushed his chair back from the table and stood, and Deacon raised his eyes to meet Kylen's.

"We've talked about this, Kylen. Time and again. You know I can't do it... I can't bring her back." Deacon folded his napkin and placed it on the table beside his empty bowl with cautious ease.

"It's not a matter of can't. It's a matter of won't."

"Yes. Won't. And you know why."

Kylen's body radiated power, and he manifested an aura, something reapers only did under extreme circumstances. Mustard-colored flames, indicating pain and anger, licked at his body as he stalked toward Deacon. Ruth held her breath.

He passed by them both without incident and stopped in the middle of the living room, looking down at the symbols of the demon trap, which were still burned into the wooden floor.

Head down, he drew the scythe from the holder that ran the length of his spine and flicked it open with a snap of his wrist. When his gaze rose to meet Deacon's, he looked like death incarnate. He shimmered and disappeared into the consecrated subway without another word.

* * *

"Shit." Nate hissed. "That guy's got issues."

"You think?" Ruth moved closer to Deacon.

"He's not stable. I don't know how we'd manage to find all of the demons without him, but I don't think he needs to be around Ruth," Nate said, giving Ruth an apologetic look.

"Again with the safety thing?" she snapped. "It's not Kylen I'm worried about. It's you two. You'll kill me with your overprotectiveness long before anything else happens to me. Kylen is fine. He just needs…time." She rose and began stacking the empty plates, smacking them together so hard a chip slivered off and fell to the floor. "He didn't even eat," she mumbled, taking the bowl she'd prepared for Kylen and stuffing it into the fridge.

"This isn't finished. He'll be back after he's had time to cool off." Deacon carried the remaining silverware over to the sink and wrapped his arms around Ruth from behind, nuzzling his face into her hair. "I have to go."

"I know," she said, relaxing into his embrace.

"I'll be back as soon as I deliver the souls to Purgatory." He pushed her hair aside and kissed the back of her neck. "I don't want to lose you, too, Ruth. Please don't do anything dangerous while I'm gone."

"I'll try."

"Try hard." He leaned his face against the back of her head and pulled her in even closer, his need pressing against her bottom.

He released her and turned to look at Nate. "You know what to do?"

"Right, burn and babysit. I'm on it."

Deacon's lips curled into a half-hearted smile as he turned back to Ruth, searing her with his gaze, both a promise and a threat.

CHAPTER FOUR

Kylen flashed into Meridian's downtown cemetery. It was already 4:00 a.m., and he needed sleep. This was his third day without any…at all. Clearly, he was unraveling quicker than usual as a result. He'd barely been able to restrain himself from tearing Deacon limb from limb in the middle of Ruth's kitchen.

His rage had leaked out visibly—he could tell from the way they'd reacted.

What he needed now was the time and space to get himself under some semblance of control.

A red neon sign flashed Vacancy three blocks down at the Marquette Hotel—sleazy was an understatement. It would do. The neighborhood was raw and dirty, but at least it would provide him with some downtime far away from the others.

He would have loved to track down another demon and take out his frustration on the damn thing. But he couldn't do that alone. He could maybe find one, but if he beheaded the host, the demon would just stream out and find another one. In this realm, only Deacon currently had the ability to dispose of them.

A fact that continued to piss him off to no end. Deacon had *everything*—power, an impressive position, Ruth. All Kylen had was cold, hard vengeance, a century's worth of bad memories… And a death wish.

He walked into the hotel lobby and leveled his gaze at the ragged young clerk who was reading a magazine behind the iron-barred, bulletproof service window. The clerk looked up, his eyes wide as Kylen paced toward him, steel-toed boots thundering across the worn oak floor. The kid backed away.

"A room." Kylen demanded.

The clerk didn't speak. He was too busy staring at Kylen's right hand.

"Did you hear me?" Kylen followed the kid's gaze to the open scythe gripped by his side.

Well, shit. He hadn't even realized he'd drawn the damn thing. Force of habit. His rage had demanded a response. Even if it was subconscious. His motivations didn't make much sense these days, even to him.

Pawing at the Peg-Board of room keys beside him, the boy kept his eyes fixed on Kylen as he pulled one loose without bothering to note its number. The key jangled against the diamond-shaped key ring in his trembling hand before he tossed it onto the counter. He gave it a shove through the tiny pay slot before backing up all the way to the wall behind him. Kylen scooped up the key and headed to the third floor without another word.

* * *

The room was humid, dark and smelled like a wet ashtray. Fitting. The bedsheets were stained and threadbare. The comforter was worse. Didn't matter. All he needed was a few hours to recharge without having to deal with the others.

He crossed to the window, parted the sheer curtain liner, and looked down into the alley below him. A working girl was giving head to some sad sack pushed up against the brick alley wall by a Dumpster. His own dick hardened against his will. *Christ.* Like he didn't have enough problems.

Satisfied that there were no immediate threats, he pulled the heavy outer curtains across the sheer liner in an attempt to block out the one streetlight glowing through the barred window. He pushed a rickety nightstand against the door. If someone wanted to mess with him, they'd have to work for it, and he'd have time to pull his weapon, which he was still holding.

Convenient.

When he reclined onto the bed, the sheath was uncomfortable beneath him, but it was so much like an appendage, he couldn't bear to remove it. Keeping the scythe in his hand, he folded it with care and settled it across his stomach.

The pillow was worthless, and he tossed it across the room toward the far wall. Arms crossed and eyes closed, he lay on the bed like the dead. He was relieved to be alone, somewhere where no one knew him, for a few hours. Here, in the dark of a strange hotel room, he didn't have to pretend to be anything other than supremely fucked up. It was downright peaceful.

Opening his senses to the night, he reached out, searching for the next demon. They were still close. All of them. They hadn't strayed as far as Deacon had expected they would. Their master was nearby as well. Instructing them, preparing them, leading them.

Yeah, Kylen could feel *him,* too.

It still surprised him that the connection didn't seem to travel both ways anymore. Of course, his own personal demon had tried to burn the bridges of communication on its way out while also attempting to destroy his physical body. But that mission hadn't been completed. Little by little, Kylen had become aware of his tether to the darkness. While he couldn't communicate with the big boss, Camael, anymore, he could still see and hear flashes of what was happening in Hell and in Meridian. Only in these revelations, in his mind's eye, was his vision still in perfect Technicolor. The demons were busy. Very, very busy.

Something big was about to go down.

Join us, Kylen. You belong here. It was Camael's voice, so very familiar to him.

Before he could tune in clearly, the transmission was severed, and his energy was too low to maintain it. The effort had sapped what was left of his reserves, managing to further deplete him, and his limbs grew heavy as exhaustion pulled him under its thrall. He would allow himself to slide from consciousness for just long enough to recharge. It was a luxury he could barely tolerate anymore. Every time he succumbed to sleep these days, he was haunted by nightmares. He couldn't decide which memories were worse: his demon's or his own.

* * *

Kara stood hundreds of yards in front of him across the battlefield, making her way from body to body, collecting the souls of the dead warriors. He'd lost count of how many she had already gathered. He had a dozen of his own, filled far beyond comfortable capacity. Kara might well have been carrying a hundred. She was a valkyrie—the ultimate reaper.

Her straight blond hair whipped wild and unkempt in the wind and her icy-gray eyes—the mark of a reaper filled with souls—shined like diamonds in the moonlight. Deacon moved downfield with swift efficiency, collecting souls as he went. Both of them were too far from her to stop what was about to happen.

Kylen heard the scream and raced toward her, reaching her before her wail extinguished. He was still too late. The warrior whose soul she'd attempted to liberate was not yet dead...and he was not alone. The demon who possessed him had been lying in wait for a reaper. As Kylen watched with horror, the warrior rose and smiled. Kara's head swiveled on her neck, blood pouring from the crescent-moon slash the demon had inflicted on her. He sliced the scythe through her body over and over again until the souls began to pour from her, streaming into his disintegrating form.

Kylen drew back his own scythe and prepared to behead the demon, but stopped when the last soul hovered, its shape becoming visible the instant before it was drawn into the beast.

Kara.

He fell to his knees before the demon, his world crumbling to a halt in a manner of seconds.

Kara was dead.

A hundred years together hadn't been enough. Not nearly. Deacon approached from behind the demon, but empowered by its consumption of Kara's soul, the demon blasted him with an orange fireball of energy that knocked him to the ground, rendering him unconscious.

The demon strode toward Deacon, intent on collecting his cargo as well, but Kylen shook off his despair and gathered himself.

"Wait," Kylen pleaded. "I have an offer."

The demon turned and considered him, the battle raging on all around them. He looked at Deacon again, hesitated and then returned to Kylen, his curiosity clear.

"What sort of offer, reaper?"

"Your ride is disintegrating around you. The strength you feel now is because you hold a reaper's soul, but in mere moments the hundreds of souls you carry will wear you thin. I'll make you a deal. You give me the reaper's soul and let me take it to Purgatory. When I return, I'll grant you access to my body. Surely you'd rather ride a reaper than a human?" Kylen held the demon's black-eyed gaze.

"Well now, that is *an offer."* The demon grinned, then gave Deacon a longing look.

Deacon carried at a least a dozen souls, too, and was as weak as Kylen. He'd be lucky to wake from his injury from the orange fireball. He had no idea if Deacon had enough light left to kick-start himself again.

"And I want the other reaper," Kylen demanded. *"He's not yours."*

"I'm not sure you have room for any further negotiations, reaper."

"I guess that depends on how much you want a new, nearly indestructible ride," Kylen added.

"Nearly would be an apt assertion," the demon taunted.

"Still sturdier than what you now ride."

"Yes, this is the third one this week. Humans are…troublesome. You have fifteen minutes to go to Purgatory and return to me. If you renege on our deal, I'll make sure your demise is nowhere near as neat and tidy as your friend's." The demon inhaled a great breath, and then forced Kara's soul from his throat in a long gray stream.

She reformed between the two men, and Kylen stepped forward to claim her. He closed his eyes and breathed in her essence before crossing over to Deacon and hoisting him up over his shoulder. The very ground he stood on had been consecrated by the sheer number of the dead this day. He didn't have to bother finding another portal to Purgatory. This battlefield had already become Hell on Earth.

"I'll be waiting for you..." the demon promised.

Kylen swirled and spun, disappearing into the consecrated subway as bodies continued to fall around him...

* * *

When Kylen awoke, he was covered in a cold, clammy sweat, his heart racing. He *hated* that dream. *That memory.* He hadn't consciously allowed it to replay in his mind for more than a hundred years, but since the demon had been forced from him, he relived it almost every time he slept.

A noise in the alley below brought him bolt upright in bed and to the window in two quick steps. He pushed the heavy curtain from the edge of the window and peered down. His heart slammed in his chest. The alley was full of imps. The gelatinous toadlike creatures sat on their haunches, patient and still, staring up at him. There was no magic circle of protection to keep them at bay here, only bricks and a barred window.

He narrowed his eyes and pulled the curtain closed, his lips thinning into a tight line. To anyone else—anyone human—it would look like nothing more than an alley full of hungry black cats. Only reapers and supernatural creatures could see them for what they really were... They would know *whose* they really were.

Demons commanded imps, but he was not a demon—not anymore, anyway—and he wanted nothing to do with these creatures. He'd already tried to command them to leave him alone. Obviously it hadn't worked. It was unclear what they expected from him.

Kin to kin.

He looked at his watch. An hour. *So much for a*

good night's sleep. It would have to do.

He shoved the nightstand aside, stepping into the dim hallway just as the screaming began down below.

CHAPTER FIVE

Kylen pounded down the stairs, taking them two and three at a time, drawn to the scream like a beacon. The bright, shrill peal of terror was coming from the alley. The silence that followed it was almost worse.

The lobby was deserted when he ripped through it, bursting out of the building's double glass doors, slamming them open against the brick walls on either side. Glass and metal shrapnel exploded with great force, scattering fragments across the pavement. He smelled the demon before he saw it. Imps smelled like baking cookies compared to the noxious, eye-burning stench that emanated from demons. Rounding the corner into the alley, the odor filled his senses.

The bastard was abandoning its wrecked host body—the skinny guy he'd seen earlier with the prostitute. The demon hovered over a different woman, definitely not the prostitute. Her eyes were wide with fear and she seemed frozen in place. Her mouth was stretched wide in a silent scream as the black stream forced its way into her.

Kylen swept forward and flicked his right wrist, extending the blade of his already drawn scythe. Seizing the woman by the throat, he pulled her back from the skinny host, who looked like a junkie, holding her upright as her knees buckled. He directed a bolt of light energy into her, the radiance exploding from his palm and fingertips, illuminating her from the inside out like a human glow stick.

The demon stalled its forward progress and began to back its way out of the woman. Hovering briefly, it gathered itself into a black ghost of its true form—a form Kylen knew all too well—before slipping back down the junkie's throat.

The decrepit man's eyes blinked once, sliding closed in a vertical slit as the demon settled back into the failing body. "Too late," the junkie mocked. "Cut off the head of one and more will take its place. You can't stop it."

"Can't stop what?"

"The war."

"I'll take my chances." Kylen slashed his scythe in a wide arc up and across the junkie's neck, beheading him.

The body fell to the ground in a heap as the head landed with a wet thunk beside it, rolling to a stop. The demon streamed by Kylen, its horrible face alone taking form from the black fog. After taking stock of his adversary, it turned and streamed down the alley, up and over the buildings.

Kylen caught the woman as she began to crumble into a pile before him. He clutched her to him. Her vacant eyes shone bright with the brilliant afterglow of the energy he'd forced through her, and then fluttered closed as she fell unconscious. Folding his blade, he slid it into the sheath down the center of his back while he held her with one arm and felt her neck for a pulse.

She was alive. Barely.

Imps gathered around his feet, circling him and the woman in anticipation. One stopped to sniff something behind the Dumpster where Kylen had spotted the prostitute. So the kid hadn't been after a happy ending after all.

Kylen scooped up the woman and cradled her in his arms. He sidestepped the seep of garbage fluids pooling under the Dumpster to investigate. The prostitute lay sprawled on the ground, unmistakably dead. From the look of things, she'd tried to crawl to safety. She had no visible wounds other than a few cuts and scrapes. Nothing mortal that he could see. But her eyes were black and vacant.

He knew what it meant.

The demons were evolving—her soul had been ripped from her still-living body. It was a tactic his demon had been fond of at the end of its days. It meant they were growing bolder, which would raise the ante for everyone.

This one had been lucky. She'd managed to die in the process. Sometimes they didn't. Sometimes they were left to wander without their souls. For sport. He knelt beside the junkie's body, the unconscious woman still in his arms, and placed his palm over the boy's chest. Two souls streamed forth: the junkie's and the prostitute's. The demon had lost its spoils in its quick departure.

Even in his current state of disgruntlement, he couldn't leave the souls unreaped.

Inhaling, he drew them into his body and cringed as they filled him, vying for purchase inside him. Now what the hell was he going to do with them? A trip to Purgatory was the last thing he wanted. Especially an unauthorized visit. But it seemed he just couldn't escape his destiny.

In *his* day—Hell, in the last twenty-plus generations of reapers—the demonic possession of a human body was extremely rare, because few made it topside. It was surprising how often humans actually summoned a demon in the *hopes* of possession, out of a craving for power, revenge or a wide variety of other selfish reasons. The host soon discovered that his or her aspiration, whatever it may have been, was hardly worth the price. Most were lucky to last the week. As time went on, the rules began to bend. Eventually the demons that found their way to Earth learned how easy it was to worm into weak-minded humans and corrupt them. Sometimes that weakness was of a spiritual nature, other times it was a mental or physical weakness; sometimes inebriation was enough of an opening to slide through. Even then it was a one-on-one proposition. One demon, one body. It was bad enough that they were poaching unclaimed souls. But if run-of-the-mill demons could rip souls from living bodies and leave the husks to wander? Those were old, old school tactics.

Lucifer's handiwork.

Kylen's demon had taken full advantage of his reaper body and skills to achieve the same results. They'd left their fair share of wanderers over the past several years, but he'd hoped the practice had died with his demon. If any demon could now do it?

Soul raping was akin to waving a red flag in front of a bull. With this development, all bets were off. While one rogue demon might not draw down the wrath of Heaven, this blatant assault on God's most prized creation wouldn't escape attention or retribution

The woman had probably been high or drunk, easy pickings, and since the demon had greedily foregone her body in search of another—the one currently in his arms—he'd left her to wander or perish.

God help them all if one of these demons

managed to possess another reaper.

The imps mewed and salivated at his feet like adoring pets. He grunted with disgust and leveled his gaze at the lot of them.

"Eat," he commanded.

The imps hissed, baring row upon row of inch-long, needle-pointed teeth in glee before they fell upon the bodies like hogs on a carcass. The wet sound of soft flesh ripping and tearing was punctuated by the crunch of bone as the fiends got down to business. Both bodies would be consumed before he reached the cemetery. They were very efficient.

Kylen left the alley, unsurprised that the raucous noise wasn't being investigated. This was not an area of Meridian that encouraged heroism. As he made his way back to consecrated ground with the woman in his arms, not a single drunk wandered out of an alleyway, and no curtains parted for a peek.

He gazed down at the woman's slender form, her face softly illuminated by the predawn light. As he walked toward the cemetery, her reddish-brown hair was drained of color before his eyes, turning a stark white. Soft and straight, it swayed like a horse's mane from her head with each step. A hand-shaped bruise began to form around her throat, making him frown.

Exhaustion poured from Kylen as he took the last few steps toward the growing sunrise, which exploded before him in pinks and reds, filling the eastern sky.

Red sky at night, sailor's delight. Red sky in morning, sailor take warning echoed in the back of his mind, reminding him of something...something important. As the realization hit, he sank to his knees in the soft turf of the cemetery, the blood rushing from his brain and blurring his vision.

What the hell?

He closed his eyes, and then opened them again, blinking rapidly, trying to make sense of something that made no sense. He could see the colors of the sunrise? Her hair? How? Why now, four months after his liberation? Too exhausted for any more self-examination, it occurred to him again that he'd only gotten an hour of sleep in the past three days. And he hadn't eaten since when? He had no idea. He was exhausted, undernourished and carrying two souls. Of course his vision was screwy.

Reckless.

Yes. He was.

He closed his eyes again and palmed the nearest headstone. Flashing with the help of a sanctified object created a more direct portal into the consecrated subway and required less energy than dissipating through a large area of consecrated ground. Right now, he needed all the help he could get.

Feeling the familiar tug, he and the woman began to swirl and dissipate into the consecrated subway. Kylen willed them to the closest thing he had to a home.

* * *

"Holy shit!" Nate leaped from the couch as Kylen and a woman landed in the middle of Ruth's living room. Kylen crumpled to his knees, holding the limp body before him like a sacrifice, the woman's white hair splayed across the floor.

"Is she dead?" Nate bent to reach for her and Kylen's eyes blazed at him with what? Rage? And the ice-gray stare of a reaper carrying a soul.

"Are you carrying a soul?" Nate rolled back onto his heels, looking at him intently.

"Yes…" Kylen ground out before falling to the

floor unconscious, the woman still lying across his lap.

"Shit." Nate scooped up the woman and cradled her in his arms like a child. "Ruth!"

Ruth scrambled out of the master bathroom with dripping hair, an oversized towel wrapped around her body. She tightened it and tucked it in as she quickly surveyed the situation.

"Oh my God!" She hurried to Nate's side. "What happened? How did she get here?"

Nate nodded toward Kylen's prostrate form as he made his way to his bedroom, which doubled as their personal hospital suite, and carefully set the woman down on the hospital bed that had mercifully gone unused for the past several months.

Arranging her on the bed, he smoothed her hair away from her face and began loosening her clothes to search for wounds or signs of distress that might explain her unconsciousness. He palpated the back of her head, too, searching for a skull fracture or other head injury. Nothing. Her pulse was slow but steady. When he checked her eyes, her pupils dilated, radiating a soft blue glow. It could mean only one thing. She'd been juiced.

Hard.

He couldn't see auras, but he could see the juice they used and its lingering aftereffects.

No wonder Kylen was so drained. Juicing the woman, carrying souls, bringing her through the consecrated subway. What had happened? And how the hell had he been able to bring her here at all? Only supernatural entities were supposed to be able to use it. So what the hell was she?

"What's wrong with her?" Ruth had followed him to the open doorway.

"I don't know. Go get some clothes on, and then gather the IV supplies for me. We'll see if we can rehydrate her and bring her around."

Ruth rushed away while Nate continued his examination. Nothing made sense. Other than the diminishing blue light in her eyes and a growing bruise along her throat, she showed no signs of trauma. Ruth returned and made quick work of gathering the necessary materials from the closet.

"Get enough for Kylen, too. He bottomed out and he's carrying souls."

"What?" Ruth looked down at the woman, clearly confused about whose soul he might have and how. Join the club, sister. There was plenty of confusion to go around.

Ruth set up the IV hook and hung the bag just like Nate had instructed. She'd become a very adept assistant. After inserting the IV needle in the woman's hand, Nate watched the fluid trickle down the tubing. He briefly considered restraining her, but decided against it.

"Nate!" Ruth cried.

"What?" Nate whipped around, looking for an attacker.

"Her aura…" Ruth looked up at him, the color draining from her own face. "It's white."

Nate sighed. White was not good. He couldn't see it. Only reapers could. But Ruth had filled him in on the meanings of the various hues and practiced on him plenty of times, decoding his every mood at her whim. It was infuriating.

White was the color of impending death.

Checking the IV again, he shook his head. He'd done all he could for now. He had no idea what was wrong with the woman. She appeared unharmed, and he couldn't find any evidence of internal injuries.

"Stay with her. I'll go tend to Kylen." Nate grabbed the rest of the supplies Ruth had prepared from the bedside table and walked into the living room to deal with the recalcitrant reaper.

Kylen was gone.

Judging from the trail of overturned furniture he'd left and the swinging door, he'd escaped to his trailer. Seriously? He hadn't even waited around to see how the woman was doing? Nate wondered why he'd bothered to bring her here at all. He wasn't exactly the nurturing type. Well, one thing was for sure—whether he wanted help or not, Kylen needed it.

Nate walked outside and knocked on the trailer door. No answer. As he turned the knob, he heard a rustling in the woods to his left, beyond the circle of protection. He had recast the circle with all four of them present, giving each of them permission to enter and leave at will, although it was strongest when they were all on site. Ruth's energy was the main engine that powered it. The rest of them were supplemental.

Lately, he had been reconsidering the wisdom of including Kylen in the spell. So far nothing troublesome had made it through the supernatural barrier...until tonight. He hoped leaving the woman alone with Ruth wasn't a mistake. She looked harmless enough, and even Kylen wasn't so far gone that he'd knowingly put Ruth at risk. Not after she'd saved his ass. Right?

He peered into the dark undergrowth at the edge of the woods. He didn't have a reaper's super-sensory powers, but something out there raised the short hairs on the back of his neck to attention.

Daylight broke over the tops of the trees, but the light still hadn't penetrated at the ground level. The line from the Robert Frost poem, "lovely, dark and deep," came to mind, except he was pretty sure there was nothing lovely waiting for him outside the circle.

At knee level, inside the undergrowth, three sets of yellow eyes glowed brightly in the still black woods. One set blinked, leaving only a vertical yellow, snake-eyed slit, before winking back to its diamond shape.

Nate squinted into the darkness, trying to make out a form, but when he refocused, the yellow eyes were gone.

His brain said cat. *Big cat.* Like a bobcat or mountain lion. His intuition and sense of self-preservation spoke of something else. Something…evil. He shuddered and pushed into the trailer.

Dead to the world, Kylen lay sprawled on the bottom bunk on the right end of the trailer. In the guy's defense, Nate was impressed with his cleanliness. The place was immaculate. Of course, the dude had no belongings. He'd been possessed for a hundred years. By a demon, not material accumulations.

Clean or not, it looked like the seventies had thrown up in here—it was all dark wood with yellow, orange and avocado floral prints on the couch and bedding.

One extra pair of black combat boots stood polished and aligned in a perfect row at the foot of the bed. Four clean changes of black fatigues were meticulously folded and arranged along the edge of the top bunk next to four pairs of black underwear and socks. Black was the prevailing theme. Seemed appropriate.

A case of gleaming blades of various lengths and shapes lay open behind the row of clothing. Dude had more blades than he did socks. Nate didn't know shit about knives unless you were talking scalpels.

He glanced around the camper. One used glass sat at the edge of the toylike kitchen sink, a toothbrush lying on the counter beside it. And that was it. Kylen didn't even have a book or magazine to read. What did he *do* out here alone all the time? He sure wasn't sleeping, and as uptight as he was, Nate struck jacking-off from the list of possibilities.

That left thinking. Alone. In a camping trailer. That was way more alone time than Nate could have handled, and he wasn't half as screwed up as Kylen. Not by a long shot. What were a dozen-plus foster homes compared to a century-long demonic possession? Small potatoes, my friend, small potatoes.

Kylen sighed softly before grunting something incoherent and kicking out with one still-booted foot. Nate shook his head and closed the short distance between them. He laid the IV supplies on the top bunk and bent to loosen the laces and remove Kylen's boots.

Freakin' reapers pushed and pushed themselves, all of them, Ruth included, and she'd only been a reaper for just over four months. Officially, anyway.

Well, they weren't indestructible. Just close.

Nate had become the family healer and magical protector by default when they'd discovered he had a few skills of his own. That and being the sole person in the house with an aura had made things…interesting. Everyone always seemed to know what he was thinking and feeling, but he had to read the others based on more cryptic clues. Well, now there was another person with an aura in the house. A white one.

What the hell is going on? he thought for about the millionth time that morning. Nate rearranged Kylen's massive body as best he could, aligning his arm to accept the nutrition IV he'd brought into the camper. He should have probably used three or four of these a week, but he always refused help when he was conscious. Kylen had been living on caffeine and hatred, for all Nate could figure. He'd been a sack of bones and determination after the exorcism, but he'd worked out like a fiend every day since. Even though he was still too thin, he was jacked, too.

For the life of him, Nate couldn't figure out how the guy was still alive. Reapers seemed to run on a different set of metabolic rules in general, but based on his experiences with Deacon and Ruth, reapers needed tons of food to fuel them. He'd witnessed Kylen eat very little. Maybe he had a secret stash of candy bars under his bed? None of it made any sense.

He plunged the IV needle into the back of Kylen's hand and stuffed the IV hook under the mattress of the top bunk. He'd prepared the IV bag with a solid sedative as well as nutrition.

Dude would have some downtime, whether he liked it or not. No one died on his watch. And that included the white-haired girl Kylen had brought home, white aura or not. He did not relish breaking the news to Deacon that Kylen had not only brought home a sick stranger but was carrying souls. Shit was about to hit the fan. They didn't have time for this nonsense. Sparing a glance toward the woods, which were now fully illuminated, he stepped from the trailer and headed back to the house.

Just another day in paradise.

* * *

Ruth was fussing around by the woman's bedside when he returned.

"How is he?"

"Out cold. I juiced him old school. He'll be a new man by nightfall. Better when he's emptied of the souls."

"What do you think happened?"

"I have no idea, but Deacon's going to freak. Bringing a civilian into the middle of your home? Carrying souls against Rashnu's will?"

Ruth ducked her head and fidgeted with her hands. "That's not the only thing he's going to freak out about."

"What do you mean?"

"I've been feeling…strange. I thought it was just

anxiety. Adapting to everything, you know? But I took a pregnancy test before my shower, just in case." Ruth smiled, but her expression filled him with dread.

"Don't tell me—"

"I'm pregnant." Her entire face lit up when she said it, but Nate felt his heart sink like a stone.

"Oh."

He was trying to process the news, turn it into something positive, but while the thought of Ruth potentially fighting demons was worrisome, the thought of her trying to protect an infant in this house with demons and imps and fallen angels on the loose was nearly more than he could bear. Nate was reasonably sure this would push Deacon right over the edge.

"That's it? *Oh,* is all I get?"

"Oh, shit? Congratulations?"

"It's not like we were trying. It just happened. Deacon didn't think it could and then…it did."

"You have to tell him, Ruth. Tonight. Don't make me keep this secret. We don't know what complications there could be with you…*and* him being reapers. Tell him."

"I will. I promise. Soon."

Nate sighed.

It wouldn't be soon enough.

CHAPTER SIX

Kylen gazed down at her in the sunlight. Her hair damp from exertion, sand twinkling like glitter on her skin, and a light sheen of moisture glistening between her breasts, Kara smiled up at him. She was so beautiful. He didn't deserve her. Didn't deserve this much happiness. She reached up and pushed his hair back from his eyes, leaning up to kiss his forehead. This was their favorite place, this stretch of beach on the coast of Haiti.

He hovered over her, stroking her fair skin and clutching a handful of her silky, straight, white-blond hair. She was visibly striking—her looks the first indication of her ferocity. Even as a child, she'd exuded an intensity that intimidated everyone around her. Everyone except for Kylen. He'd accepted her strength as a challenge and somehow managed to tame her. Or so he kidded himself.

If Kara was tamed, it was at her inclination. Not his. He could live with that. And in this moment, in the afterglow of making love to her, as her green eyes searched his, it was more than enough. It was everything. He bent to take her mouth, and she moaned, raising her hips to him. He'd never get enough of her body. Of her. Never. Not here on this beach. Not anywhere.

Kylen jerked awake to a laser beam of sunlight streaming through his trailer window. His heartbeat pounded in his ears as he realized it was only a dream, a memory. His cock thought otherwise, however, and was hard as a billy club in his fatigue pants.

He needed curtains to block out the sunlight…and for privacy. But he'd be damned if he was going to go all domestic and pick some out at Wal-Mart. No telling what he'd end up choosing. After all, his vision had returned to shades of gray as soon as he got back to the trailer.

Perfect.

If he had any clothes or linens to spare, he'd hang a shirt or a towel over the windows. He had neither. His level of maintenance was below low. Whatever the hell that was.

Raising his arm to cover his eyes, something sharp stabbed at the back of his hand.

What the hell? Fucking Nate.

The resident witch had doped him. No telling with what. He tore the offending sliver of steel from his flesh and threw it toward the door. It snapped back on the end of its tube and nearly took his eye out.

Wouldn't that be perfect?

He slapped his head back against the thin camper mattress in frustration and grabbed the couch cushion he used as a pillow to cover his eyes.

How late is it? It felt late. Real late. Afternoon late.

But it wasn't late enough. He still had an entire day to burn. They hunted demons at night. The cover of darkness made things a little easier to hide from the civilians, and the demons were more active after sunset.

Lots of bad things could happen in the darkness. He should know. He *did* know. Last night in fact…*the woman!* He bolted upright, slamming his skull into the top bunk, nearly knocking himself out.

Stars exploded behind his eyes in bright white flares. More careful this time, he rolled out from under the top bunk and settled his feet on the floor. He'd tried to sleep in the larger bed on the opposite end of the trailer, but it seemed too big, too exposed. He slept better—when he did sleep—cocooned in the cavelike bottom bunk. The souls fluttered inside him, reminding him he still had work to do. After tugging on his boots, he pounded out of the trailer toward the house. The bright afternoon sun spiked into his eye sockets, and he had to close them, running half-blind to the back door.

He raced up the back steps and into the kitchen. The entire family was sitting around the table eating something that made his stomach twist and demand attention. It smelled wonderful. He squinted his eyes as they slowly adjusted to the less intense light of the kitchen, and he surveyed the room. Yep, the whole lot of them were present and accounted for. Kylen scowled, confused.

Where's the woman?

"You looking for Snow White?" Nate asked.

"Is she…alive?" He realized he was terrified to hear the answer. His hands were sweating, and a trickle of perspiration ran between his shoulder blades.

"She's alive. But still unconscious." Nate gave Ruth a wary look.

What aren't they telling me?

Kylen stalked past the table with purpose, but stopped when Deacon stood in his pathway. Placing a hand on Kylen's shoulder, he said, "First, let's talk about why she's here. Then you can tell us why you're carrying souls. What happened?"

Talking was the last thing Kylen wanted to do. What he wanted, as rage built up inside him, was to break Deacon's arm. He barely managed to tamp his emotions down.

"Take. Your hand. Off of me."

Deacon held his hand in place for an eternity before lowering it to his side, slow and easy, never taking his eyes off Kylen's. Stepping around him without another word, Kylen walked into the bedroom.

He sucked in a hard breath when he saw her. Her white hair was fanned out beneath her, surrounding her head like a halo. Her skin was pale, almost luminescent. He found himself memorizing her features, and he reached out a hand as if to touch her face. She looked like a goddess.

Fuck me.

Shaking his head, he tried to clear his betraying brain and restore his senses. Then he saw it. Faint at first, but the more he concentrated, the more obvious her aura became.

What the hell? What color is it? Why is it so bright?

He didn't want to ask the rest of them what color it was. They already knew he was damaged. No need for them to know he could no longer make out colors.

Still frozen in the doorway, he eased forward, tentative and unsure, reaching for her on autopilot. She was so cold. As he closed his hand around her fragile fingers, warming them with his own, he felt a small charge of energy building between them without any conscious effort on his part. The glow, dim at first, built and changed—from nondescript brightness it transformed into cobalt-blue fire, leaking out between his fingers.

Blue?

When he looked back at her face, he was certain of what he saw this time. Her light was white. Bright white, save for the blue charge building between their touching hands.

What the hell?

Her hand warmed in his, the warmth drawing from his body into hers of its own accord. Her eyelids fluttered open for a moment before shutting again. His heart constricted in his chest.

Wake!

He wanted to scream it at the top of his lungs, but the word wouldn't come.

Wake! he demanded again in his head. Suddenly, she arched off the bed, her neck bending back as she thrashed her head side to side, her hair whipping across her face.

A seizure?

He wanted to call for Nate to come and tend to her, but he was paralyzed, his hand attached to hers as his energy poured into her. When her eyes opened again, she stilled stiff as a cadaver, and her obvious terror almost destroyed him. His throat swelled and the lump there threatened to suffocate him. He sucked in another hard breath and closed his eyes to keep her gaze from searing his soul. What was he doing to her? And why couldn't he stop himself?

"Shit. Nate, come here!" Deacon called from the doorway as he crossed over to Kylen and attempted to pry him away from the woman.

It took both men to break Kylen's hold on her hand. When they did, Kylen slumped to his knees between them, completely exhausted. The woman had relaxed, melting back onto the bed, where she lay loose and boneless, her head turning to the side. Her eyes closed again, and perspiration beaded on her forehead.

"Her aura! It's changed to blue. Deacon, do you

see it?" asked Ruth, who had run into the room after them. She was gently stroking the woman's forehead.

Deacon looked from the woman to Kylen, then back again.

"Let's talk, Kylen. Now." Deacon helped him to his feet, and Nate joined them as they walked back to the kitchen table, leaving Ruth to attend to the woman.

CHAPTER SEVEN

Nate set a full bowl of stew in front of him along with half a loaf of French bread, and Kylen's stomach betrayed him with a loud growl. He picked up the spoon in one hand, the bread in the other and went at the meal like a man on death row.

Ironic.

Deacon sat across from him while Nate leaned against the kitchen wall. Both of them waited less than patiently while Kylen stalled, shoveling food into his mouth as he tried to collect his thoughts. Finally, Deacon succumbed to curiosity.

"Spill it, Kylen. How exactly did you manage to come by the woman? And what's with the blue light?"

Kylen groaned, resigned to the inevitable interrogation that was to come. At least he felt a little better. A lot better, actually. He didn't know whether to attribute his sudden good feelings to Nate's interference with the IV or the stew. *Or her,* whispered an insistent voice in his head. For a few fleeting seconds, he almost allowed himself to feel…what? Relaxed? Peaceful?

No need to get carried away. He'd settle for rested. Anything else would be extravagant, all things considered.

"Kylen?" Deacon pounded on the table, snapping him out of his jumbled thoughts.

Kylen leveled his gaze at Deacon. God, he was a pain in the ass.

"I found her downtown. A demon was trying to possess her, and I stopped it."

Deacon studied Kylen hard. "You mean the demon tried to take her soul before she had even passed?"

"Yes."

"How is that possible? There are rules."

"My demon stopped playing by those rules long ago, but he was an aberration. If any run-of-the-mill demon can do it now… Well, things are escalating and they're only going to get worse. The lucky victims will die. The rest…"

"What?" Nate asked.

"The rest will wish they were dead."

"What a freakin' mess." Deacon splayed his palms across the kitchen table and hung his head, eyes closed. "You killed the demon?"

"I stopped it. I killed the host."

"Dammit! We can't leave a trail of bodies around the city. Where is it? Nate and I will have to go clean it up." Deacon pinched the bridge of his nose.

Kylen shifted in his chair. The last thing he needed was for them to know he still controlled the imps. They knew of his link to his dark side because of his ability to track the demons. That, along with his recent history, was reason enough for his loyalties to be questioned by the higher-ups, and he could see in Deacon's eyes that their once rock-steady trust had evaporated.

"I took care of them."

"Them? As in more than one? Demons or bodies, Kylen?"

"Bodies."

"Shit." Deacon rose from the table and splayed his hands on either side of Kylen's bowl, leaning in close. "Did you kill them both?" His eyes practically threw off sparks.

Kylen looked up, rage boiling inside him at the insinuation. "No."

"Explain. More than one word at a time, please."

Angry anew at being treated like a petulant child, Kylen managed to repress his urge to rip his best friend's head from his shoulders.

"I saw a junkie and a whore engaged in a transaction in the alley. Later, I heard a scream. When I went to investigate, the demon was fleeing its host and attempting to possess the woman who's now in Nate's room. I stopped it. She collapsed, and when I picked her up, I noticed that the whore was also dead behind a Dumpster. Since this one seemed to be salvageable, I decided to bring her back here so Nate could patch her up, as he's been requesting to do for months now. He's the one who thinks we can stop killing the hosts. His wish has been fulfilled. You're welcome."

"How exactly did you prevent the demon from entering the woman?"

Kylen exhaled, exasperated, and tipped his head back to stare at the ceiling. "I pushed it the hell out. I used my Reiki, and it fled."

"And the souls you carry?"

"Without a vessel, the demon left them behind. I didn't think you'd want me to leave them for the next available ride. Or did you?"

Deacon rubbed his forehead as if he were trying to erase an unwanted thought. "Of course not. Can you find it again? The demon?"

"Yes."

Nate pulled out a chair and sat at the table beside Kylen. "Is the woman supernatural?"

"I have no idea." Kylen pushed his bowl away and clenched his hands together in front of him. His knuckles turned white as bone with the effort of self-containment.

"How could you have transported her through the consecrated subway otherwise?"

"I don't know." Kylen shifted again, uncomfortable.

"I think I know," Ruth offered, walking up behind Kylen. She placed a hand cautiously on his shoulder, giving him a gentle squeeze. "Her light is white, Kylen."

Kylen flinched under her touch.

"You may not have noticed it in the confusion, especially if you juiced her. But her light is bright white, except—it seems—when you first arrived back at the house and when you were with her a few minutes ago. Her aura turned bright blue, but then it began to wear off. She's dying, Kylen. Whether from the attack or something else, she doesn't have much longer. That may be why you were able to take her through the consecrated subway.... She's almost gone." Ruth squeezed his shoulder again, and he fought the urge to tear away from her touch. Violently.

So much for his peaceful, easy feeling. Rage boiled up inside him again.

Screw the whole lot of them.

The one time he made the effort to save a host...*potential host*...it was exactly as he'd predicted: a colossal failure. They might as well put her down now. At least Nate wouldn't push him on the issue again. If this didn't prove there was method to his madness, what would?

He cringed at the thought of harvesting her soul.

Deacon could do it. He wasn't supposed to, anyway, and besides, he was done with the whole supremely effed-up situation. He considered bolting again, except he had his own soul issue to resolve and there were still six hours to go until full dark, when they could resume hunting. What the hell was he going to do? With the souls, with this situation? Sit around and rehash this entire debacle?

"Tell me about the bodies, Kylen. How do you know they won't be found?" Deacon crossed over to Ruth and pulled her into his arms.

"I took care of them." Kylen looked up at the ceiling, and then turned to face Deacon. "Don't you trust me?"

"Not anymore." Deacon stared him down.

Well, well, well. There it is—out in the open at last.

Relief washed over him, cleansing the pain of the past few months that they had spent dancing around the obvious.

"Do you plan to take the souls to Purgatory?" Deacon asked.

"I'd rather not."

"Purge them. I'll take them."

Kylen bristled at the command. While he didn't want to take the souls, he also didn't like being told what to do. Under any circumstances. He'd been forced to follow orders for far too long. About a hundred years too long. Resigned, he gathered the souls inside him and forced them from his body. They streamed out through his mouth and swirled around his head for several long seconds before Deacon consumed them. His relief was immediate but temporary. The hollow feeling inside returned along with a fresh wave of anger.

Kylen rose from his chair with slow deliberation and headed to the back door without another word. This conversation was over. As far as he was concerned, all of their talk had accomplished nothing. Six hours until he could hunt the demon who had basically killed the woman in the next room.

He'd be ready.

CHAPTER EIGHT

"That went well." Ruth stroked a hand along Deacon's face, and he leaned down to kiss her.

"I'm trying, Ruth." He trailed three quick kisses down her neck.

"Try harder."

"I don't know how much more I can do for him. He's reckless and now his behavior is putting you in danger."

"She seems pretty harmless to me." She wrapped her arms around his waist and he pulled her in for a long, slow kiss.

"Ahem!" Nate picked up the empty bowl and silverware from the table and carried them to the sink. "Get a room already."

The tension broken, Deacon smiled. "Sounds good to me." He scooped Ruth up into his arms and swung her around the kitchen.

"Deacon!" she squealed.

"Come with me. I'll take the souls to Purgatory and then..." he whispered in her ear. "I'll take you."

He flung her over his shoulder caveman style. "Nate, can you…"

"Babysit? I live to serve." Nate rolled his eyes. "I think I'll take some blood samples from the woman and get the lab guys to run some tests under the radar…. You know, in case we can turn things around for her."

"Good idea. Someone should be around in case she wakes up. When you're ready to leave, have Kylen keep an eye on her. He got us into this mess, so he can help take care of it…and her." Deacon slapped Ruth's behind with a playful swat and carried her to the center of the living room. "We'll be back before dark. Be ready to go demon hunting." They swirled and shimmied into the consecrated subway.

* * *

Nate had no idea where they went when they vanished like that. Of course they were heading to Purgatory first, but then? He assumed it was to some secret lover's hideaway. At least he wasn't going to have to listen to them going at it like rabbits in the next room. That had gotten old really quickly the first week he'd been here.

Finished with the dishes, he hung the towel and dishcloth over the basin. Time to check on their patient again. When he walked into his room, she was still sleeping. She looked peaceful, her shocking white hair disconcerting with her dark eyebrows. Wondering what exactly had happened between her and Kylen with all the blue spark action, he wished he could see her aura, if only to gauge her health.

As it was, he couldn't manifest the Reiki mojo without Ruth's help. She seemed to be the catalyst to activate his powers in that regard. Since returning from Hell, they'd practiced a few times together. Their combined energy had strengthened the circle of protection immensely.

He smiled. She might have the Reiki mojo down pat, but he could travel without consecrated ground. It was a trick he'd only recently learned how to control.

Even Deacon couldn't explain the anomaly that was Nate. Deacon himself had obtained the ability to flash anywhere, anytime when he was promoted to Powers. Every other reaper could only use the invisible supernatural subway to move from consecrated ground to consecrated ground. Since there was a cemetery, church, hospital or funeral home every few blocks in most cities, small towns and even rural areas, it made things pretty damn fast and convenient for the reaper set.

For Nate, flashing was an unexpected perk. Hell, he hadn't used his Honda in weeks except for grocery shopping. A guy could only carry so much with him, and popping into the middle of Smillie's Grocery would have caused more than a few problems. He'd used his skills judiciously.

Great power equals great responsibility and all that.

And the demons? They used entrance and exit portals, straight to Hell unless the demon was riding a reaper or some other being that could cross consecrated ground.

The woman's vitals were steady and her pulse was a bit stronger, but her pale skin had grown ashen—the Reiki energy from Kylen already absorbed by her body. Drawing two vials of blood from her arm, he wondered if she needed a transfusion. He still had two units of O- negative in the fridge he could use, depending on the CBC panel results.

He wasn't a doctor. He was an EMT, but he'd been pressed into more demanding service time and again over the past few months. Over the course of a week that spring, he had discovered he had bizarre untapped supernatural powers, besides his witch abilities, and traveled to Hell…and back.

His mind still reeled with the discovery, and he'd had to make a lot of adaptations to his life. Like going part-time at his job and moving in with Ruth and Deacon out here in the middle of nowhere. It wasn't like he could have kept living in an apartment building in the middle of town, given the threat that any number of supernatural beasties might find their way to him. Of course, the changes weren't all bad—that is, if you could get past the demon hunting, beheadings and body burnings.

The buzzing on his nightstand drew his attention, and he picked up his pager. The hospital. He was getting called in. With luck, he could have them run the blood work while he was out on call. He might have the results by the time he returned home for demon hunting. He grabbed his EMT bag and placed the blood vials into the side pocket. Pulling an icepack from the freezer, he slid it down next to the vials, and then slung the pack over his shoulder as he headed out the back door to call Kylen into babysitting service.

* * *

Kylen stared unblinking at the white-haired angel lying motionless on the hospital bed in Nate's room. Why the hell had he brought her here?

He hadn't even stopped to consider it.

He'd just reacted.

Instinct? Doubtful. His primary instinct these days was to destroy, not protect.

The house was silent with the exception of the various beeps and pulses from the monitors Nate had attached to the woman. She looked like a space traveler tethered to Earth by plastic lifelines.

Is she really dying? The thought brought on a peculiar twinge in his chest. He was in the business of death. It was his calling and his duty.

Contrary to urban legend, reapers weren't creatures of Hell. Reapers were conduits, ferrying souls to Purgatory, where the angel Rashnu sorted them and sent them to their final destinations. Reapers were unaffiliated with either team, although most of them chose to retire in the upper regions rather than the lower. But then Kylen had welcomed his possession, becoming an unwitting pawn in an eternal battle.

Once a venerated archangel, Camael had been the Chief of Powers and leader of an all-but-defunct group of elite reapers. Only Heaven and Camael knew why he fell, but soon after, he pledged himself to Lucifer and began building an army for the dark one's assault on humanity, planting the seeds of war by releasing demons at every opportunity.

It had been an effective strategy until Ruth and Nate destroyed one of his lead demons to free Kylen. In the meantime, Camael had detained Deacon, the reactivated Powers, for long enough to launch a more concerted effort, freeing dozens of demons. And that was the mess they were even now attempting to clean up.

As Kylen watched the gentle rise and fall of the woman's chest and the steady zigzag of her heart on the monitor, disquiet roiled inside his own vacuous chest.

Woman?

She had a name. He wondered idly if he'd ever learn it.

She doesn't have much longer.

Ruth's words pinged around his brain. He had no ties to this woman except for the fact that they had both been in the wrong place at the wrong time. Two wrongs make a right, right?

His brain was fried. Nothing made sense anymore.

Pressing his rough palms over his closed eyes, he tried to push the thoughts out of his head. He needed a reset. A do-over.

How many times had he replayed his choices in his mind since he'd been freed? Hundreds? Thousands? Free will was a bitch. On that one thing he and Camael agreed, but for such different reasons. Kylen's one remaining desire was to make the choices that would somehow lead him back to Kara.

His real home.

Exhausted by too much self-reflection and coming off his IV high, his heavy lids fell shut. In seconds his head canted to the side and his body sank low in the chair beside her bed.

Kylen stalked down the alley. He'd lost track of how many souls the demon had poached this night, but he cringed when he saw where it was taking him. The warehouse district was infamous for the unofficial gatherings that took place in its abandoned buildings. On any given night, there were hundreds of inebriated souls getting their fixes within the brick buildings. This wasn't the first time Orithidon had brought him here. Dread crept into Kylen's consciousness, but he quickly stuffed it down. The demon reveled in any emotions he could entice from his host and constantly prodded and poked at his memories. Memories Kylen had quickly learned to protect by purposely burying them.

For years he'd stayed dormant inside his own body, consumed with his private grief while the demon rained terror and destruction on humans, stealing their souls before ferrying them to Hell. Kylen hadn't resisted at all, hoping that the demon would quickly burn through his body and abandon him to death.

No. Such. Luck.

The demon was able to manipulate his reaper powers enough to heal his body over and over again. He couldn't use Kylen's reaper Reiki for external manipulation of humans, but he could keep Kylen going and hoover up a hell of a lot of souls in the process.

Humanity overall was so morally bankrupt, so far from spiritual purity, so consumed with consumption and unholy matters that it made the demon's work ridiculously easy.

Through Kylen's eyes, he could see the auras of his prey, and he sought out the ones with dirty, mixed-colored auras first. Brown indicated the presence of a dark side to one's personality—a quality that suited Orithidon's purpose perfectly.

Until this night.

As they climbed through the broken warehouse window and surveyed the room's occupants, Kylen felt a shift in him as Orithidon formed his plan. He felt his own face twist against his will into an evil grin and heard laughter erupt from his mouth as all eyes turned his way. His eyes closed briefly, hiding his view as he sensed Orithidon summon power from below the earth. The floor trembled and began to split beneath his feet. Screams erupted in the chaos as fear and sulfur flowed through the room like a thick smog, making it impossible for anyone to find the single exit.

One by one, Orithidon pulled souls from the frantic bodies of half a dozen late-night revelers, leaving their shells to stumble and clamber into one another in the darkness. Systematically, he reached out with his senses and tore them loose from their moorings, consuming them all.

When the screaming ceased, the fog dissipated. Many of the humans had not survived the premature extraction of their souls. The ones who did wandered—

unseeing, unthinking, unknowing— about the room. All that they had been was contained in their soul.

Now, they were the walking dead.

From that day forward, Orithidon didn't bother waiting for "donors" to die. No chasing ambulances or scouring hospitals and graveyards for him. He took what he wanted and found pleasure doing so.

A sharp gasp snapped him to attention. Temporarily untethered, he tensed and searched the room for danger. His eyes locked on to hers. They were open. She reached for him and without thinking his hand shot forward to take hers.

The room exploded into sharp, vivid colors, threatening to slam his eyes shut with their brightness. Pain lanced through his sockets, but he couldn't tear his gaze away from the piercing demands of her arctic stare. Her eyes were the blue-gray of deep-frozen ice. The color of a reaper's eyes when they carried a soul.

Brilliant blue energy glowed between their palms, leaking around the edges of their hold. Kylen watched as her bright white aura saturated into a sparkling blue, enveloping her in an iridescent halo. Alive and strong, his energy filled her and her pale color began to transform into a radiant healthy glow.

Warmth burst somewhere deep within Kylen, and it felt...good.

Her cheeks pinked and her eyes grew large. As her hand became overly warm in his, he pulled away, releasing himself from her grasp. Her hand fell to the bed, and she raised it to clutch at her thin covering, pulling it snug over her breasts and under her neck for protection.

Kylen swallowed hard. Inappropriate thoughts of peeling that blanket down her body and opening her like a gift threatened to choke him.

"Where am I?" Her trembling hands worked the

edge of the blanket in a worried frenzy. "Why am I here?"

Even though he was no longer touching her, Kylen's color vision lingered this time. Sharp and focused, everything seemed new and shiny. Her hair was such a brilliant white that her blue eyes seemed even brighter in contrast. They radiated an innocence and beauty that staggered him.

To think that the demon had nearly… Her gaze darted around the room, finally landing on Kylen's face again.

"You? What happened?" She relaxed slightly, lessening her grip on the top of the blanket.

Kylen cleared his throat in an attempt to reclaim the voice in which he no longer held confidence.

"You're safe." He straightened, leaning against the hard back of his chair.

"Safe?" Her eyes blazed, searing into him, and blue energy skittered along his skin, searching for a receptacle. He wanted to touch her again. So much so that he gripped his thighs to stay the ridiculous impulse.

"Yes." Well, wasn't he just the master of one-word conversation. He cringed at the memory of his earlier talk with Deacon.

Bit by bit, she pushed herself up into a sitting position. Ruth had dressed her in a sleeveless blue satiny gown that had already worked its way off one shoulder. She was so thin and fragile. She wouldn't have lasted a day as a host. Hell, not even an hour. She was easily twenty pounds lighter than Ruth, who was petite herself.

"Are you ill?" Kylen held his breath, not sure what he wanted her to say. If her weakness and frailty were the result of the attack, he had no idea how to proceed. They hadn't tried to "rescue" anyone before, and the Reiki energy they exuded was way too powerful to be used at will on humans. If her condition wasn't a result of the attack, then maybe it was his fault for juicing her… Hell, he was screwed either way.

She folded her hands in her lap and looked down at them like she was searching for answers of her own. "Yes. I have cancer."

His heart paused, skipped a beat and then kicked up again, resuming its treacherous function. "Where?"

"Everywhere," she answered, meeting his gaze. "It's end stage."

His head pounded. Her pale countenance and frailty could be explained away with that one word. *Cancer.* His eyes burned, and he rose unsteadily to his feet. Turning away from her, he tried to control the ridiculous flow of…what?

Emotion? Oh, hell no.

She flinched like a frightened animal at his sudden movement. He froze, and then eased himself back into the chair, extending his palms in a calming gesture.

No more sudden movements.

Couldn't blame her. After what she'd experienced, it was no wonder she was jumpy.

"What were you doing in that alley?" he asked, unable to keep the chastisement from his voice.

"I volunteer at the shelter next door. I cook for the homeless. I was on my way in for the breakfast shift when I saw a kid dragging someone behind the Dumpster."

He heaved in a breath and closed his eyes, hoping for patience he wasn't capable of manifesting.

"And you thought you could do what?" he asked, amazed and disgusted by her lack of self-preservation.

"Help?" she whispered.

"That worked out great. You could have been killed, too. Did that not occur to you?"

She looked down at her hands again, twisting them together, working her thumb in a circle inside her palm. "I'm already dying. What did I have to lose?"

What the holy hell? His brain erupted in an explosion of expletives in a variety of languages.

CHAPTER NINE

Kylen's gut twisted into a knot of anger as the blue energy zinged through him, threatening to immolate him.

He needed to get out of her room.

He should not be caring for anyone; he should not be trusted with this woman. A woman whose name he realized that he still did not know.

His head twitched her way again. "What is your name?"

She pulled her knees up against her chest beneath the covers, curling herself into an upright fetal position. Tilting her head to the side, she rested her cheek on her knees, her gaze lasering through him.

"Olivia."

He pushed abruptly against the chair with the back of his legs as he stood, scraping it across the wooden floor like fingernails on a chalkboard.

"I'll be back."

Air, he needed some damned air. *Now.*

Stumbling from the bedroom like a drunk, he

staggered to the back door, desperate for the sweet relief of the late September afternoon…and his trailer.

* * *

Olivia realized she was not afraid. Perplexed? Concerned? Confused? Yes, but not afraid.

Her hero was intense, but there was something reassuring about him nonetheless, betraying his harsh exterior. She was more concerned with finding out who had undressed her and where her things were.

It was so quiet here…wherever here was. And why was she in a hospital bed hooked up to machinery when this clearly wasn't a hospital or hospice center? It was all so disconcerting. This wasn't the way she'd envisioned her last day at the homeless shelter.

One by one, she'd been ticking off the items on her bucket list. She was down to the last fourteen. Of course, they were the most frightening ones, which was exactly why they were last. Cooking at a homeless shelter was nothing compared to #53 and #58: *get drunk* and *have a one-night stand.*

She shuddered.

The idea of a bucket list had seemed so wonderful at first. Essential even. As she'd ticked her way through the list, she was surprised by how easy most of them were to achieve. Of course, her wishes weren't too exotic. No running with the bulls in Pamplona, swimming with sharks in South Africa, or other such craziness. And she had no intention of leaving a trail of unpaid debt behind despite her former coworker's suggestion that she charge everything to a credit card, Visa be damned. Her parents would have been so disappointed with her if she'd even considered such a thing. In preparing for her death, she'd proceeded as cautiously as she always had in life, with the notable exception of # 53 and #58.

She'd never been drunk. Ever. Not even one drink. She'd always felt the need to be the responsible one. And so she had. But it looked like so much fun! As for the other thing, well, sex was fun, but there were always complications.

She was proud that she'd managed to accomplish so many tasks in such a short time. Her focus had crystallized after the initial diagnosis, even though it hadn't come as a surprise. Both of her parents had already passed—her mother from the same rare genetic form of cancer, her father from heart disease. Her fate had been all but sealed years ago. Twenty-six years ago, to be exact.

Expecting her life to be short from the beginning had instilled her with a maturity and intensity that had set her apart from most of her peers. Then again, she didn't consider anyone her age to be a real peer. She'd always gravitated toward older mentors and acquaintances. None were close friends, but that was okay. In fact, it rather pleased her that she wouldn't be leaving a trail of broken hearts in her wake. Having never experienced true love was her one regret, but her current situation wasn't in any way conducive to that. Her life was a done deal. Well, almost. There were still a few loose ends to tie up.

Fourteen of them.

Olivia pulled herself back to the present.

He hadn't answered any of her questions. And where had he run off to?

Scrutinizing the room, she tried to imagine its inhabitants and the reason for the odd setup and unusual furnishings. She could form no reasonable explanation except that someone with a severe handicap or in need of long-term care must have resided here at some point. How odd that she'd ended up here. She was grateful for the rescue—that young man had been attacking her, hadn't he?—but it was all so bizarre.

Her own hospice plan had been established long ago, but she wasn't ready for it yet. *Especially right now!*

She stretched her arms above her head and leaned back, luxuriating in the complete lack of pain. Ever since her doctor had muttered the words "metastatic Ewing's sarcoma in your bone marrow," she'd known nothing but pain and nausea.

She knew the drill. Her mother had suffered through the disease, dying a slow and painful death. Olivia had refused treatment with the understanding that she'd be lucky to see the beginning of fall. Well, she was a few short days away from September 22, the equinox and the first day of fall, and at the moment, she felt wonderful. Who knew why? She just wanted to take a few moments to enjoy it.

At first, she'd planned to shoot for a top-one-hundred bucket list, but ultimately she'd settled for sixty. Sixty gave her one task to complete every other day. A few she'd even stretched out for a bit longer, like her work at the homeless shelter. Cooking there was so rewarding—her favorite thing in the world if she had to pick.

She doubted she could actually complete the list now; she was nearly out of money and almost certainly out of time.

She smoothed her hand across the satin covering her hips, feeling the sharp, protruding bones there. She looked anorexic. No matter how much she ate, she continued to waste away. At this rate, her metabolism would kill her before the cancer did. She needed to get out of this place—wherever it was—and try to make a final effort to finish her list.

The list!

Where was it? Panic bloomed behind her ribs and burned its way up her throat. Her heart thundered against her chest as she scanned for her clothes. The list was in her jeans pocket.

Flipping back the covers, she let her legs dangle over the edge of the bed, her feet still hovering several inches above the floor. With care, she let herself slide from the bed until her soles landed flat on the cool wooden floor. She gingerly tested her balance, and then began to shuffle around the edge of the bed, the IV pulling at her hand. She reached up to turn off the drip before peeling back the tape and removing the needle. She frowned; she was determined it would be the last time she was hooked up to anything.

Free at last, she extended her arms, trying to regain her balance as she shambled her way to the bathroom to search for her clothes.

She needed to find that list.

Tears stung her eyes at the unfairness of losing it so close to her goal. The last fourteen tasks were burned into her memory, but the list itself was still a tangible talisman.

Her lifeline.

She knew—*knew*—she wouldn't die until she'd marked off the last item. Without it, she felt herself losing control of her destiny. Illogical, perhaps, but who said a dying person needed to make sense?

An eternity later, she made it to the bathroom that was attached to the bedroom.

No clothes. Where could they be?

She caught her reflection in the mirror and gasped.

Her formerly auburn hair was pure white. Still soft and straight but shockingly white. She ran her hands through it, not comprehending the sudden, severe change.

Did he dye my hair?

A trickle of fear passed through her but dissipated just as quick. If he'd meant her harm, he wouldn't have rescued her and cared for her. Right?

Unless he plans to keep you as a pet, a voice inside chided.

She shook her head, not willing to consider it. Somehow, she managed to relieve herself without passing out, which was a small miracle considering the pounding of her heart.

Where did he go?

She needed help, dammit. If she didn't find her clothes, her list, and a ride home in the next ten minutes, there was a very high probability her sudden healthy glow was going to be wasted on a full-scale meltdown.

She peeked around the frame of the bedroom door. She searched for him, taking in all the details of the small living room. Catching movement to her left, she realized that the back door was swinging gently in the breeze. She crossed through the kitchen area, passed through a small mudroom and stepped through the open door.

Pausing to orient herself, she peered around the house's backyard. An old Lincoln Continental and a newer Honda Accord sat in the open-front garage behind the house at the edge of the woods. A camping trailer was parked beside it. The afternoon sunlight dappled through the treetops, and the huge globe of the sun sat perched on top of an impossibly tall pine tree like a lollipop. The house was surrounded by forest.

Something scurried in the undergrowth at the edge of the woods, just beyond the camper. Thinking it might be her captor, she picked her way through the tall grass and pushed her way toward the movement. Two sleek black cats, their eyes glinting green in the sunlight, were nosing around in the pine needles beyond the trailer.

Oh! They're beautiful!

Forgetting her anxiety, she continued to approach them, bending low and extending her hand in a gentle greeting.

"Here kitty, kitty," she coaxed, but they wouldn't come any closer.

She eased her way toward them, moving farther into the woods. Pleased that they didn't seem frightened of her, she closed the distance between them, murmuring soft reassurances. When she was within arm's reach, she squatted on the soft bed of pine needles behind the camper and settled back on her heels, waiting for them to come to her of their own free will.

Which they did. Both of them.

"Good kitties!" She smiled. Another task she could mark off her list: *#50 have a pet.* She was going to have to be a bit more flexible with the rules at this late date. She knew there wasn't much time left. Playing with two cats definitely counted as "having a pet" at this point.

The cats purred and rubbed their silky heads against her hands, nudging her for more petting.

Oh, they're so soft!

They couldn't be strays. Their coats were much too slick, healthy looking and luscious for them to be feral. She longed to know their names. Two toms from the looks of them. She laughed. It figured—they were charmers.

If they were hers, she'd name them Lucky and Charm.

How perfect!

They purred, loud and aggressive in their affection and desire for attention, their entire bodies vibrating with their happiness. Either they didn't normally get much attention, or they were playing her.

She relished their easy company, wishing for the millionth time that things could be different, that she had time to fulfill her bucket list the right way if nothing else.

She should have adopted a pet long ago. A pet might have helped ease some of her loneliness. It would have given her someone to curl up with each night. Now it was much too late to get a pet. Poor thing wouldn't even have a chance to settle in before it would have to go somewhere else.

She liked caring for others—and especially liked feeding them. That's why she'd put the gourmet-cooking seminar and the baking classes toward the top of her list. Before starting the classes, she took an indefinite leave of absence from her job at the newspaper. Only a couple of coworkers knew she was ill, and only one knew she was terminal—the one who'd suggested the list and the Visa ditch.

One of the cats climbed into Olivia's lap. Smiling, she settled down on the forest floor, making a more comfortable bed for it across her thighs as it circled and pawed around before curling into a ball. The other cat climbed in next to it.

They were so lovely, and she felt indescribably peaceful sitting there snuggling with them.

Gazing up into the cerulean-blue sky, she closed her eyes as the sun dappled through the canopy of loblolly pines and settled against her face. It felt like heaven.

Maybe she was already there.

CHAPTER TEN

"What the hell are you doing, Olivia?"

Olivia yelped and jumped, scaring the imps from their lap nap. One bared its long fangs, hissing to show its displeasure as it slid from her lap. Its eyes blinked, closing in a vertical slash. The other scrambled out of Olivia's reach.

Kylen tore across the gap between them, grabbed Olivia under the shoulders, and wrenched her back inside the circle of protection, well away from the two imps. He lost his balance, and she landed on top of him with a huff.

"What's wrong? My God, I was only playing with the cats!" She pushed off him and stood, dusting pine needles and dirt off of her suddenly ridiculously revealing nightgown. Her pert little breasts pushed against the material and her nipples rounded like two perfect pearls beneath the fabric as she tugged the hem down, hopelessly trying to recover her modesty.

No amount of tugging was going to make that gown any longer.

Things stirred in him. Low. Things he didn't want to think about. He reached for anger instead. Hell, he left her alone for twenty minutes, and she was out here playing with imps?

"Those aren't cats, Olivia." He extended a hand in front of him, indicating that she should return to the house. Her eyes crinkled and a tiny fan of frown lines spread between her dark brows as she stared at him like he was a slow child.

How much should he tell her? He knew the answer to that—he shouldn't tell her anything. He should take her home. Wherever that was, and let her… die? Could he do that? Of course he could. What was with this sudden flare of conscience?

Jesus, he was getting soft in the head. Okay, softer. His eggs were way scrambled already and now it seemed like they were being served up with a side of toast.

Fantastic.

"Where were you?" she asked. "I came looking for you. I don't know what's going on here, but I want my clothes, I want my list and I want to go home!" Her voice cracked on that last demand, but it was the only sign of weakness she allowed—her eyes flared, her mouth set in a tight line, her hands perched on her too-bony hips.

The girl needed to eat.

No sooner did he think it than her stomach growled loudly.

Confirmed. She was hungry.

Instead of hiding in the trailer, he should have been feeding her. He felt like someone had left a helpless newborn on his doorstep, and he had no idea what to do with it. He was so not nurturing material.

He groaned. "Come inside. You need to eat. I'll look for your clothes."

She didn't budge. Hands still on her hips, her vulnerability vanished, replaced with utter defiance.

"Where were you?" she asked again.

"In the trailer," he answered, confused by how the balance of power had shifted so suddenly and why she was so damn bossy.

"Why exactly am I here? And what were you doing in there?"

His heart did a little flip-flop, and he staggered back from her. He wasn't used to answering to anyone, let alone a pushy little hundred-pound vixen.

"I needed to do something," he said, the answer sounding weak even to him.

"What?"

Damn but she was persistent. "Something personal."

"Oh." Her hands slid off her hips and ran smoothly along her gown on either side of her thighs, her cheeks pinking in embarrassment. His eyes tracked every slippery twitch of her fingers as they started worrying at her hem.

She lowered her eyes, resigned, and walked barefooted back across the grass to the back steps. Kylen spared a sneer for the imps, which were all but rolling drunk with their small victory on the soft earth in the fading evening light, baring their teeth at him in mockery.

The fiends were getting bold. Too bold.

The circle of protection Nate had cast prevented them from coming any closer. It kept supernatural entities out unless they were excluded from the spell, like the four of them were. It didn't do shit to keep humans in or out.

Nate was a powerful witch, and Kylen didn't discount his usefulness, only his lack of experience with the hidden supernatural world. Unfortunately, Nate still couldn't see most creatures' true forms, like Ruth and every other true reaper could. He wouldn't have seen the imps for what they were, either.

Imps had the perfect camouflage as cats. Because of their superior attitudes, independence and general pissyness, humans didn't even question their behavior when they went all medieval on someone or something. If Olivia could see what they really looked like, she sure as hell wouldn't have been cuddling with them.

He shuddered at the thought of the imps clearing the bodies in the alley. They could have turned on Olivia in a heartbeat. She could have been shredded on that forest floor while he was sulking in his trailer.

He couldn't let her out of his sight again. That much was clear.

She turned as she ascended the top step and pulled open the back door. "What's your name?"

Stunned, he nearly tumbled into her.

"Kylen."

She nodded and turned her back to him, her sweet ass flouncing under the satin as she walked toward the kitchen.

Sitting at the table, she folded her hands primly in her lap.

"My clothes? Or at least a robe?" When he didn't answer quickly enough, she sighed. "Please, Kylen. I need to know what's going on, but I don't feel comfortable wearing this."

That one word—his name—was his undoing.

Defeated already, he walked past her, scooting along the small bank of cabinets and the refrigerator to give her a wide berth. He'd seen Ruth wear some sort of fluffy robe thing from time to time. Maybe it was in the bathroom she shared with Deacon? Who knew where women kept things like that?

Stomping toward the bedroom, he hesitated inside the doorway. He'd never been *in* their bedroom before, let alone their bathroom. A quick sweep around the room revealed no fluffy garments. He was not digging through any drawers. God knew what he'd discover in there. The room was neat, and a fat overstuffed comforter covered the king-sized bed they'd dragged home a few weeks ago.

The place was downright nauseating.

Thank God for Craigslist. Dragging his trailer home with a rented truck was the one thing he'd done right over the past few months. It made him feel a little more like his own man rather than one of Deacon and Ruth's pets. The piece of shit would only be better if it had a motor, and he could drive it away. Like right now for starters.

Either that or fall into a giant hole somewhere because his thoughts were spiraling out of control. One minute he was ready to take her home and drop her off, and the next he was admiring her ass? Misfiring brain circuits was his only explanation. He had one mission. Hunt and destroy the demons. All the rest of this? Not important.

Frustrated, he thrust his head into the bathroom doorway. He heaved a sigh of relief. The fluffy monstrosity was hanging on a hook beside the shower. He snatched it up and carried it back to the kitchen like it was on fire.

He presented it to Olivia.

"Thank you." A slow, sweet smile spread across her face.

"Welcome." Yep, a one-word miracle, that was him.

He moved to the fridge and extracted a giant covered pot full of leftover stew. Realizing he had no idea where the bowls were kept, let alone the silverware, he started on the left side and began opening cabinet doors and drawers, searching for his prey.

Success.

Inordinately proud of himself, he found a measuring cup and began hoisting great scoopfuls of stew into two bowls. Grabbing them up, he spun in a circle, searching for the microwave.

Where the heck was the thing?

He knew the others had used one. He'd heard it humming.

"Above the stove," Olivia offered.

Jerking at the sound of her voice, he nearly sloshed the stew onto the floor as he turned to face her. Completely swallowed up by the robe, she looked like a pink Sno Ball snack cake with the creamy filling exploding out the top.

Edible.

A shy smile spread across her face. She was beautiful. The last rays of sunset penetrated through the window behind her, bathing her in a glow that had nothing to do with magic or Reiki energy. The red-orange light from the window created a halo around her white hair. Humor sparkled in her blue eyes, and while he had no idea how or why she'd triggered his color vision, still, he was grateful.

An angel, that's what she was.

He swallowed hard and turned back to the stove. Yep, there was the microwave—right where she'd told him it would be. After shoving the bowls inside, he jabbed at the keypad, slammed the door shut and stood guard, watching the bowls spin around on the carousel.

When the microwave dinged, he removed the steaming bowls, burning a layer of fingerprints off on his way to the table. He set them down a little harder than he'd intended, brushing his painful fingertips down the side of his fatigue pants.

He retrieved two spoons from the third drawer he tried, and then sat across from her, pushing a bowl toward her. "Eat."

She frowned at him. "You are very bossy."

Funny, he'd been thinking the same thing about her only a few moments ago. He spooned in a great gulp of steaming stew.

"Where are my clothes, Kylen? What happened to my hair?" She crossed her arms over her chest, the sleeves of the robe so fluffy it was difficult to take her seriously. "Where are we, and how did we get here? What was in that IV? Were you drugging me?"

"Eat."

"Not until you answer my questions."

"You have too many questions." He took another bite. "What are you, a reporter?"

She sat up a little straighter in her chair and gave him a surprised look. "Yes. Or at least I was...before I took a leave of absence."

Figured.

"What beat did you cover?"

"Food...cuisine."

He eyed her, suspicious of her story. Wasn't there a saying about never trusting a skinny cook, or something like that?

"Don't look at me like that. I don't need your pity. I do eat. Just not as much as I used to."

He pushed the bowl in front of her, nearly touching her crossed arms as he tapped a finger on the rim. "Eat, and I'll look for your clothes."

Tilting his own bowl toward his mouth, he let the rest of the stew slide down his piehole. Damn, it was good. It amazed him how his own appetite had returned.

Spoon in hand, Olivia brought a tentative bite to her mouth. When her eyes drifted closed as she savored the taste, he was lost.

CHAPTER ELEVEN

"This is very good." Olivia said between rapidly accelerating bites.

Pleased to see her eating, Kylen stood and started the search for her clothing.

Where in the world would Ruth have put them?

He combed through Nate's room, searching without success until it occurred to him that Ruth might have *washed* her clothes. He knew where the washer was, since everyone in the house was responsible for taking care of their own laundry. Ruth did a lot for them, but she drew the line at being the "house mother for a bunch of reaper frat boys."

Her words, not his.

His personal goal had been to avoid fraternizing altogether. He had no desire to relive the glory days with Deacon or make any new memories with Ruth or Nate. He had a job to do, plain and simple, and an end-goal in mind. Once the demons were finished, he would be, too.

He was counting the days.

Opening the dryer door, he peered inside and

recognized the jeans and green T-shirt that Olivia had worn in the alley. He gathered the bundle in his arms and piled it on top of the dryer before nudging the door shut with his knee. He shook out the shirt before folding it.

Cooks Spice It Up was emblazoned with red and yellow flames on the green background. He was not impressed with the double entendre.

She should know better than to wear something like this around a bunch of men.

Homeless *men, no less.*

As he folded her jeans, he felt a lump in the pocket and reached in to extract it. It was a piece of paper that had been folded over several times. The washer and dryer had compacted it down to a frail lump of pulp. He carried it back into the kitchen.

When she saw him returning with her belongings, her eyes lit up.

"You found them! Oh, thank you!" She leaped up to claim them and pressed a chaste kiss on his cheek. Electric-blue sparks snapped between them, and she sprang back with a yelp, pressing her fingers to her lips.

"What was that?" she asked, her eyes a more brilliant blue as the energy flickered behind them.

"It's complicated," he said, rubbing his cheek and trying to ignore the heat radiating from her unexpected nearness.

"Explain it to me. You haven't answered one of my questions yet. When can I go home? There were others here earlier, where did they go? Is this your house? If so, why do you go to the trailer outside? What happened in the alley? What—"

"Stop!" he shouted, with more force than he'd intended to use.

She cringed and stepped back from him, and he immediately regretted his reaction.

Ah, hell.

Raising his hand, he opened his palm between them and presented her with the wadded paper from her pocket instead of the answers she'd requested.

"Ruth washed your clothes."

Unexpected tears sprang to her eyes as she took it gingerly from his hand. Blue sparks crackled like lightning across the surface of his palm as her fingers brushed it, and his cock twitched in response.

He couldn't decide whether to bolt again or bend her over the table. Twisting his head side to side, his neck popped, and the familiar habit helped ground him.

Get a grip.

He watched as she tried to unfold the melted pages, tears trailing silently down her cheeks. The pages tore and crumbled. In defeat, she crossed over to the back door and pitched the lump into the trash can. Pausing with her back still to him, she swiped her eyes with her fluffy pink forearm.

At least the damn thing is absorbent.

"I'm going to go put my clothes on now." She walked past him without making eye contact. "Thank you," she whispered, her voice a broken thing.

Inexplicably, he wanted to reach out to her, wanted to scoop her up and comfort her. What he didn't want was any more tears.

He ran his hands through his hair, raking it across his scalp.

Kara had not been a crier. Ever. Ruth sometimes shed a few tears in anger, but these? These were— heartbreaking.

Or they would have been if he'd had a heart.

He cleared his throat. "Welcome."

As she walked away, her long white hair and bare feet were the only parts of her that were visible above and below the pink fluff of Ruth's robe.

Brilliant, dumbass. Another one-word epiphany.

* * *

Olivia stared into the mirror. She didn't even recognize herself. Of course, her hair was...well, shocking. But her coloring was even more shocking, because her pallor was gone. She glowed and looked downright healthy. As in, two-years-ago healthy, before the diagnosis that had cracked and crumbled her world.

And her appetite! She had eaten that entire bowl of stew, and if the ruined list hadn't upset her so much, she probably would have had more. She knew what the final items were, but the list itself had been the one tangible thing left that had meaning to her. Now it was gone.

Ruined. One more sign that she was on her way out, too.

There was no way she could recreate the entire list. No way to remember all forty-six tasks that had already been completed.

In the long run it didn't matter, of course. Losing the list didn't discount her achievements or experiences, but the list had been a sort of eulogy. Proof that she'd lived—*really lived, dammit!*—even as she was dying.

She pulled off a piece of toilet paper, blew her nose into it and tossed it in the trash. The pink robe had to go. She looked like the Stay Puft Marshmallow Man in drag. Not that she had anyone to impress, and she was thankful for the modesty it provided her in front of Kylen, but still. A girl needed some dignity.

God, that man was infuriating!

Why had he even bothered saving her if he was going to be such an ass? And why couldn't he be bothered to give her the simplest of explanations?

Sliding off the robe and satin gown, she tossed them onto the countertop next to the sink and eyed the shower. A shower would feel wonderful. Since Kylen didn't seem to want to answer any of her questions, she wasn't going to consult him on her every move. She reached out and turned on the water, letting the room fill with relaxing steam.

* * *

Kylen paced around the kitchen.
What was taking her so long?

Darkness had fallen, and none of the others were back yet. He itched to get after the demon who'd attacked Olivia. This one was a sure bet. As soon as he got back to the alley, he would be able to track it straight to its hole like a fish in a barrel. Killing this particular demon was personal now.

He could barely wait.

The water began to run in the bathroom.
The shower?

His cock hardened as a picture popped into his head of her dropping that pink robe to the floor, her body bare beneath it, and...*a whole lot of shut the hell up! That's what.*

He spun around and barreled toward the back door. While she was showering, he'd have time to get weaponized and prepared for hunting. Surely, she couldn't get into too much trouble if he left her alone for ten minutes.

When the others made it back, he was going to make Deacon and Nate leave for the hunt immediately. Ruth could look after Olivia. She'd certainly do a better job of it than he could.

As he opened the back door, his eyes landed on the wadded paper on top of the trash can. He stuffed it into his pocket on a whim and headed for the safety of his trailer.

* * *

Nate flashed into the living room and a seemingly empty house.

Where the hell is everyone?

It was well after dark. He'd figured they would be pissed that he'd been gone for so long. He'd had to be at the hospital longer than anticipated, but the guys in the lab had gotten the test results back to him in record time. She had some crazy, rare bone cancer.

It was a very disappointing prognosis.

She has to already know. Right?

He hated to be the one to tell people crap like this. She was probably in the system somewhere, but since he didn't know her name, he couldn't search for her chart in the online records. He'd managed to research the cancer from the medical database, though, and all signs indicated it was *bad*. Since she still had all of her hair, he assumed she either recently found out or wasn't taking chemotherapy treatments.

He couldn't wait to hear her story when she woke up, *if* she woke up. Deacon and Ruth had already explained to him why they couldn't use their reaper Reiki to heal her. Apparently one-hundred-percent humans were too fragile for that sort of intervention. Occasional light jolts of energy were okay, but heavier, more extensive usage would fry their circuits like an egg.

Still, it seemed to him like it might be worth the chance, experimental though it would be. From what he'd seen in the cancer center, radiation and chemo weren't much better. Sometimes the cure really was worse than the disease.

Walking into the bedroom, he stopped abruptly. The woman was gone. The IV was still hanging from the drip, but it had been turned off.

Where the hell was she?

What if she was wandering the woods alone? There was no telling what was waiting out there.

The bathroom door suddenly swung open and Nate spun around, hackles raised. His mouth dropped open and relief flooded through him. The woman stood in the bathroom doorway, blue eyes wide, and gaped at him.

She was dressed in the clothes she'd arrived in—jeans and a T-shirt. Only now did he notice the slogan on the shirt.

He smiled. "Well, hello there."

"Uh, hello." She crossed her arms over her chest, her eyes moving past him to search the living room. "Where's Kylen?"

Nate stopped smiling. Hell if he knew where the bastard was. Not watching the patient, that was for sure.

"I just got home, so I haven't tracked him down yet," he said, moving toward her with his hand extended. "I'm Nate."

She hesitated before taking his hand and shaking it. "And do you live here, Nate?"

"Yep, with Ruth and her...man, Deacon." Boyfriend seemed like a ridiculous word for Deacon. The man was too much of a badass. *Baby daddy?* He hoped to hell Ruth had told him. He was so done with other peoples' secrets.

"So Kylen lives here, too?"

"Uh, yeah. He was supposed to be watching you." He smiled at her again. "How are you feeling?"

"Good," she frowned. "Fabulous, actually. So, does Kylen live in the house or in that trailer out back? Why did he bring me here? When can I go home?"

What was up with her giving him the third degree about Kylen? No doubt he'd stayed holed up in the camper for most of the afternoon. Couldn't he even be trusted to watch a mostly comatose woman? How freakin' hard was that?

"Was everything okay while I was gone? With Kylen I mean? He didn't... he wasn't..." Nate wasn't sure how to proceed. He didn't even know how much he was supposed to tell her. One thing was for sure: they were going to *have* to tell her something.

"A complete ass most of the afternoon? Yes, he was," she offered.

Yep, that was Kylen in a nutshell.

Welcome to our world.

Nate chuckled. "Sorry about that. He's all about being the lone wolf. Sounds like he saved your life, though. We didn't exactly get a detailed story, either. Since you were there, we were hoping you could tell us what happened."

Her eyebrows rose as she looked past Nate. He swiveled around to find Kylen standing behind him in all his "I am here to fuck you up" reaper glory.

Dude was loaded for bear.

That is, if you planned to do hand-to-hand combat with a bear.

He had two long knives—the word *machete* came to mind—strapped to both his thighs, and two more six-inch blades strapped to his inner forearms. Nate had no doubt the scythe was sheathed down the middle of his back.

If there hadn't already been a dude named Blade, Kylen could totally have rocked that.

He looked intimidating as hell and was obviously scaring their guest.

"Going all out tonight, I see."

"You need to get ready. As soon as Deacon and Ruth get back, we're leaving." Kylen said. Though he was addressing Nate, his eyes were locked onto their guest. Nate realized he still didn't know her name.

Ignoring Kylen, he turned back to her, "So, Ms. Doe, what do we call you now? I was thinking of nicknaming you Snow White, but I guess I'm the only one who thought that was funny."

"Olivia," Kylen answered for her.

"Let's go, Olivia, this is Nate's room, and he needs to get ready."

Obediently, she walked past Nate, heading into the living room to join Kylen. Now it was Nate's turn to gape. Things around here were just getting weirder and weirder. What the hell had he missed? He'd been gone for a few hours, and now the situation he'd left was almost unrecognizable. The previously comatose girl was up and about, and Kylen had uttered more than a one-word sentence?

Had to be the apocalypse.

Before he could shut the door so he could change out of his scrubs, Deacon and Ruth appeared in the living room, right in the middle of the demon trap.

* * *

Deacon held a laughing Ruth in his arms, and he leaned in to kiss her behind the ear before lowering her feet to the floor.

As soon as the room came into focus around her, Ruth gasped and clapped her hands. "Oh! You're awake! Thank God!" She rushed past Kylen and drew the white-haired woman into a quick hug. "How are you? We were so worried for you!"

The woman pulled away gently and cut a swift look to Kylen. "I'm feeling much better. I had a shower, and I'm happy to have my clothes back. Thank you for washing them."

"Oh honey, you're welcome. Come. Sit." Taking

the woman's hand, Ruth led her to the couch.

"Kylen let me borrow your robe. I hope that was okay. I left it in the bathroom."

Ruth looked over at Kylen, not bothering to conceal her shock—it seemed like the last thing he'd think to get for her. "Of course!" She took the woman's thin hand in hers. "What's your name? We've been dying to know."

"Olivia," Kylen and Nate, who was leaning out of his doorway, answered at the same time.

Both women jumped at the force of their combined helpfulness.

"Okaaaay," Ruth said, wondering what she'd missed. Nate and Kylen always seemed to be bickering about something.

"Welcome, Olivia," Deacon said. He narrowed his eyes at the other men. "You two ready?"

"I will be as soon as I change. Rambo here has a hard-on to go." Nate laughed and shut his bedroom door in Kylen's face.

"Ruth?" Deacon asked.

"I know, I know. Stay here. Hold down the fort. Yada, yada, yada. You're lucky Olivia is here to keep me company."

Deacon walked over and bent to kiss the top of her head. "Thank you for staying."

"Keep living the dream," she said and smiled up at him. He just shook his head as he walked toward their bedroom to gather his own hunting gear.

Ruth looked up at Kylen, who looked even fiercer than usual, "Are you feeling better, Kylen? You were a mess this morning when you brought in Olivia."

"Fine," he mumbled. Another Kylen special.

"Olivia. That's such a pretty name. Well, I'm so glad you're here. This house is swimming in testosterone if you hadn't noticed." Ruth laughed. "When did you wake up? I'm sure you were terrified. But don't worry, this is a safe place."

"So I've been told." Olivia shot Kylen another glance.

"Oh good, so Kylen has brought you up to speed?"

"Not exactly. In fact, he hasn't answered any of my questions. Not one."

Ruth laughed again. "Well, that's Kylen all right!" She winked at him, hoping to goad him into some sort of response.

The man was like a stone statue of some war god. And just as mute. Except for the frown lines crinkling his forehead, he was completely unanimated.

Always so serious and intense.

Something was going to have to lighten the guy up, or he was going to combust.

She'd tried to cheer him up for months, flipping through satellite channels and trying to get him caught up on pop culture. She'd even coaxed a few private smiles from him with her elaborately detailed reenactments of old *Seinfeld* episodes. Kylen had missed so much quality television.

"Don't worry, Olivia. I talk far more than he does, and I'll have all night to get you caught up. By the time these guys get back, you'll know more about us than you ever wanted to know."

"Do you think that's a good idea?" Kylen asked—the longest question she could recall him asking for at least a few weeks—taking a step forward.

"Yes. I do. I've already spoken with Deacon about it. Considering…well, we think she deserves to know."

Kylen shook his head and walked over to wait on the demon trap, but his eyes never left Olivia. Something big was going on here.

Nate emerged from his bedroom wearing his backpack and joined Kylen on the demon trap without comment, staring a hole through Ruth. His message was clear. She had almost told Deacon about the baby, but for some weird reason she liked the idea of doing it at home. Tomorrow. She'd definitely tell him tomorrow. Ruth shrugged her shoulders in answer to his silent question.

Mercifully, Deacon emerged from their room moments later, breaking the tension.

Grinning like the Cheshire cat, he laid a big kiss on Ruth's mouth. "Later, baby. Be good."

"Always am."

Deacon stepped onto the demon trap and stood in the middle of the other two, setting his hands on their shoulders. "Lead the way, Kylen."

The three of them swirled and shimmied until they dissolved into the consecrated subway.

"What the hell was that? Where did they go?" Olivia asked, jumping up and reaching out toward where they'd been standing seconds before, her face a mask of confusion.

Ruth looked up at her. "Lesson one: supernatural travel can be fun."

CHAPTER TWELVE

A light mist was raining down when the men landed in the downtown cemetery. Kylen shrugged from Deacon's hold and made his way to the street, not bothering to see if they were being followed. He could already smell the sulfur from the nearby alley where the imps had dispatched of the bodies. Following the demon's trail would be easy. What disturbed him was the *intensity* of the trail. More than one demon had been through here since he'd left…and recently.

Nate surveyed the alley. "Is this where you found Olivia? What was she doing here? What were *you* doing here?"

"She was volunteering," Kylen said sharply.

"Volunteering for what? To be possessed?" Nate asked, confused.

"No, asshole. Cooking at the homeless shelter next door."

"And you?" he pressed.

"None of your business."

Deacon looked down at the ground where the

prostitute's body had been gobbled up by the imps. A black stain, muddied by the rain, ran across the pavement and under the Dumpster.

"And the bodies? Here?" Deacon asked, pointing to the stain.

Kylen sighed. Enough with the inquisition about the bodies. "I've got a bead on more than one demon. Let's concentrate."

That got their attention. Deacon drew his scythe, and Nate pulled out a tiny BC-41 knuckle-duster.

Kylen shook his head. "Are you kidding me with that?"

"What?" Nate asked, sounding genuinely puzzled.

Kylen had let him select something from his own personal stash of blades, and that was the one he'd chosen. The idiot didn't even know what he was holding. It was *vintage.* Kylen had picked it off a British commando on some WWII battlefield after his demon poached the grunt's soul. He should probably feel a little worse about that than he did.

Thankfully, Nate was at least proficient enough with the piece to keep himself alive...so far, anyway. The jury was still out on whether or not he healed like a reaper.

"Lay on, Macduff," Deacon said, ignoring their bickering.

* * *

They made their way through the alley, Kylen leading the way. Three-quarters of the streetlights were broken along their path. Kylen noticed with regret that his vision had once again faded back to gray. Of course, in the misty darkness, he doubted the other two were faring much better.

They walked several blocks before he caught a glimpse of an imp peeking over the rooftop ahead of him before vanishing. Another scurried straight up a wall across the street and then slid through a broken window. A third hung precariously off the corner of an abandoned bread factory like a gargoyle. Soon, they were popping up everywhere like gophers.

"Company," Deacon said. "And considering how many of them there are…it may be a nest."

"A nest?" Nate asked.

"Sometimes demons hunker down in a hole somewhere together," Deacon explained.

"They're social?" Nate asked, flexing his grip on the BC-41.

"Not exactly. They're consolidating their power. It means they're expecting us." Kylen said, tuning in to Hell's network with the demon's residual connection. "There are five of them in the basement. There." Kylen pointed to a small, street-level window. He was pleased that Olivia's attacker was among them.

It was a poor point of entry. He'd have to go around and find the main door. It wasn't consecrated ground, so Kylen couldn't flash into the building alone or he'd already be in there. Either that or he'd have to tag along with the other two.

"We'll flash in together. A back-to-back formation will give us the best angle for our attack," Deacon said.

Yes, thank you, Captain Obvious.

God, he wished he could do this without them. Unfortunately, Deacon was the only one who could kill the damn demons. And oh, how Kylen wanted to kill them. All of them. With his luck, one of the hosts would be some teenage girl, and Nate would get all squishy about killing it. Nate was the biggest bleeding heart he'd ever met.

Nate and Deacon turned and pressed their backs together, preparing to flash. Kylen forced himself to turn and do the same. They formed a triangle, their backs touching enough that they could travel together in formation and immediately spring into action upon entry.

"Ready? On three. One, two...three."

* * *

Olivia could not get over her shock. The men had disappeared before her eyes. It was the craziest thing she'd ever experienced. Until Ruth started talking, that was. She discovered that she remembered very little of what had happened in the alley after seeing the skinny boy drag someone's limp body behind a Dumpster. Had she spoken to him? Yelled at him? Cried for help?

She didn't know. All she did know was that she'd experienced a choking sensation and a horrible upwelling of terror, and then...?

Then she'd awakened here wearing some strange girl's nightgown in a bed and a house she didn't recognize. And that had been the normal part.

The explanations Ruth had been giving her for the past hour went way beyond normal: supernatural highways, demons, reapers, angels? It was surely all a bad dream. No wonder Kylen hadn't wanted to answer any of her questions.

Yes, that must be it. It's a dream. I've fallen into a coma from my illness, and this is the end. It's the result of the really good drugs the doctors have pumped into me. Or bad drugs?

Except.

Except. Every time Ruth grabbed her hand, explaining some new horror in an excited voice, Olivia was jerked back to this new alternate reality.

"So, Kylen didn't tell you any of this?" Ruth asked.

"No. He's not very…verbose."

Ruth clapped her hands together and shook all over with laughter.

"Oh my God! That's the biggest word anyone has used in this house since the guys moved in. God bless you, Olivia. And no, he is definitely *not* verbose."

"What's wrong with him? Why is he so angry? And grumpy? And bossy?" Olivia asked, worrying the hem of her T-shirt.

Ruth smiled, an almost sad look playing across her face. "Kylen would hate it if he knew I was talking about him. But he's been through so much, Olivia. Believe it or not, he's a thousand times better than we had any right to expect. Up until four months ago, he was possessed by a demon. That's what he saved you from, Olivia. A demon was trying to enter you, and he stopped it from happening." Ruth shifted on the sofa, breaking eye contact with her. "You're the first one who's survived… other than him."

Well, wasn't that ironic. Kylen had saved a dead woman. What kind of hero did that make him?

She laughed.

"What?" Ruth smiled.

"I was thinking how funny it was that he saved a dead woman from dying."

"I knew you were ill the moment you arrived. Your aura is white, Olivia. White means impending death." Ruth reached for her hands, taking them into hers.

"You aren't telling me anything I don't already know, Ruth. I have end-stage cancer. And I'm at the end of my prognosis. The autumnal equinox is my six-month date, so anything past that is… a bonus. I'm at peace with it, so there's no reason for you to feel bad."

"The equinox? Oh, Olivia! Let's have a party. Nate is Wiccan, a real witch. He was already planning a Mabon celebration tomorrow night for the equinox. We'll celebrate your life, too."

It all seemed a little over-the-top for a group of folks who had just met her, but considering she didn't have any close friends or relatives to throw her a wake or a funeral...why not? Why shouldn't she enjoy a party of her own? At least this one she'd be able to attend.

She'd been so careful to let the emotional ties of her life slip away, so eager not to cause wounds in those she left behind. A friend here, a coworker there had faded away over the past six months. People had busy lives, and if you stopped calling, emailing and texting, it was surprisingly easy to fall off the radar. Only one coworker knew the ins and outs of her situation and had stayed in touch.

"Um, okay...I guess. I'm still not sure I believe in magic, although seeing the men disappear before my eyes was certainly compelling evidence." Compared to all of the other insanity Ruth had told her, magic seemed pretty tame, actually.

"Ha! My first supernatural travel was to Purgatory. But that's a story for another time. You don't have to believe. It's like prayer, Olivia. It can't hurt you. It can only help. Think of it as a party if you want and nothing more. Enjoy it. Nate already did most of the shopping. All we have to do is cook and bake!" Ruth jumped up from the couch, as eager as the bunny in those battery commercials. She seemed as starved for human connection as Olivia was.

"Well, I'm good at both of those things." Olivia smiled and followed her into the kitchen.

* * *

They landed in the center of the nest. The room was nearly pitch-black, and only the thinnest rays of light illuminated the north wall from the dirty basement window. Kylen's eyes adjusted within seconds and his grayed-out vision crystallized the sharp contrasts provided by the bit of light. He drew a six-inch push blade from his forearm, wielding his scythe in his other hand. Doubly armed, he surveyed his quarry. All of the demons were contained in male hosts, he noticed. The observation gave him some comfort as the enemies approached. They were outnumbered, five to three.

The demons had not only been expecting them, they'd also prepared by stockpiling substantial weaponry. Knives slashed through the dappled darkness, preceded only by grunts of exertion and the whisper of air as the demons attacked. Hand-to-hand combat was very satisfying in general, but this battle was feverish— facing five adversaries in this small, unfamiliar room, they were at a decided disadvantage.

Kylen targeted Olivia's demon and drew back his arm, his forearm and biceps coiling until his shoulder reached its limit, and then slashed forward in a long arc, drawing his weapon through the neck of the host in front of him. The blade of the scythe sliced through flesh, tendon and bone easily and without resistance. The host stood motionless, not even realizing he was dead until Kylen planted his boot in his chest and kicked him across the room, the head falling forward as the body flew back. Vindication bloomed in the black void of his heart. This was almost too easy.

The next two hosts approached, and he oscillated the scythe left then right, felling both of them without ever leaving the original formation. Having run out of adversaries, Kylen turned to check on the others. Deacon and Nate were not faring as well as he had. Deacon had bested his host, but Nate was struggling with his, blood running down his arms from the demon's attacks.

Black smoke roiled from the necks of the fallen hosts, and Deacon sent out a burst of light, filling the room with illumination and power. One by one, the demons streamed toward Deacon's sternum, drawn in by the black hole of his power. Still struggling, Nate slashed and stabbed the BC-41 toward the last host, slicing through little else but air.

Kylen stepped forward and finished the job for Nate, and then watched with satisfaction as the last of the demons entered Deacon.

"Thanks," Nate gasped.

"You're gonna need a bigger knife." Nate nodded. Maybe he'd take Kylen's advice more seriously next time. The glow intensified, drawing their eyes back to Deacon. Dozens of light gray streams poured from the bodies. Souls. There had to be at least thirty of them, and they were flowing into Deacon's mouth and through his throat chakra. They would meet a very different fate from the demons.

Deacon fell to his knees. It was the most demons—let alone souls—Kylen had ever seen him consume. He'd only ever seen a Valkyrie carry more. Deacon's body bucked and convulsed before settling to the ground. He dropped his head in exhaustion for a moment, but then pushed to his feet. Nate rushed to his side to help steady him.

"Holy shit," Nate said. "What was that all about?"

"There were more than thirty souls poached by the demons. Deacon consumed them all."

"Whoa. You Scooby-Snacked five demons *and* thirty souls? Isn't that a new record for you?"

"Yes," came the weak reply.

"Impressive." Nate held Deacon's shoulders, blood dripping off his elbows from his own injuries.

"The bodies," Deacon said. "We need to clean them up."

"We'll take care of them," Kylen said. "Go to Purgatory. We'll meet you at… Ruth's." Even now he was hesitant to call it home.

Nodding, Deacon withdrew from Nate's hold and pulled himself to his full height. He closed his eyes and flashed to Purgatory, leaving Kylen and Nate alone with the dead hosts.

* * *

The place was a bloodbath. Black ooze spread across the concrete floor like oil, making walking a hazard. Nate sighed and eased off his backpack, removing yet another tarp and tape.

Knives lay scattered around the floor of the basement room. Kylen collected each one of them. If he had a hobby, collecting knives was it. Sharp knives were the weapons preferred by most supernatural entities, since guns generally just managed to piss them off. Beheading was the one way to ensure that a beastie or reaper wouldn't rise again. Demons were the exception—behead a host and the demon could stream out and find another host, perpetuating itself for eternity if it so desired. But now they had Deacon to take care of that little problem.

He was their ace in the hole, the Dyson of demon cleanup.

Still, he and Nate had a roomful of dead bodies and blood to take care of before they could declare this mission a success. Kylen had a way to take care of that, but he didn't want to fill Nate in on the imp situation.

"Well, that was…" Nate hesitated.

"Satisfying?" Kylen finished.

"Messed up," Nate corrected. "I can't take you back along with all of them."

"Take one at a time, I'll stay with the rest."

"You sure?"

"Yes."

"All right. It's going to take a while, but I'll go ahead and get this one started," Nate said as he surveyed the carnage. "Christ, it's going to take days to get rid of this many."

Nate unfurled the tarp, rolled the first body onto it, and taped up the ends while Kylen sensed the imps were gathering outside through the small, street-level window. There were dozens.

Hoisting the body over his shoulder, Nate gave another frustrated sigh. "No, no, don't bother helping. I've got this."

"Good," Kylen answered, not bothering to make any other form of acknowledgment. After all, Nate might not know it, but he was going to save him plenty of work.

"Whatever. Back when I can," Nate said, and then vanished into the consecrated subway.

As soon as he was gone, Kylen summoned the imps. They burst through the street-level window in a shower of glass, and streamed in—a muddy river of black, oily flesh and teeth. Landing with a wet thud on the concrete floor, they descended on the bodies like piranhas. Kylen was confident there wouldn't be anything left for Nate to take back on his second trip.

He squatted, leaning back against the cool concrete wall—the one place in the room that was illuminated by the sole streetlight left on the block—and watched for a while as the imps went about their work. Satisfied with their progress, he pulled the wad of paper from his pocket and picked at its folds, careful not to tear it more than necessary as he worked it open.

It was a list.

Several words were no longer legible, but most of it was still decipherable.

She had given up too easily.

He read it in order, taking note of each item that had been scratched through with a ruler-straight line. He scowled, listening to the hosts' bones crack and crunch, as he considered the final fourteen items, which hadn't been crossed out. A few were especially troubling.

Like #58.

The words *hell* and *no* came to mind.

* * *

Olivia screamed and bolted upright on the couch in Ruth's living room when Nate appeared before her with a rolled tarp over his shoulder. She jumped to her feet and backed away from him, her heart all but exploding from her chest.

"Sorry," Nate said, a lopsided smile forming on his face. He shifted the package and took a step forward. "Do you know where Ruth is?"

"Shower," Olivia answered, as soon as she'd calmed down enough to speak.

"Okay, I have to take care of this... um...just tell her I'm back. She can find me in the basement." He smiled again and headed toward the back door.

As he walked away, she noticed that the package seemed to be shaped like a body. What had she fallen into here? Were her last few days on Earth really going to be spent with *unearthly* beings? Or worse...murderers? Didn't that make her an accessory?

Either way, it was the most interesting thing that had ever happened to her. She was tempted to stay, if they'd have her. The reporter side of her was intrigued.

If only she had more time! She'd stumbled upon a career-making story here—one that could catapult her well beyond the "Food & Cuisine" page.

But that was the one thing she didn't have.

Time.

None of this was on her list. Reapers? Nope. Demons? Nope. Supernatural travel through invisible subways? Nope. In fact, her time was running out for the things that *were* on her list.

Of the fourteen that were left, she could only mark off *#49 volunteering at a homeless shelter, #50 have a pet* and, with any luck, *#51 make the best dessert ever.* She'd baked an apple pie crumble dessert that was even now cooling on the kitchen cabinet. Hopefully it would be good enough for her to knock that item off her mental list. Ruth had shown her all the ingredients Nate had assembled, giving her the Wiki version of the Mabon celebration they'd already been planning. The box of apples had all but begged to become a dessert.

Still, the question of what was rolled in the tarp wouldn't leave her…

Fatigue settled heavily upon her, though, making her thoughts slow and sluggish. She lay back on the couch and closed her eyes. The energy that had flowed through her all afternoon was long gone, and weariness pinned her to the couch like concrete blocks on her chest.

She was *so* tired.

Her eyes refused to open even when she commanded them to do so. She felt herself slipping into unconsciousness, but was helpless to stop it. A nagging wish played in the back of her mind that Kylen had been the first to return home instead of Nate.

Vaguely, she wondered why.

Chapter Thirteen

Deacon had never been as happy to deliver his cargo as he was tonight. When he stepped into the main terminal of Purgatory, Rashnu caught sight of him and stepped down from his platform, motioning the long queue of reapers waiting to unload their quarry toward the other end of the tunnel. There, at another platform, stood…Rashnu. The angel had split himself in twain many millennia ago so he could sort souls at a more expedient rate.

He didn't trust anyone else to do the job.

The place was rocking tonight. There were thousands of reapers from dozens of species milling around the station. Some were waiting to deliver souls in the now-enormous line, and others had already deposited their cargo and were enjoying some bar-side camaraderie. The same creatures that would eat one another alive top-side drank and bullshitted down here.

Tonight, none of them looked even remotely human.

Which meant that a lot of humans must be dying

tonight, keeping the reapers of humans too busy to socialize. But Deacon had too many pressing problems to ponder that one closely.

Purgatory was the no-man's-land of reapers. It was a forced détente, and no violence or discord was tolerated. Cross the line and Rashnu would smite you to oblivion. Deacon had witnessed it happen more than once.

A thing like that made an impression. When Deacon caught Rashnu's eye, the angel nodded to the door at the outermost end of the terminal. This was not Deacon's first rodeo. He'd been through this door and down this particular hallway several times now—each time he'd consumed a demon.

Grim—yes, *the Grim*—had ascended to Seraph, leaving the opening for Deacon to become a Powers. So far, things had not been going his way. It was infuriating. They knew Camael was responsible for all the recent demon activity on Earth, but so far they hadn't found a way to shut him down permanently. The power it took to make a release portal large enough to free dozens of demons left a mark and Grim could locate and close those quickly with Deacon's help, but the smaller exit portals were trickier to find and shut down. One demon sliding through an exit portal was like a piece of sand in the bottom of the sea, a small and insignificant presence.

Deacon didn't even want to know the politics behind it all, but he would have appreciated a little more help from up top. Grim was still his mentor and would be for the indefinite future, but some days it seemed like he was being left to hang. If the higher-ups weren't motivated enough to help track down and destroy all the demons that were currently tormenting the citizens of Meridian, Deacon didn't even want to know how much worse it had to get before their attention was piqued.

Deacon followed Rashnu down the brilliant white stone hallway to Grim's chamber.

* * *

Grim was not the black-robed character of storybooks.

Never had been, in fact.

Still, he inspired a healthy respect among the Purgatory crowd. And now that he was a Seraph? The guy was even more intimidating. He was standing—or, rather, levitating—on the far side of the chamber when they walked in.

Deacon was grateful the guy had found a way to tone down his overwhelmingly bright glow, but his eyes were still searing when he looked directly at the Seraph. Three sets of wings peeked out from behind Grim, but Deacon could only see the feathered shoulders of the wings that were folded against his back. The first time Deacon had laid eyes on him, the wings were fully extended, stretching a good twelve feet on either side of Grim's body.

"Good luck," Rashnu said, pulling the door closed as he left the room to wait in the hallway.

It was hard to get a fix on Grim's actual appearance, since there was no way to properly study him without going blind. As it was, Deacon would be seeing spots for the next few hours.

Grim's face morphed between a man's visage and a child's, sometimes becoming almost animalistic. He tried not to dwell too much on the animal part. A long white flowing robe covered the rest of the Seraph's body.

"Deacon," Grim greeted. "Come, let us dispatch of this unpleasantness."

Grim had taught Deacon to consume the demons

and eat their power, but it was a tricky task when he was also full of souls, particularly this many of them.

He welcomed the help.

Deacon closed his eyes as Grim approached. A warmth enveloped him as the Seraph enclosed him in a sphere of purple light. The light pressed against him, pushing the souls and demons from him. He opened his eyes, watching as the souls streamed from his mouth in a long line, one after another for what felt like an eternity. They passed through the light, circling around Grim's head with reverence. The demons were expelled from Deacon's heart chakra in a long black stream, but they couldn't pass through the field energy.

Grim helped him free the souls but retain the demons. Grim had promised that with time he'd be able to do it himself. Deacon had no doubt that he was right. The power he'd pull from consuming these demons might be enough to push him over the edge.

Doubtlessly understanding their fate, the demons churned like dervishes, beating against their purple cell.

Grim waved his hand above his head, pointing to the chimney in the center of the room. The souls hovered, reluctant to leave his light, but they eventually streamed toward the tunnel, up and away.

That particular chimney, Deacon had learned, was a one-way street to Heaven. Like Hell, there were various levels and circles. This tunnel was a fast track to redemption.

They were the lucky ones.

Deacon didn't like to think too hard about how many souls the demons had already taken straight to Hell. And he especially didn't like to think about how many his friend Kylen had been responsible for poaching over the past hundred years. Deacon shuddered. He'd been to Hell. He hated to think of innocent souls being marooned there for eternity.

* * *

Deacon's body trembled, craving the power just within his reach.

"A bit more business, I see. Energize the sphere, Deacon."

Desperate for relief, Deacon pushed out a long cleansing breath, and then drew in another. Spreading his arms wide, he sent the force of his light into the sphere. The black streams of smoky haze coalesced into one tremulous mass before being drawn back into his sternum through his heart chakra.

The purple sphere of light surrounding Deacon went supernova and flashed, diminishing even Grim's radiance to a weak glow before winking out. There was an explosion of bright white fireworks behind his lids when he closed his eyes.

Deacon's chin fell to his chest briefly, and when he opened his eyes, a triumphant grin spread across his face.

This was what success felt like.

"Well done," Grim praised.

He lifted his gaze to Grim's. Power leaked from him as purple light sizzled down his arms and out the tips of his fingers. He was the Potentiate, the Powers. And at this moment, he felt like it.

"Impressive, Deacon. Five demons is a notable haul. How were you able to capture so many?"

"Kylen can track them, sir. We're not sure how or why, but he's been invaluable."

"That one is on a precipice, Deacon. Watch him. He has not yet chosen his path, and nothing is predestined." Grim floated toward a long bar and poured himself a drink. The amber liquid filled his tumbler, flakes of gold floating and swirling inside as if it were alive.

"If he could see Kara, I'm sure she could set him back on the path to righteousness."

"Kara is well on her way to the fourth Heaven. You know what it would cost her to meet with him. We've discussed this." Grim sighed.

"Isn't every soul worth saving if it can be redeemed?" Deacon continued, hoping he hadn't crossed some unseen barrier of angel etiquette.

"Deacon," Grim crossed the gap between them until Deacon had to close his eyes against the harshness of his light. "Your intentions for your friend are pure, although he may soon be beyond redemption. Even now he dabbles in the darkness of his previous life. The residue clings to him. He made a choice once, and soon he will need to make another."

"He made that choice to save someone he loved," Deacon pointed out.

"Damning himself in the process."

"At least consider it?"

"Your request has been noted. It's really up to Kara."

CHAPTER FOURTEEN

Nate returned to the concrete basement downtown to find a whole lot of nothing. No Kylen. No bodies. Not even a pool of black blood on the floor. Things were going from weird to weirder. As if that were even possible.

He'd stuffed the body into the furnace after cleaning out the ash and bone from the previous one, and then stoked the fire until the newest addition was well on its way to cremation. He was getting way too good at burning bodies. Maybe he should have been a mortician. Despite the gruesomeness of the task, something about returning the bodies to ash was…rewarding.

By the time he made it upstairs to flash back to the basement, Olivia was asleep on the couch and Ruth was in her bedroom. Now that the first body was on its way to consumption, he had planned on flashing the remaining ones back one at a time, leaving them in a stack. He would bring Kylen home last. Now that he was here, though, there was nary a sign of either the reaper or the hosts.

He spun around at the sound of scuffling in the dark corner behind him, drawing his knife. Yellow eyes winked in the darkness, and then inched toward him. He backed out of the puddle of light shed by the broken basement window.

What happened to the window?

A black cat emerged from the darkness and hunched down to lap at a shiny spot on the concrete floor, but it let out a sudden growl and bolted from the room. Nate released a relieved breath. He didn't like being here alone. A cold shiver rolled down his spine as the light behind him sputtered then dimmed. Someone or something had crossed by the window. He moved deeper into the shadows from where the cat had emerged and waited. He could flash back if need be, but something felt...off.

A second growl was followed by a sharp crack and thud. It sounded like someone had dropkicked the thing across the alley just outside the building's doorway. He held his knife down at thigh-level so that the light wouldn't glint off its blade, giving him away.

Nate couldn't believe his eyes. A woman had walked into the room, and she was...breathtaking. Dressed in black leather pants and a tight, black wifebeater tank, she had even more knives strapped to her body than Kylen carried around. Every visible inch of her was steeled muscle. She turned to face him and smiled, her white teeth glowing almost iridescent in the pale column of light. Long, straight, ink-black hair swayed to one side as she tilted her head to look at him. He knew who she was instantly:

Maeve, the replacement reaper.

Even though she'd been around for months, only Deacon and Ruth had actually met her. Ruth worked with her most nights and Deacon had crossed paths with her on his many trips to Purgatory. Because of Nate's inability to harvest or carry souls, he was left out of the Purgatory loop, and Kylen's Purgatory card had been revoked. Despite his infraction with the souls in the alley, Kylen was still on soul probation, and would be until Deacon decided otherwise.

"Are you gonna hide in here all night, or do you want to come out to play?" she asked, clutching a knife in each hand.

Nate took a tentative step forward. "Maeve?"

"Who are you?" She tensed and her eyes flashed in the moonlight.

"I'm Nate."

Recognition crossed her face. "Deacon's friend? The non-reaper?"

"Right." Nate held his ground, waiting for her to back down.

She continued to work the switchblade in her right hand, assessing him as she flipped it open and shut, open and shut. The other knife she slid into the sheath on her left thigh.

"What's going on here? I found an imp in the alley, and this place reeks of death and sulfur." She walked the perimeter, inspecting the floor and corners before pausing beneath the street-level window.

Searching for his voice, Nate cleared his throat. "We found a nest of demons. We killed them all, and Deacon brought the demons and the souls they were carrying to Purgatory. Kylen and I were going to take care of the bodies. I took one home, and this is what I found when I got back…"

"Nothing?" she finished.

"Nothing. Unless you count a cat… And get this, the place was a bloodbath when I left. How could it be this clean now? And what happened to Kylen?"

Maeve toed several shards of broken glass into a pile against the wall with her boot. "Was this window broken the last time you were here?"

"No."

"Didn't think so," she dragged her index finger across the window ledge and held it up in the light. Black blood glistened on its tip. "This is from an imp."

"An imp? They must have been the demons' imps..." Nate suggested.

"Not necessarily," Maeve swiped her hand across her pants, wiping it clean. "Once their demon dies, there's no master left to command them. They wouldn't stick around, unless..."

"What?" Nate asked, taking a step closer to inspect the window.

"Unless they were summoned. They are hungry buggers. And thorough. They could have cleaned up the bodies.

"Isn't that convenient?"

"Yes. But it's dangerous, too. They are indiscriminate and insatiable. Unless they're commanded, they can easily get out of control. I'm surprised you didn't see the one in the alley." She tilted her head at him again in question.

"I'm not a reaper, remember? I can't tell a cat from a hell beast. They all look the same to me." He had seen them in all their glory in Hell, but he didn't feel like offering up that little nugget of intel.

"Well, that's damn unfortunate." She kicked the pile of glass, scattering it back across the floor as she continued to circle the room. He had no idea what she was hoping to find.

"How many were there?" she asked, her brow crinkling.

"Demons? Five."

"Five? You killed five demons here?"

"Deacon killed one. Kylen took care of the rest."

Maeve whistled through her teeth, obviously

impressed. "Well, what merry little nightmare you three are. Nice work." She walked to the doorway and peered out into the alley, looking both ways.

"Gotta run. There are still plenty of demons out there waiting for a girl to take a break and steal some newly departed souls. No rest for the weary or the wicked." She grinned at him. "Watch out for cats. All of them." With that final comment, she stepped through the doorway, vanishing into the darkness of the alley.

Nate hesitated, wondering if Kylen was still nearby, and if so, whether he'd had anything to do with the imps. Could it be a coincidence that six bodies had vanished in the past twenty-four hours, all in Kylen's wake? One thing was for sure—Deacon needed to know what was going on. If Kylen was responsible for this, Deacon might be the only one who could do anything about him.

CHAPTER FIFTEEN

The first light of dawn broke across the horizon as Kylen stepped onto the consecrated ground of the downtown cemetery in Meridian. Nine hours had passed since they'd left to hunt the demons. His clothes were crusted with blood and worse things, and his chest was filled with a crushing weariness that he feared he might never beat back.

It had been a long night, and he'd spent the past few hours laboring to recreate Olivia's list while drinking the contents of the now-empty fifth of Jameson that was perched on the headstone behind him.

It boggled and amazed him that she had completed nearly everything on the crisp new list that was carefully folded in his cargo-pants pocket. He hadn't done any of those things, and he'd been alive for more than two hundred years. Of course, the past hundred hadn't exactly been his own, but still... He couldn't help feeling like he'd squandered most of his life.

There hadn't been much free time to pursue any personal interests not related to his vocation. His parents had been reapers, his friends had been reapers, and his lover had been a Valkyrie. The very human pleasures and dreams on Olivia's list were oddly appealing to him as a testament to the true power of free will, of choosing one's path and living it.

Life and death had always been intertwined with his existence, but now they felt closer than ever before. The veil had become all but transparent after Kara's death, and now he felt...what? Why was he even wasting his time considering anything as trivial as his feelings? They didn't matter. He had a mission and that was all.

That was all.

Maybe if he kept repeating that as a mantra, he'd begin to believe it.

He lifted his eyes toward the eastern sky. The horizon had split into layers of gray and bright white light. He wondered—briefly—what colors it was.

With dread and anticipation, he allowed himself to be drawn back to the house through the consecrated subway.

* * *

The *house* was in chaos.

Confused by the yelling emanating from Nate's bedroom, he drew his scythe instinctively, certain they were under attack. He raced to the doorway, assessing the threat.

Nate leaned over Olivia's limp body, which lay on the hospital bed once again, his mouth pressed over hers. All sane thought left Kylen's brain, and he drew the scythe back without even realizing what he was doing. Ruth's scream brought him back to his senses.

"Kylen! No!"

He hesitated. Lowering his weapon, he realized

with fresh terror that Nate was attempting CPR on Olivia.

What the hell is going on?

"Ruth, the AED, now!" Nate cut through Olivia's shirt with a pair of surgical scissors, shearing it up the center. He cut through her black bra as well, exposing her breasts and the translucent white skin of her chest.

All of the blood drained from Kylen's brain, pooling in a clump in the center of his own chest.

Nate ripped open the box containing the defibrillator and powered on the device. After tearing the backing from the two yellow pads, he slapped them roughly across Olivia's chest, and then stood back while the machine kicked into gear.

"Shock advised. Please stand back. Charging," the machine directed.

Nate and Ruth backed away from the bed and raised their hands, poised to act once the AED delivered its jolt of energy. A light blinked rapidly as the machine activated.

"Shock advised. No one should touch the patient. Please stand clear. Press the flashing orange button now," the machine advised in its mechanical voice.

Nate pressed the button.

Olivia convulsed on the bed, her back arching off the table before falling back again.

"Shock delivered. It is now safe to touch the patient. Continue CPR for two minutes," the machine continued.

Nate immediately resumed compressions.

"Stand back. Reassessing heart rhythm," the machine directed.

A lifetime passed before the machine proclaimed, "No heart rhythm detected. Resume CPR until help arrives."

Kylen's legs threatened to give way beneath him.

Nate continued administering CPR to Olivia for several more minutes, pumping her chest and breathing for her, until Ruth placed a hand on his shoulder.

"She's gone, Nate. There's no aura."

Kylen's own heart stuttered to a halt, and he sucked in a rasping breath. It was true—the glow surrounding her had diminished to nothing.

No! It isn't time yet!

Nate backed away from the bed, bending forward in exhaustion, pressing his hands into the tops of his thighs. Ruth led him over to his bed and helped him lie down.

"What happened to her?" Kylen managed to choke out, his throat tight, his eyes fixed on Olivia's frail body.

Ruth's hands shook as she pulled a light blanket over Nate. "She was on the couch. I thought she was still asleep." The words caught in her throat and tears welled in her eyes. "When Nate got home a few minutes ago, we tried to wake her. Her heart had stopped. We weren't sure how long ago. I guess she was already gone, Kylen."

Kylen walked over to Olivia's prostrate form and stared down at her, his chest tightening.

You're giving up too easily! You still have work to do.

With his back to Nate and Ruth, he reached into his pocket and pulled out the list. Reaching forward, he took her small hand in his, turning her wrist until her fingers rolled open. He uncurled her tiny hand and placed the list in her palm, closing her fingers around it with his. Like before, electric blue sparks danced unbidden from his hand, traveling through her fingers before following a path up the veins of her arms. Kylen watched with awe as the energy moved beneath her translucent skin, filled her chest cavity and then burst outward in every direction like a star.

"What the hell are you doing to her?" Nate asked, rushing to the bedside.

Kylen couldn't tear his hold from her hand if he'd wanted to... The room flared to life as his vision erupted into brilliant color once again. He gave Olivia what little energy he had left, allowing her body to pull from him what she needed.

He fell to his knees, still gripping her hand, his cheek pressed against the coolness of her sheets.

The AED beeped to life. "Normal heart rhythm detected. Cease CPR. Await further medical assistance."

The last thing he remembered was Nate physically trying to break his hand free from Olivia's.

Then, blessed darkness.

* * *

Kylen was in Hell, weaving down the long, torturous stone hallways that grew progressively more claustrophobic and darker the lower he traveled. There were many levels of Hell, and Orithidon, his particular demon, was highly enough ranked that he was welcome everywhere except for the private chambers of Lucifer. A fact that Kylen knew caused the fiend dismay. It was a point of contention between them, the one tool Kylen had that could incite the demon to something akin to an emotional reaction. It drove the bastard out of his mind when Kylen taunted him with the unfairness of his position. After all the souls he'd personally retrieved for the greater evil, he was still not welcome in the innermost circle?

It was maddening to the demon.

As they trudged down, level after level, the sounds grew softer. The sharp keening from the sea of the dead in the entry-level arena was muffled this far down. But the misery here was palpable.

The demon's excitement at being this close to the threshold of his king and commander began to ebb the nearer they got, but he still pressed on. He wanted praise for his accomplishments. Wanted acknowledgement for a job well done. He craved the attention as a child would from a parent.

The temperature grew warmer, and sweat beaded across Kylen's forehead and trickled down his back. The demon's second thoughts were betrayed by a shiver that shimmied up Kylen's spine. The demon hesitated. Turned around. He'd meant to walk right up to the chamber door and demand an audience. A plan Kylen had silently encouraged because the chances of a swift physical death were all but ensured.

Kylen's soul would never make it out of Hell, but at least he wouldn't be an active participant in helping to propagate it.

The door within sight, the demon's resolve crumbled, and he retreated.

"Coward." Kylen prodded.

The demon didn't answer. He just made his way back, up and up and up, bursting into Hell's receiving area.

So much for a swift death.

* * *

Olivia opened her heavy, heavy eyelids before letting them fall shut again. The quick glimpse confirmed she was once again on the hospital bed in Ruth's house. Although her eyes refused to obey her commands, her ears worked fine. She could hear voices in the living room. They were talking. About her.

"How could this have happened? She's human. That much energy should have killed her," Deacon said.

"It was amazing. It was like she drew it from him, Deacon. He wasn't doing it *to* her. Maybe that's the trick." This time the speaker was Ruth.

"She's steadily improved since it happened," Nate interjected. "I can't do any blood work here, but her vitals are good. She should wake up soon."

"And Kylen?" Deacon asked.

"He's in the trailer. I hauled his ass out there, juiced him up with a nutrition IV—again—and he's sleeping like a baby. He was wiped, and he smelled like he'd been swimming in whiskey," Nate said.

"He was drunk?"

"Drunk? Hard to tell since he was unconscious as soon as it was over, but he sure smelled that way."

Olivia tried to force her eyes open again.

Babysteps, she reminded herself. *Come on! You can do this.*

She drew in a deep breath and tried again. Her head felt dizzy, and when she opened her eyes again, it was as if the room was rolling by in still pictures with every other frame missing. When she brought her hand up to steady her aching head, the IV needle shifted under her skin.

People need to stop poking needles into me already!

She reached over to grab the edge of the bed, hoping to maneuver herself into a sitting position, and her hand brushed something that had been tucked under her hip. She closed her fingers around it and, with a herculean effort, brought it to her chest. It was a folded piece of paper. Rolling gingerly onto her side, she unfolded it.

Her vision began to steady as she scanned the

neatly lettered page, and tears filled her eyes unbidden. It was her list. Someone had rewritten all sixty items.

The completed ones were crossed through with a ruler-straight line of black ink, exactly as they'd been on her original copy.

How?

Kylen was the only one who knew about the list. Or about the paper, at any rate. She hadn't actually told him what it was. She felt her cheeks redden when she thought of him copying down some of the items.

Like #58.

She folded the paper carefully and tucked it into the pocket of her jeans as her stirring caught the attention of those gathered in the living room.

"Olivia!" Ruth cried, rushing to her side. "Oh, Olivia. You've got to quit scaring us like that."

Nate followed Ruth, easing her aside so that he could tend to the IV. He backed the needle out, and the relief was instant. She was so going to have to impose a no-more-needles policy with these people. And maybe a do-not-resuscitate at some point. They might never let her die in peace at this rate.

"Thank you. Again," Olivia said.

"You're welcome," Nate said. "But I think Kylen did more for you than we did."

"How?" Olivia asked. "And where is he?"

"Sleeping off a long night—and now day—in his trailer," Deacon offered.

Olivia pushed herself into a sitting position with great effort and glanced out the window. The sun was setting. "What time is it?"

"It's evening, nearly dusk," Deacon said.

"And what *day* is it?" She'd lost track.

Ironic that I can still lose track of the days when they've become so precious.

But she had.

"Saturday, September 22," Nate answered.

"The equinox," Olivia sighed.

"Well, now we have all the more reason to celebrate, Olivia. Do you feel like a shower? Can I help you with that? And maybe find you some more comfortable clothes?" Ruth offered. "I'm afraid some of yours got destroyed during the whole saving-your-life thing." Olivia peeked under the light blanket she hadn't realized she was clutching to her chest. Her shirt and bra were shredded.

Good grief. At least she had pants on this time.

"A shower would be good. And a shirt. And maybe some help walking to the bathroom, I think," Olivia said.

Ruth gave the others the heave-ho, and they scattered without further comment. They were well trained. Taking Olivia's arm, she helped ease her off the bed. Olivia sighed with relief. It appeared as if her legs were actually functional, and the fuzziness in her head was starting to ease up as well.

They walked slowly to the bathroom together. "Don't worry, Olivia. I'll go find something for you to wear while you clean up. You'll feel like a new woman after this shower."

"Thank you."

Olivia sat on the edge of the tub while Ruth started the water for her and laid out a fluffy towel and washcloth like the ultimate concierge.

They had treated her well...when they weren't sticking needles into her. Even then, she knew it was because they were trying to help her. But she also knew that she was a stray they wouldn't be able to keep.

"There you go. Back in a jiffy. I'll set the clothes on the vanity for you. If you leave the rest of your clothes out, I'll wash them again." Ruth smiled and leaned forward, giving her a gentle hug. She pulled the door closed behind her when she left.

Olivia removed the list from her pocket and slid it under the tissue box, lest this one suffer the fate of the first.

Another day gone! And tonight is the equinox?

She'd already missed the light half of the day. At least she'd be awake for the darkness. Tonight, she would complete #55 *sleep under the stars on the fall equinox.* Nothing could stop her. She was determined.

She stepped into the shower and adjusted the temperature, letting the cool water rush over her body and hair. Goose bumps prickled her skin, but she already felt more awake—stronger. How she could go from unconscious to strong in a few short minutes, she didn't understand. This cancer was such a roller-coaster ride. But for now, she was strong Olivia once again. Something about the light Kylen continued to share with her was prolonging her life in a way no drugs ever could have, but she couldn't even let herself hope that it might be a cure. What she could hope was that she could hang on for a little while longer. And that would be enough. Washing her hair and body, she wondered at the stickiness on her chest. Was it from some medical intervention they'd tried on her? She scrubbed off the gluey residue and finished with a hot blast of water to warm her skin.

Stepping out of the shower, she spied the clothes Ruth had left for her, and toweled off. Black yoga pants, a black long-sleeved T-shirt, and a bright blue fleece jacket. Ruth had even thought to bring underwear and a too-big sports bra.

Weird, but better than nothing, she thought, thankful that she wouldn't have to go commando. The bra wasn't all that necessary, though. She'd lost so much weight that she had the profile of a preteen boy.

As she reached for the clothes, the steam cleared

in the bathroom, and she caught a glimpse of herself in the mirror. Once again, she was startled by what she saw. Her hair was the most shocking until she saw something truly strange—a faint trace of light blue ran beneath the surface of her skin from the hollow of her neck to the top of her pubic bone.

What is that all about?

She was falling apart, disintegrating before her own eyes, and now her body was starting to resemble a roadmap.

All the more reason to finish that damn list.

CHAPTER SIXTEEN

Deacon stood outside Kylen's trailer, fist raised, ready to knock. "You sure this is a good idea?"

"After what he did? Yes. Is he the best guy for the job? Absolutely not, but apparently, that's not up to us," Nate said.

"How long do you think her heart was stopped?" Deacon backed away from the door so that he could look at Nate.

"I have no idea. But she was dead and gone. Ruth said her aura was gone, and the AED detected no heart rhythm. We thought she was toast. We shocked her… then nothing. I'm telling you, Deacon—he saved her life. Again. Without his energy? I don't know how long she'll last. At least we know that his energy won't kill her. We don't know that about the rest of us. Considering how weak she is already…"

Deacon tipped his head back, looked up at the sky and sighed.

He rapped on the door. "Kylen, we're coming in."

When there was no answer, he pulled it open and went inside.

Kylen was crammed into the bottom bunk, snoring like a freight train. Deacon could smell the alcohol fumes from the doorway. If he lit a match, they'd blow sky-high.

Dumbass.

Like the guy needed to compound his problems by getting drunk with so many demons still on the loose. At least he was safe now. The fact that he came home at all was a blessing. Kylen had been unpredictable at best and dangerous at worst. At times Deacon saw glimpses of the Kylen he'd known in his youth, but lately? Two Kylens raged within his friend, and Deacon wasn't sure which one he was with most of the time.

He loved the guy, but it sure wasn't easy.

He poked Kylen's shoulder with a little more force than was necessary. "Kylen! Wake up!"

When he didn't stir, Deacon looked at Nate, "Did you drug him?"

"Nope, he ran out of juice and passed out. There's just nutrition in his IV."

Deacon laid his palm on Kylen's chest and pushed a jolt of orange light into him. They tried to keep themselves healthy and energized the natural way—food and rest—because juicing someone else was draining. Most days, Deacon had plenty to spare with the upgrades and all, but it wasn't a good idea to make a habit of it since they never knew when they would be pressed back into action.

This would be a night off. They'd downed a good score yesterday, making a significant dent in the remaining population. The battle was half-won. Now they needed rest. Besides, Nate had set up everything for his whole Mabon celebration. Given the latest developments and Olivia's miraculous discovery, it seemed like they might actually have something to celebrate.

Deacon gave Kylen another jolt, and he jerked to life, cracking his head on the bed above him.

Serves him right.

"Welcome back, sunshine," Deacon said.

Kylen looked around the trailer, eyes wild, trying to figure out where the hell he was. Whiskey would do that to a guy.

"Take it easy, killer. You're good," Deacon affirmed, wondering how much liquor he'd actually consumed.

Kylen kicked his still-booted feet over the side of the bed and rubbed his newly bruised head. The guy was suffering all right.

Deacon felt a pang of satisfaction. Kylen had been a Class-A asshole ever since they returned from Hell. They'd given him tons of latitude and coddling. More than they probably should have. As he watched Kylen struggle back to reality from wherever he'd been for the past few hours, the word that came to mind was *broken.*

"Get your shit together. We have to talk." Deacon walked the length of the trailer and sat at the little banquet table. Nate closed the door behind him, shutting the three of them into the tin-can house on wheels, and took a seat on the edge of the full bed on the opposite end of the trailer.

"Where's Olivia?" Kylen asked, head still in his hands.

"She's cleaning up. I hear she had a rough morning. You did, too, from the looks of things. Still think getting drunk was a good idea?" Deacon asked.

Kylen didn't answer. If experience was any indication, it would be like pulling teeth to get any kind of response out of the guy. Of course, this was going to be more of a lecture than a conversation. Lucky for him, Deacon was in a lecturing sort of mood.

"Olivia was dead, Kylen. Nate says he doesn't know how long, but somehow...someway, you brought her back. Nate thinks something about *your* energy in particular is sustaining her."

Kylen raised his head to make eye contact with Deacon, then flicked his gaze to Nate, clearly skeptical.

"I know. Go figure. None of us wants to risk juicing her, Kylen. She has some tie to you. Maybe it's because you forced the demon from her. I don't know why. But what we *do know* is that we all want to keep her alive for as long as you can." Deacon leaned forward, elbows on his knees. "Do you think you can help with that? Keeping her alive?"

Kylen lowered his gaze and studied his boots like they were a map, and he was lost in a dark wilderness. "Yes."

"Good. I was hoping you would say that. You do realize it means you'll have to take better care of yourself. You can't feed her if you don't feed yourself. Right?"

"Yes," Kylen assented.

Nate shifted like he was uncomfortable, and then lifted the side of the thin mattress to reveal a dozen more knives in various lengths and sizes. "Nice use of storage."

Deacon stood and walked to the door. "Get yourself cleaned up. You reek. Dinner will be ready in half an hour. Nate wants us all in the backyard for the bonfire and celebration afterward. I'd appreciate your company. You used to like a good party."

"I used to like a lot of things."

Deacon started down the stairs, Nate following, but he turned back after a couple of steps. "Go easy with her, Kylen. Don't break her."

With that, they left the camper, shutting the door behind them.

* * *

Kylen's head felt like a legion of imps were beating the shit out of each other inside his skull. No, the Jameson had decidedly not been a good idea, but it was the only way he could have gotten through that list.

Both dreading to see Olivia again and craving it, he couldn't shake the image of her lying on that bed. Exposed. Vulnerable. Dead.

He'd seen a lot of bad shit in his life.

Done a lot of bad shit. But that was the worst thing since…Kara.

Fuck.

How many times had he relived her murder in his head?

His mind was a jumble of death and destruction and darkness. How could he have anything to offer Olivia? But it sounded like it was too late for him to make that call. Was he tied to her now? What about when the electric-blue juice stopped working? No way was he watching another woman die on him. His shirt was stiff and crunchy, still caked in blood and gore from their confrontation with the hosts. He was a wreck and he needed a shower.

Walking over to the sink, he took slow, determined steps, careful not to jostle his aching head any more than necessary, and managed to brush his teeth, a minor miracle in itself. Grabbing a change of clothes from the top bunk, he opened the door to the full dark of evening. He'd missed an entire day… again.

How many more days did Olivia have left?

CHAPTER SEVENTEEN

Nate and Ruth had prepared a feast while Olivia was out for the count. There was so much food, and she felt a special appreciation for the abundance.

She also felt...good. And hungry.

Somehow they all managed to crowd around the small kitchen table, and Nate insisted on serving them. Two large pillar candles sat in the middle of the table: one black, one white. Nate placed a heaping bowl of what he declared to be autumn stew in front of her. It was different from the stew she'd shared with Kylen the previous night.

Just last night?

Her inner timetable was so confused. She couldn't even remember how long she'd been here anymore.

Deacon and Ruth whispered and laughed across from her while Kylen sat to her right, stoic and silent, like he always seemed to be.

She hadn't even had a chance to thank him for redoing her list. The yoga pants Ruth had given her didn't have pockets, so she'd stuffed it into her sports bra.

Finished with the preparations, Nate joined them, taking the empty chair next to Olivia's after lighting the candles.

"Let's join hands for a prayer," Nate said.

He reached for Olivia's hand, and Olivia searched under the table and took Kylen's hand in hers. A jolt coursed through her palm and up her arm. She jumped and Kylen tried to tear his hand away, but she held onto it, refusing to let him go. She smiled at him, but he didn't return the expression.

It occurred to her that she hadn't seen him smile in the entire time she'd known him. However many hours that was now. She'd have to see if she could change that.

"Kylen?" Deacon reached across the table for his other hand.

You would have thought the guy was going to come unglued by the thought of touching another person. Reluctantly, he took the proffered hand. For Kylen's sake, she hoped Nate would be brief. Otherwise the big blond badass might just spontaneously combust.

She suppressed a giggle.

Nate sighed and closed his eyes. "Equal hours of light and dark, we celebrate the balance of Mabon and ask the gods to bless us. For all that is bad, there is good. For every feeling of despair, there is hope. For the moments of pain, there are moments of love. For all that falls, there is the chance to rise again. May we find balance in our lives as we find it in our hearts. Let it be."

"Is this where I get to say 'pass the bread'?" Deacon joked as Kylen pulled his hand out of his grasp like it was on fire.

Everyone dug into the feast eagerly. And it truly was a feast, in every sense of the word. Dark bread, stew, and a corn and red pepper casserole were passed around while four bottles of wine sat open and ready on the table.

Nate filled his own glass and offered the bottle to Olivia.

Why not? She still had *#52 get drunk* to complete. Time was short and from the looks of things, the wine was plentiful.

She nodded, and Nate filled her glass to the top with sparkling white wine. Only when she went to reach for her glass did she realize that Kylen was still holding her hand under the table. Her reflex made him release his hold, and she immediately regretted it.

Raising her glass, she took a tentative sip. It was cool and refreshing, with the tiniest bite at the end.

Delicious.

No, #52 would not be a hardship at all.

* * *

Deacon pushed back from the table. "I wish every day could be Mabon. That was an awesome meal. My compliments to the chefs."

Nate stood and cleared away the dirty dishes, piling them into the sink.

Ruth beamed. "Nate orchestrated it all and even bought the groceries. I just helped him assemble everything. And wait until you see the dessert Olivia made."

Olivia shifted in her chair, her cheeks blushing at the attention. "It's the first time I've made it. I hope it's good."

Kylen watched as Nate carried a pie plate from the kitchen counter and placed it in the center of the table with a flourish, giving a nod to Olivia. "Would you do the honors?

Normally not tempted by sweets, Kylen found his mouth watering as she cut into the top of the oozing apple pastry.

It smelled so damn good.

She served him first, and to his surprise, he realized he was already holding his fork in anticipation. Her hand brushed his as she placed the pie in front of him and sparks flew between them that were clearly visible to everyone.

"Whoa!" Ruth said. "You two are a fire hazard."

Kylen forked a bite of the pie, ignoring the others as Olivia served them dessert. He neither wanted nor needed the condescending look that Deacon was sending his way. This whole *family-dinner* fiasco had been exhausting. He was not family. Or if he was, he was the black sheep or the third cousin twice-removed who'd recently been paroled from prison.

"Oh. My. God. This is the best dessert ever, Olivia," Ruth said, closing her eyes as she wrapped her lips around her second forkful of pie.

"She's right, Olivia. It's very, very good." Deacon offered, punctuating his praise with a smile.

"Amen that," Nate agreed.

Kylen shoveled in his first bite, and for a horrifying moment, he felt like making a Valley-girl proclamation of his own. It really *was* the best dessert ever. And that was saying something from a guy who'd been around for more than a couple of centuries.

The girl could bake.

He finished his piece, and then rose from the table to escape outside, away from the supernatural Brady Bunch, away from the love-fest that was threatening to dull his edge.

Olivia's list came to mind as he walked out into the chilly fall night—*#52 make the best dessert ever.* Her list was getting shorter.

And so was her time.

* * *

"Thank you all," Olivia said, carrying the empty pie plate to the sink.

"For what, hon?" Ruth stacked the remaining dishes into the soapy water.

"For helping me enjoy my last few days. It's been…interesting. But I really am ready to go home now. Tomorrow, I'd like to leave. I have…commitments to fulfill."

Deacon came up behind Ruth and slid his arms around her waist. "Olivia, I know it's difficult to accept or even believe what you've learned these past few days, but all things considered, I think it's for your own good to stay with us a little longer."

"Deacon, there are things I still want to accomplish before it's too late. Things I can't do out here in the middle of the woods no matter how kind or intriguing you all are." She searched his face for understanding, fully realizing that he was the one in control of this group.

"You might be a target for the demons again now that they have you on their radar. Please consider staying here a little longer."

"That's what I'm trying to explain to you. I don't have 'a little longer.' It's my life. I understand the risks more than most. I'm not going to spend the rest of my time under lock and key. If you won't help me leave, I'll find another way. But I *am* going home. Tomorrow."

Nate dried his hands and set the last clean dish in the cabinet. "Maybe Kylen could go with her? Protect her while she does what she needs to do, and then bring her back here?"

"We would all be safer if we just stayed here,"

Deacon said.

"Of course, but we made a big bust last night. It should take the demons at least a couple of days to regroup. Besides, none of us likes living in a bubble, Deacon. I'm pretty confident that Kylen can handle himself and protect Olivia."

"Would you send Ruth out there with him?" Deacon asked.

"After what I saw him do last night? Yeah, I would. He may be a social train wreck, but he's damn efficient at exterminating demons," Nate said. "And keeping her alive."

"I don't like it."

"Deacon, Nate is right," Ruth said, turning in Deacon's arms to give him a light kiss. "She's a big girl. She can make her own decisions. Have you learned nothing about women over the past four months? We'll find a way. It's easier if you help us instead of fight us."

She smiled up at him.

"If you can convince Kylen to go with you, I'll back off." He gave Olivia a smug smile. "Good luck with that."

Nate headed to the back door. "Come on," he said. "Let's start a fire."

CHAPTER EIGHTEEN

Olivia wasn't sure if it was the starry night, the warmth from the last smoldering logs on the fire or the bottom of her second glass of wine, but she felt utterly content sitting in the canvas sling chair beside the dying bonfire.

Nate added the final touches to a beautiful Mabon altar full of gifts from the woods nearby, including acorns, three huge oak leaves, pine needles, apples from the farmers' market, pumpkins of various sizes and a full glass of wine. He'd encouraged them all to consider what they were thankful for as he lit the bonfire, but he'd spared them from having to recite their blessings aloud when Kylen threatened to retreat to his trailer. Their prayers were supposed to float straight up to the gods from the fire. She'd sent up several, including a request for a few more days.

Deacon had promised he'd withdraw his objections to her leaving if Kylen went with her. Since Kylen hadn't said even one word to her since dinner, she was less than hopeful about his answer. She barely knew him at all, and yet she already knew better than to ask him in front of everyone else.

He would not be happy to babysit her while she was on her list-completing mission. Considering the remaining items on her list, the whole prospect was rather mortifying. Still, she was determined to see it through.

Across the fire pit, Deacon took Ruth's hand and pulled her to her feet, leading her toward the house.

"Good night," he said. "Olivia, please don't leave the mowed perimeter of the yard. You'll be safe as long as you stay within the circle of protection, but it ends at the perimeter." He directed a hard stare at Kylen, which felt like a warning, even to Olivia.

As they crossed the lawn, she wondered why there was still so much animosity between the two friends. Ruth had explained some of their history, but there were some missing puzzle pieces, and she was pretty sure she wasn't going to get answers from Kylen. To say that he wasn't a talker would be the understatement of the century. He'd said less than a hundred words to her.

Most of those in one-word sentences.

Nate followed. "I'm going to turn in, too. Olivia, I'll sleep out on the couch. You can have my bed if you'd rather not spend another night in a hospital bed."

Olivia felt her cheeks redden and was thankful for the cover of darkness. "That's very kind, Nate." She decided not to tell him that she'd be sleeping out here, under the stars.

She watched as he disappeared into the house, too.

The fire crackled and popped, and then winked out, leaving her alone in the growing darkness with Kylen and one more bottle of wine. The vacuum of silence was overwhelming as she leaned forward for the bottle. She was reasonably sure she'd succeeded quite well in fulfilling #52, but her anxiety about making a request of Kylen—about being alone out here with him— demanded more fuel.

As she fumbled for traction on the wine bottle, she lost her balance and fell forward. Kylen flashed in front of her, pulling her away from the fire just before she fell onto the smoldering coals. Blue sparks raced up her forearms where his hands were touching her flesh. Her head was fuzzy and swimmy, her legs unsteady beneath her.

"Oops. I guess maybe I've had enough?" She shivered.

He looked amazing in the moonlight, which made his hard features seem softer despite the scowl on his face. His blond hair all but glowed in the darkness, and the desire to touch his face was so strong she curled her hands into fists to resist the impulse. She couldn't help but wonder what his smile might look like.

"Yes, you have. You need to go inside to bed. You're cold."

"No…I mean, yes, I am cold, but I'm not going inside to bed. You read my list. Tonight is #55. Do you remember #55?" Emboldened, she reached into her shirt and down her sports bra, retrieving the list. Unfolding it with meticulous precision, she turned it toward his face and pointed to #55.

"Sleep under the stars on the fall equinox." She wobbled again. "And that's what I'm going to do."

"You can't sleep out here. You'll freeze to death," he said, keeping his fingers curled around her forearms.

"Well, that would certainly speed things up."

He frowned at her again. Did the man have any other expression?

"Sit," he said. "Don't move. I don't want to find you up in flames when I come back."

Pushing her back into the camp chair, he hesitated for a moment, and then pulled her to her feet again, scooting the chair another three feet away from the coals. "Sit."

She complied, feeling like a chastised dog. Seriously, she was fine.

Drunk, but fine.

Leaning her head back against the chair, she looked up at the night sky. Now that the fire was down to a few glowing embers and her eyes had finally adjusted to the darkness, stars started popping out of the sky like jewels dangling from invisible chains. She blinked. It was almost as if she could pluck one from the sky. Reaching up, she batted the air above her head in a half-hearted attempt.

"What the hell are you doing?" Kylen asked, appearing beside her with a sleeping bag and an armful of blankets.

"There are so many stars…"

Kylen looked up at the sky, and then back at her. Either that or he was rolling his eyes at her, which seemed unimaginable even in her drunken state.

She watched as he dropped the sleeping bag, and then spread the blankets on the ground beside her chair, well away from the fire.

"If you're sleeping outside, you're going to need this." He unfurled the bag on top of the blankets and unzipped it.

He moved in front of her and stood there, towering over her. She stared up, up, up his torso. He'd pulled on a black fleece, which completed his dark ensemble.

The man in black. She giggled again.

"What now?"

"Is black the only color you wear?"

"Yes." He reached for her hands and pulled her

to her feet. She rose too quickly for her head to catch up, so she wrapped her arms around his waist for balance. He stiffened in her hold, his entire body as rigid as a mannequin's, and stared into the forest behind her, purposely avoiding her gaze. She admired the sharp angle of his jaw and chin, and then leaned in for a more thorough ogle.

The wine was making her brave…or stupid.

Didn't matter.

"You're very handsome," she said, expecting him to push her away.

"You're very drunk."

"Yes, I think I am. Another list item successfully accomplished. After tonight, I'll only have ten left."

He crinkled his forehead, his lips forming a tight, white line, and then looked down at her.

"Nine."

"Nine?"

"You'll have nine things left on the list after tonight."

Confused, she tried to process what he'd said with her wine-drenched brain.

"Make the best dessert ever. You did that. #51."

She felt a slow smile extend across her face as her heart raced in her chest. "You think so?"

"Ruth said so."

"But do *you* think so?" she asked, all but begging him for the compliment.

"Yes."

The electric blue sparks arced between them again, and she felt his energy flowing into her, filling her with light. It wasn't painful or unpleasant. It never had been. But it was surprising and unexpected each time.

She swooned, and he wrapped his arms around her, pulling her against his hard body. A sudden heat built between them, and she pressed her lips to the hollow of his neck. Kylen scooped her into his arms and carried her over to the makeshift pallet in the grass. He lay her down on the sleeping bag, hesitated for a moment and then backed away from her, looking more than a little spooked.

Confused, she asked, "What's wrong?"

"Nothing. You need sleep."

"What about you?"

He lowered himself into the camp chair where she'd been sitting, crossed his arms over his chest and stared at the now nonexistent fire. "I'll keep watch."

"Watch for what? Deacon said we were safe inside the perimeter, and I don't plan on sleepwalking."

"You have a way of finding trouble."

She smiled. "Deacon seems to think so, too." She snuggled down into the sleeping bag, lying on her back so she could look up into the sea of stars. "He doesn't want to let me leave tomorrow to complete my list unless you'll go with me. To protect me."

Silence. Crickets. More silence.

She closed her eyes, willing him to respond. "Did you hear me? Will you go with me?"

Her voice sounded desperate even to her own ears. It felt like he held her future in his hands, like he'd be the difference between the success or failure of her mission. Yet another aspect of her life that was not under her control.

"Kylen...please." She hated pleading, but it was the only weapon she had left.

She wouldn't ask him again. Assuming she had her answer, she rolled away from him and closed her eyes. A tear slid down her face as she curled her knees up into her stomach, the ground cold despite the sleeping bag and the blankets underneath.

What felt like hours later, as she was finally drifting off, she heard Kylen rise and walk toward her.

His steps crunched in the dry grass, but she stayed perfectly still, feigning sleep. She felt him draw another blanket over her. And then he did something unexpected—he reclined on the ground beside her.

She debated for only a moment, and then pushed herself against his stony length, soaking up his warmth. His blue energy flowed into her even through the many layers of cloth, seeming to saturate to her very soul. He was like a human electric blanket, and the heat between them seemed to promise so much more than a warm night under the stars. There was something between them, and even Kylen couldn't deny it. Otherwise he never would have joined her on the ground.

He stayed as still as the dead behind her, feeding her with his energy and light.

She knew his answer. He would take her. He would protect her. Now it was up to her to follow through on the last items on the list.

CHAPTER NINETEEN

As the birds began to wake in the morning woods, Kylen opened his eyes to the first rays of pink light streaming through the opening in the trees. The sky was vibrant with soft layers of violet, pink and orange. He didn't know if he'd ever seen a more beautiful sunrise. Certainly not in the past four months while his vision was grayed out. He only hoped the colors would last this time.

The fact that Olivia lay curled against him, her snow-white hair fanned out behind her, made his heart feel slightly lighter, almost buoyant. Good God, he was going soft.

Get a grip.

He rolled out from under the blanket and stood, staring down at her. At least Deacon hadn't come out to look for her yet. He didn't care to explain why he'd spent the night in the backyard with her. The questions would never stop. He headed behind his trailer to relieve himself, and then went inside to brush his teeth. That was pretty much the extent of his personal maintenance routine these days.

Once inside the trailer, he decided to change into a clean set of clothes since his smelled like campfire smoke. Not that he minded, but...*whatever.* As his stomach let out a loud growl, he realized with surprise that he was starving. Olivia had drained a lot of energy from him over the course of the night. She still didn't really know what was going on or how he was prolonging her life. Hell, he didn't know much more than she did. All he knew was that every time they made any sort of contact, she drew energy from him like a current...without him even *trying* to juice her.

Well, as long as she needed him, he would help her.

He slid a fresh T-shirt over his head and tucked it into his black fatigue pants. Sliding his belt through the loops, he realized he needed to buckle it one notch looser. He'd been eating a ton lately. Or at least much more than he had been over the past few months. It looked like he was finally filling back out.

Rolling up his pants one leg at a time, he strapped a sheathed push blade onto each calf. He would have liked to wear more, but he'd discovered that it sent the locals into fits of panic when he walked around in the daylight that way.

Whatever.

He wasn't about to go anywhere unprepared.

Adjusting his belt yet again, he found himself thinking about how wispy-thin Olivia was. He'd watched her consume several good meals over the past couple of days, but it was going to take a lot more than that to get her to a healthy weight. Six meals a day, seven days a week, and a steady supplement of blue energy and maybe... Then came the sickening realization: time was the one thing she didn't have.

A timid knock at his door spun him around.

"Kylen?" Olivia asked.

He cracked open the door, and she stepped back so that he could swing it wide enough for her to come through. She entered timidly, like she was slightly disappointed with the whole thing. He looked around his trailer, trying to see it through her eyes.

Yep, it was pathetic.

His entire life fit into one hundred and ninety-two square feet.

She sat on the edge of the big bed and folded her hands in her lap. "This is nice," she lied.

"It's a dump. But it's mine."

"Well, it certainly requires minimal maintenance. You could use some curtains, though."

"Yes."

"Thank you, Kylen." Olivia looked down at her hands.

"For what?" he asked, confused.

"For sleeping with me last night. For recopying my list. For helping me complete it. It means a lot to me. You're the only one who even knows about it."

"I didn't *sleep* with you." And he hadn't. He had just lain there beside her with a rock-hard cock and bad intentions, looking up at the stars as they slid across the sky. All. Night. Long.

"You know what I mean," she smiled coyly. "So, when can we leave? I'd like to get started early."

Kylen ran a hand through his hair. "Breakfast first. Yes?"

"Sure."

"Then I thought maybe I could help you with another list thing."

Olivia swallowed hard, her eyes big as cue balls. "Which one?"

"Number 56."

She smiled. "Learn to use a weapon? What did

you have in mind?"

Kylen turned and reached behind the neat stacks of black clothing on the top bunk, retrieving a long scabbard. He drew the scythe from the sheath carefully, and then flicked his wrist, brandishing it with a flourish.

"Oh my!" she squealed with delight. "Yes, that will work!"

Olivia reached for the weapon but he kept a firm grasp on it. She traced her thumb across the engravings on its handle. "It's beautiful. Is it old?"

"Very."

"Where did you get it? It looks like something out of Dungeons and Dragons."

"It's Valkyrie-made."

"What does that mean?"

"It means it's valuable. So don't break it." Kylen folded the blade and slid it back into the scabbard, placing it behind his wardrobe. He hadn't even looked at it since stowing it on the bed a few months ago. He told himself it only made sense to let Olivia use it. The weapon was stronger but also more lightweight than the scythe he carried himself. It was a woman's weapon. It had been Kara's and the demon had kept it as a souvenir, a taunt really, but Kylen had secretly found it a comfort and shielded his need for it in his heart. The weapon was his only remaining physical connection to Kara.

"Are you going to let me use it?"

"You have to eat breakfast first." He walked to the door and pushed it open. "After you."

* * *

Raised voices in the house brought them both to attention. Kylen drew the push blade from his leg sheath and shoved Olivia behind him as he entered the house through the laundry room, making as little noise as possible.

"Why did you wait so long to tell me?" Deacon thundered. "Dammit, Ruth, you've been putting yourself in danger. You've been putting the baby in danger."

Kylen came to an abrupt stop at the word *baby* and surveyed the room. Nate sat on the couch, his hands pressing into his knees as if he were trying to hold himself down. Ruth was standing in the doorway to her bedroom, hands on her hips in defiance. The words *domestic disturbance* came to mind, and Kylen wanted to bolt for the trailer more than anything in this world or the next.

Olivia put a gentle hand on his back, and he felt the spark of her touch. They stood frozen in place together. Not sure whether to stay or go.

Deacon loomed over Nate, his finger pointed out like a weapon. "And you're no better. You've known for how long? You're a *medical professional.* This isn't a game. Our job—our lives—are not conducive to creating or sustaining life. Or haven't you two noticed?" He directed his anger back at Ruth. "I don't even know how this happened. We've both been traveling the consecrated subway constantly...*carrying souls...*" He shook his head like he was trying to shake some sense into it. "It shouldn't be possible to conceive a child that way. It hasn't been done before. There's no telling what horrors we're in for now. Good God."

Deacon sat down hard on the hearth, dropping his head into his hands.

The room was deadly silent.

Ruth walked over to Deacon hesitantly and came to a stop when she reached him. She took his head in her hands and pulled him to her stomach, holding him there as he wrapped his arms around her waist.

"Deacon, I didn't know that traveling the subway while pregnant was dangerous. You didn't tell me. I still have a lot to learn. We both do." Ruth rubbed his back in slow circles.

His shoulders heaved once, twice, and then settled as he tried to pull himself together.

Nate walked over to them and put a hand on Ruth's shoulder. "I have a friend who's an OBGYN at the hospital. She'll take a look at Ruth and make sure things are okay. I'll drive her there now. She isn't more than a few weeks pregnant, Deacon. If it's meant to be, it will, no matter what the rules are. Nature finds a way."

Nate walked into his room, nodding to Kylen on the way, and closed his door behind him. Ruth whispered to Deacon, her words too soft to be heard from Kylen and Olivia's vantage point.

Kylen took Olivia's hand and led her to the kitchen. "Looks like we're eating out," he said in an undertone.

He grabbed a box of cereal from one of the cabinets and handed it to Olivia, removing a gallon of milk from the fridge next. After taking two bowls from the cabinet and spoons from the drawer, he quietly left the house—Olivia behind him—and returned to the trailer.

* * *

"That was intense." Olivia chased her last Cheerios around the bowl with her spoon.

"Yes."

"Deacon didn't seem very excited about the baby. How long have they been together?"

"Four months."

"Oh. I guess that's sort of sudden."

"In our time, it's not even a moment." Kylen tipped his bowl to his mouth to drink his cereal milk.

"What do you mean? In your time?" Olivia

leaned back in the small eating nook and looked at him quizzically.

"Ruth didn't explain this to you?"

"Guess not. What is there to explain?

Kylen sighed. This is exactly why they didn't mix with humans except while working. And the dead didn't ask questions. Thank God.

"We have an exceedingly long life span unless we're killed."

"How long?"

"Centuries."

"Oh."

He could see her wheels turning as she tried to calculate how old he might be. "Two hundred and eight."

"But you look like you're in your late twenties, maybe early thirties." She perched her elfin chin on her hands, studying his features in uncomfortable detail.

"We stop aging as soon as we harvest our first soul. There's an extensive training period from birth until the first reaping, and then time basically stops for us. As long as we avoid a beheading and make sure we fuel up enough, we can live indefinitely."

Her eyes blinked rapidly as she processed his words. "Wow," she said.

"You'd be surprised how boring living so long can be."

"Well, I'd be willing to give it a try."

"Why are you smiling?"

"You need to learn to appreciate what you have. And that answer was the longest sentence you've ever said to me." She smiled up at him, her tone playful.

Kylen felt something dangerously close to a smile pull at the corners of his mouth, but he narrowed his eyes at her instead.

"Let's go slice and dice something."

CHAPTER TWENTY

Olivia sat in the camp chair near last night's fire ring, enjoying the play of the morning sun on her face while Kylen gathered materials for her lesson. When she'd added *#56 learn to use a weapon* to her list, she'd figured she'd probably go target shooting or something. Frankly, learning to use a scythe hadn't even been on her radar. Who even used a scythe as a weapon?

She certainly had an answer now. Reapers.

It occurred to her that Kylen or one of the others might need to reap her soul. It was oddly comforting to know that it would be a friend who did the deed. She wondered if they felt the same way. Did they like knowing the people whose souls they carried or did they prefer to keep it all business?

As a direct result of her family's health problems, she'd always wondered what happened to a soul after death. She'd sought answers from a variety of religions over the years before finally settling on her own cobbled version of faith and an afterlife—one that gave her solace and peace. Over the past few months the question had become especially pertinent. What happened to a soul after it was reaped? If she could get lucky enough to have another full-sentence conversation with Kylen, she'd ask him what would happen after she passed.

A commotion at the back door caught her attention, and she rose to see what was going on. The others were leaving the house in a group.

"Hey, Olivia," Ruth said as she headed for the Lincoln.

"Where's Kylen?" Deacon asked, holding the back door open for Ruth.

"He's around the front of the house," Olivia answered, keeping her answer purposely vague. She wasn't at all sure they'd approve of her scythe lessons.

"How are you feeling today, Olivia?" Nate asked.

"Great. Better than I have in a long time." She smiled at him as he slid behind the wheel.

Kylen walked around the side of the house, the pumpkins from the front porch stacked in his arms. Deacon gave him a puzzled look, but didn't ask for an explanation. Kylen didn't offer one.

"We're taking Ruth to Meridian for a checkup. I have no idea when we'll be back. You got this, Kylen?"

"Yes."

Deacon looked from Kylen to Olivia. He shut Ruth's door and walked around to the back passenger door. "We'll see you later tonight?"

"I guess that depends on Olivia's business."

"Really?" He shook his head in obvious frustration. "Keep your head."

Olivia watched as they drove off, leaving her alone with Kylen once again.

* * *

"Planning to make a pie?" Olivia asked, amused.

"You're going to practice on these since we don't have any demons handy."

Olivia frowned at him. Demons. Kylen had saved her from one. She knew that now. He was a hunter, or at least that was what Ruth had told her. She still couldn't wrap her mind around the idea, and she had no clue how she'd recognize a demon if she saw one. Obviously, she hadn't identified the one in the alley.

Kylen walked around the back of the garage and returned with an armful of logs. Taking meticulous care, he placed them upright around the fire pit, positioning a pumpkin on top of each of the ten perches.

Once he was satisfied with the setup, he walked to his trailer and returned with the scythe he'd shown her earlier. Kylen drew it from the scabbard and presented it to her. "Hold it. Carefully."

Olivia took it with both hands. It was heavier than it looked. Her right hand grasped the smooth grip, just below the engravings, as her left cradled the folded blade. She held it before her like she would a lovely but poisonous snake.

"Not that carefully." Kylen moved behind her, enclosing her scythe-hand in his. Blue sparks sizzled as skin touched skin.

He adjusted her grip on the blade, holding her tightly to his chest as he helped her find the correct balance with the weapon. "Loosen up," he demanded.

Olivia laughed. "Maybe I would if you didn't have me trapped in a bear hug."

Kylen gave her a little more space, but he kept his right hand firmly wrapped over hers, helping her hold the blade with one hand. "To open the blade, flick your wrist. Hard. Like you mean it. When you hear the click, it's locked in place, and you can swing it."

"Show me," Olivia said.

Kylen took the scythe from her and backed away. In one fluid motion, he flicked open the blade, brought it even with his shoulder, and then slashed the first pumpkin in half horizontally. The top half lifted slightly before falling back into place on the bottom half. Not even a seed spilled out, and a hairline cut sliced completely through the pumpkin.

Olivia clapped and laughed. "Amazing!"

Kylen rolled his eyes upward and folded the blade shut again. "Your turn."

After taking hold of the blade, Olivia made an attempt to flick it open. The scythe flew from her grasp, hitting the ground behind her with a clatter. "Sorry! Let me try again."

She picked up the blade and held it in her hand again. Flexing her wrist, she tried to determine the appropriate amount of force to exert. Satisfied with her calculations, she folded the weapon in against her chest. Using her elbow as a hinge, she extended the blade in a swift forward motion. Sure enough, the blade unfolded and locked into place.

Taking a step toward the next pumpkin, she swung the scythe back and then slashed through the pumpkin with such force that the scythe nearly sliced through her leg upon its exit. She spun with the momentum of the stroke.

The top half of the pumpkin glided off its bottom half in slow motion, sliding to the ground with a wet splat.

Olivia couldn't keep the smile off her face. "Well?"

"Adequate. Again. Try not to cut your leg off this time."

Olivia closed the blade, advanced on the next pumpkin in the ring and repeated the process, this time without the ballerina moves on the follow-through. She glanced back at Kylen for approval.

"Next," he instructed.

She narrowed her eyes at him before snapping the blade shut and shuffling to the next pumpkin. As she lined up to take on the fifth pumpkin, Kylen stayed her hand and took the blade from her. "Let's try something a little more difficult."

He took the volleyball-sized pumpkin from the log and backed away from her.

Holding the pumpkin in his left hand and the scythe in his right, he tossed the gourd into the air, flicked open his blade, and sliced through it midair. It split in half—its entrails leaking out as it tumbled to the ground.

Cocking his head to the side, he handed her the blade and retrieved the next pumpkin. "I'll toss. You slice."

Nervous that she might lop off one of his appendages, she backed away from him. He tossed the pumpkin high into the air, giving her plenty of time to open the blade and bring it slashing back through the projectile before it smashed to the ground.

"Huh," he said, a hint of a smile turning up the corners of his mouth.

So close to a smile, yet so far from it! She couldn't slap the smile off her own face. She couldn't believe she'd hit the pumpkin like that on the first go. It was very…satisfying.

"More!"

Olivia sliced and diced the next five pumpkins midair. She didn't miss once.

"Nice," Kylen complimented.

Olivia felt her cheeks redden as the warmth of that small compliment filled her from head to toe. She was happy she'd pleased him and impressed with herself for accomplishing such a bizarre task. "Another one bites the dust. Number 56 is history!"

Kylen frowned and gathered up the pumpkin carnage, piling it into the center of the fire pit. The remains would probably be scavenged by raccoons—or perhaps the cats she'd seen in the woods—by nightfall.

It was only a quarter to ten but her stomach growled again loudly. Kylen heard it and whipped around to look at her. "You're hungry?"

"Guess so! I've been eating way more over the past couple of days than I have in months."

"Good. I know a place. We'll eat first, and then..." He walked over to the spigot by the back of the house and starting cleaning his scythe.

"Then you'll help me work on my list. Right?"

He dried and buffed the blade before folding it and sliding the weapon into the concealed scabbard on his back. "Right," he mumbled unenthusiastically.

Olivia walked toward the Honda.

"Where are you going?" Kylen asked.

"Aren't we ready to go?"

"Yes, but we aren't traveling that way."

Confused, she stopped. "What do you mean?"

"Come inside, we're going the easy way...maybe."

She followed him into the house, and then into the living room. When he was standing on the strange markings that were burned into the floor, he reached for her hand. A jolt flashed through her as she took it and allowed him to pull her in next to him.

He wrapped his arms around her from behind, and energy crackled up her spine where their bodies touched. Leaning in, he said, "If this works, we'll be there in a few seconds. If not, I'll come back to get you, and we'll take the Honda."

"If what works?" she asked, as the room began

157

to shimmer and spin around her. Her stomach lurched, and for a moment she thought she was going to be ill. It was like they were on a crazy amusement park ride, but everything was speeding by so fast it was a blur. Her head swam far worse than after the second glass of wine last night.

When her world stopped spinning, she found herself standing inside an elaborate stone crypt, still locked in the grip of Kylen's arms. Her legs crumbled beneath her, and she was sure she was about to pass out when Kylen's blue energy began to seep into her through his hands, which were clutching her back. The warm light raced through her, restoring her to her senses.

As her head swooned back, she drew in a gasping breath, making eye contact with Kylen. He pulled her to her feet again and took a step back, energy still flowing between them.

"How did you do that?" she asked, relieved by how much better she felt.

"The travel or the energy?"

"Both."

"Let's go eat, and I'll tell you."

CHAPTER TWENTY-ONE

He took her hand and led her from the crypt into the most beautiful cemetery she'd ever seen. Century-old oak and maple trees created a shady canopy, and the grass was clipped low to the ground, edged to perfection around each marker. A variety of stones and markers were arranged in neat grids across the grounds. In fact, it really seemed much more like a park than a cemetery. Stone benches were scattered throughout, too, and there was even a picnic table under a gazebo in the center of the grounds.

They left the cemetery and walked in silence, Kylen leading her several blocks down the busy main street in Meridian. White-collar workers hustled across the sidewalks in their shiny shoes and crisp suits, in and out of office buildings surrounding the bustling historic town square.

Kylen pulled her down a narrow alley, darkened by the height of the buildings that surrounded it. He stopped at a heavy wooden door and pulled her into a tavern advertising Stag beer above it. As lunch destinations went, this would not have been her first choice. She'd visited several lovely bistros in the area for her "Food & Cuisine" column. Gilardis or The Aviary would have been delightful, although she had trouble picturing Kylen sitting at one of those tiny round tables eating a cannoli or crepe.

After surveying the bar, filled with just a few hardcore patrons scattered throughout, Kylen led her to a booth against the back wall. Motioning for her to sit across from him, he took a seat that put his back against the wall and gave him a full view of the one visible door. A busty waitress sashayed over with two glasses of water, ready to take their orders. Kylen ordered for them both without making eye contact with the waitress: two cheeseburgers, a basket of fries and a beer for himself.

"You got it, sugar," she said. "You're here awful early today. We usually don't see you until the wee hours."

Kylen ignored her, and she left to turn in their order.

"A friend of yours?" Olivia asked.

"No."

"Well, I would hope not. You were very rude to her."

Kylen grunted and leaned back in the booth, stretching out his legs under the table and crossing his arms over his chest in an I-am-relaxed-but-don't-mess-with-me pose.

Unintimidated, Olivia continued, "I need some answers, Kylen. Ruth told me a lot, but it's so different to have actually experienced it.... I still don't get how you zapped us to the cemetery. And more importantly, why every time you touch me you shock the crap out of me...in a good kind of way," she added shyly.

"We're not human, Olivia. Not entirely. We can travel through the equivalent of a subway from consecrated ground to consecrated ground. Most supernatural entities can move this way. Some have more restrictions, some have less. Demons and the minions of Hell move through different portals. Deacon and Nate don't even need to enter the subway through consecrated ground. They can access it from anywhere."

"That's amazing! How is it that no one knows about this? Humans, I mean. And how come you can take me with you?"

"Humans can't see most aspects of Heaven or Hell. You can imagine the problems it would cause if they could. Reapers can see…everything."

"And me? How is it I can travel with you? Can you take anyone? Anything?"

"We can take any physical objects that we can carry. As for you…Ruth thinks it's because your aura is white."

"The death aura."

"Yes." Kylen frowned at her. "Ruth explained what the colors mean?"

"Only the white. Is mine still white?"

Kylen drank from his water glass and stared toward the door like it was the most interesting thing he'd ever seen. "Mostly."

"What does that mean? Mostly?" She'd get answers from him if she had to pry each one out—which, at this rate, she'd probably have to.

He sighed and rubbed the bridge of his nose like he had a bad headache. "It seems to alternate between white and blue."

"How?"

"Good God, do I look like Doctor Oz? I don't know how all of this works. All I know is that every time we come into contact, you draw energy from me. And somehow that seems to be… prolonging your life."

"You're keeping me alive?" she whispered.

"Yes."

She searched his face, looking for... something. Something to explain why a reaper, *this* reaper, would want to keep her alive when it would be so much easier for him, for all of them, to let her die as nature intended.

"What happens to my soul when I die?"

The waitress brought their food, along with Kylen's beer, and set it all down on the table. Kylen picked up the beer and took a long pull.

"Anything else, sugar?" she asked.

"Bring me two more of these," Kylen said, tilting back the beer and finishing it.

"I will. But it's awful early, sugar. Pace yourself."

Kylen scowled as the waitress left and Olivia pressed on, "What will happen to me, Kylen?"

"After you die, a reaper will collect your soul and take it to Purgatory for processing. You'll be sent to Heaven or Hell, and then you'll begin the process of ascending or descending through the various levels of wherever you're sent."

"Who decides where I go?"

"An angel, Rashnu, does the initial sorting."

"And the demons? What do they have to do with all of this?"

"The demons work for Camael. Camael is...*was* an angel. Now he's classified as a fallen angel. He's a duke of Hell, and he commands legions of demons on Lucifer's behalf. The demons collect souls and take them straight to Hell. They don't get sorted, and they can't be retrieved. We think that the more souls he has, the stronger his demon army becomes. A war is coming. We're trying to prevent it."

"And if you can't?"

"The term *Hell on Earth* will become a real thing."

Olivia pushed her food around her plate, her appetite gone. Kylen's studious appraisal of her made her self-conscious and uncomfortable. She knew she still didn't understand the extent of what they were up against, but she was secretly grateful she wouldn't be around to see it. She had her own battle to fight.

"Eat," Kylen demanded, his own plate already empty.

"I'm not really hungry anymore."

"We are not leaving here until you've eaten everything on your plate."

She smiled at him. "You're not the boss of me."

"I am for today."

Amused, she bit into the hamburger to placate him. It was delicious.

* * *

It was almost eleven when Kylen led them back to the crypt in the cemetery. He surveyed their surroundings. Things probably wouldn't get too dicey until after dark, but that wasn't a given. Imps, demons and worse things could move about in the daylight, but they preferred the darkness because of the protection and anonymity it offered. They would have eight hours of peace. If they were lucky.

"Will you take me home now?" Olivia asked as she followed him through the door of the crypt.

"Where do you live?"

"An apartment in Maple Wood."

"Is that near Maple Park Cemetery?"

"Yes, it's a few blocks away."

"Good," he said. Sometimes a guy really could get lucky.

"Come." He pulled her into his arms. His blue energy danced across her skin as they shimmered and spun toward Maple Park.

There was no crypt where they landed in Maple Park, but the cemetery was much smaller and, thanks to the almost unbroken canopy of old-growth maple trees, it was shady even in the midday sun. There were so many big trees that the stones were set at random around them instead of in a neat grid like in the downtown cemetery. The trees had probably been here long before the first corpses.

"Which way?" Kylen asked, glancing around the small expanse of the cemetery for any potential threats.

"Follow me," Olivia said, taking his hand this time to lead the way.

They walked down a broken sidewalk through a quiet neighborhood of brick buildings and Victorian homes. It was Meridian's historic district, and many of the houses were probably about as old as the maples.

"There." Olivia pointed to the top floor of a renovated Victorian.

She keyed in a code on the security pad, and they walked through the shared entry door before winding up three sets of stairs to her small suite of rooms.

Kylen had noticed a shared kitchen and laundry room on the bottom level. "How many people live here?" he asked.

"There are four separate apartments. Mine's the largest because it spans the entire top floor."

When they reached the top of the stairs, Olivia unlocked her door and pulled him inside. Her entire apartment could be viewed from the doorway. It consisted of a spacious 20 by 24 living room, a small bathroom with a claw-foot tub and wraparound shower curtain, and another 20 by 24 bedroom with a small study and library arranged between the two dormers on the front-side of the house.

A Victorian gothic theme characterized the decor, from the rich burgundy walls to the heavy damask- striped curtains hanging from the side windows. The two dormered windows, which were surrounded by shelves and shelves of books, were paned with stained glass.

A sofa table with ornately carved legs stood behind a red velvet couch in the living area. Two mahogany wing chairs squatted on the corners of a richly detailed Persian rug. An intense wallpaper pattern of ridiculously large velvet-embossed flowers covered two walls of the living room.

The entire apartment was such an incredible mishmash of patterns and dark colors it bordered on horrendous.

It reminded him of Hell. At least it smelled better.

"It came furnished. And decorated," Olivia said, acknowledging his look of abject horror. "None of the decor is mine. Only the books and clothes, really...and a few other things."

He nodded. Speechless.

He caught a glimpse of the decoratively draped four-poster bed in her bedroom and broke out into a cold sweat. The room looked remarkably similar to the suite they'd rescued Deacon from in Hell.

"I have some housekeeping to do. There's a club my friend from work told me about. Tonight is karaoke night, and I'd like to go. Will you take me?"

His head said no. But his heart said that this is what he'd signed on for. He'd agreed to help her, although against his better judgment. The sooner she got this ridiculous list finished the sooner he could get back to his job—his *real* job—and get her back to the safety of the compound.

"Yes."

Her smile settled into his chest and pushed his heart down into his stomach.

This was a very bad idea.

Returning to the living area, he sat on one of the stiff wing chairs as Olivia went to her bedroom. When he heard the shower turn on, he got up to pace the room. He hated this place. It was impossible to secure and with only one door, the place was a fire hazard. Probably didn't even have a fire escape. Drawing back the dark burgundy drapes, he looked out the window. There was no fire escape and only the shallowest overhang, which slanted too severely off the roof to use for an escape.

He hated everything about the place. Movement in the alley between homes caught his eye. Three imps sat hunched against the side of the neighboring house, staring up at him, waiting like jackals.

He found himself hoping he wouldn't have anything to feed them tonight.

Kylen wasn't sure how long her chores might take, but a crazy plan began to form in his own mind. If he was going to help her in this ridiculous quest, maybe he could help her to achieve at least two of her bucket list items in short order. As an added bonus, they'd take them far away from the dangers of Meridian...for the time being at least. *#47 swim in the ocean* and *#49 fly over a volcano* could both be accomplished in one place and within a few hours. It had been a long time since he'd been there. Too long. She'd love it.

When the shower stopped he called out to her before he lost his nerve.

"Olivia."

The door opened and she peeked through the crack in the door, her hair dripping with water. "Yes."

"Put on a swimsuit. We're going to make a detour."

When her face lit up with anticipation, Kylen's

heart cracked a little.

She was going to be the death of him.

CHAPTER TWENTY-TWO

Winter meant nothing in Hawaii. While Meridian, Arkansas was in the 40s, Hawaii stayed a balmy mid-80s year round. It was the nearest place he'd been able to think of where Olivia could swim in the ocean and fly over a volcano in two hours.

They landed in a small cemetery on the island of Kauai. Not exactly secluded, but one of the most amazing sunrises Kylen had ever experienced had been at Shipwreck Beach. He hoped they'd have a chance to see one equally as spectacular.

"Where are we?"

"Hawaii."

"What!" Olivia spun around in a circle, taking in the tropical foliage. The water was still well beyond their line of sight. The five-hour time difference and the short walk from the cemetery down the dirt path would put them on the beach just in time.

As they emerged from the forest and onto the edge of the pristine white beach, Olivia gasped. "Oh, Kylen. It's…"

"Number 47. The sunrise is a bonus."

Olivia sank to the sand on her bottom, wrapping her arms around her legs, and rested her chin on her drawn-up knees. She kicked off her shoes and dug her toes into the sand.

"I've always wanted to see the ocean. Where are we? Exactly?"

"Kauai."

"You've been here before?"

"Yes."

"You're so lucky to be able to travel like you do. You must have been to thousands of places this lovely. Is this your favorite?"

"No."

"Then where? I can't even imagine anywhere better than this. Look at those colors!"

Kylen did look. But it had been too long since he'd last exchanged energy with Olivia. His color vision had faded again, and he would have to trust her assessment.

"Come. You can sit by me to watch it," Olivia said.

This wasn't a vacation, and they didn't have time to be leisurely, but he couldn't deny the appreciative sparkle in her eyes. She was practically glowing with happiness. It didn't escape him that he was the cause, a fact that pleased him more than it should. But while he didn't want to ruin this for her, they needed to knock these items off the bucket list and get back to Meridian to finish the rest.

He sat.

His scythe scabbard was rigid and unyielding against his back, so he was uncomfortable at first, but he soon found himself lost in the gray shades of the Shipwreck Beach sunrise. Olivia's bright aura was almost a physical presence between them.

She reached for his hand, taking it into hers and held it without words.

He let her.

He watched as his electric blue energy leaped up her arm, turning her white aura a pale shade of blue. From the corner of his eye, he caught a glimpse of the colors of the sky, and he watched in awe as the sun rose over the craggy rock projection that had given the beach its name.

As the colors finally faded to the brilliant blue of morning, he pulled his hand away.

"If you're going to swim, now's the time."

Olivia smiled and rose to her feet. She pulled her sundress up and over her head, dropping it at his feet.

"Will you join me?"

"No."

"Chicken."

She ran to the surf and let the water roll in against her, wave after wave until she was properly drenched. He watched as she made her way out into the deeper water. With her white hair floating all around her and her head bobbing to the top of the waves as she made her way to the beach, he couldn't help but think of Kara and their special place in Haiti. Which made him feel all the guiltier for the ridiculous position he now found himself in.

What was he doing here, flouncing around a tropical paradise with a human girl? No matter how much she needed him. What would Kara think if she could see him now? Betraying her this way.

It wasn't long before tourists started to make their way down the long boardwalks to the very public beach. Kylen caught Olivia's eye and motioned her in.

It was time to wrap this thing up.

One more quick stop, and then it was back to reality.

* * *

Olivia couldn't believe she was in Hawaii, which was beautiful beyond words. She'd really had no hope of completing either of these items on her bucket list and had written them off as a lost cause.

She waited on the helipad as Kylen finished making arrangements inside the tiny little hut office. They were going to fly over not one but two volcanoes. Kilauea, one of the world's most active volcanoes, and Mauna Loa, the world's largest volcano. She was so excited she couldn't even think straight.

Kylen approached her with a ticket in his hand.

"You'll be gone about an hour," he said as he handed it to her. "We'll leave when you get back."

"You're not going to come?"

"No."

Olivia's heart sank. She'd accomplished all of her other list items alone, but this one? It didn't seem right for him to go to all this trouble if he wasn't going to enjoy the experience right along with her.

"You have to come with me."

"No. I don't."

"But why? Is it the money? I can pay you back. I can pay for my own ticket."

Kylen shifted uncomfortably, refusing to make eye contact with her.

"What is it, Kylen?"

"It's not the money. I have plenty of money."

"Then what?" She reached for his hand, imploring him to look at her.

"I'm afraid of flying."

She almost laughed. Almost. But that would have put the nail in the coffin. There would be no talking him into it if she did that.

"You mean to tell me you travel all over the world, even to Purgatory and Hell and back, through an invisible consecrated subway that's scary as hell, and you're afraid to fly in a helicopter?"

Kylen's jaw tightened. She could tell he was grinding his teeth together, considering his response.

"Yes."

"Well, if you're not going to go, neither will I."

"I already bought your ticket. I brought you to a freaking volcano. You are going up in that helicopter."

"Not without you. Your choice."

She waited for his decision, wondering if at any moment cartoon steam might start blowing out of his ears. He was clearly furious.

After several long moments and a stare-down of epic proportions, he turned and headed back to the ticket office. He returned with two tickets.

The blades of the helicopter began to whirl behind them.

* * *

Kylen had a white-knuckle grip on the armrests in the back of the helicopter. Flying above the Earth in a man-made machine was just plain unnatural. He was starting to wish he was doing just about anything else as the death trap canted a hard right toward the rising plume of smoke belching from Mauna Loa. Massive was an understatement.

The pilot told them about the history of the volcano while they circled it. Olivia was sitting in the passenger seat in front of him, and she seemed to actually be listening to the pilot's nonsense. Kylen decided to keep his attention locked on her instead of looking into the fiery crater and imagining his death, which suddenly wasn't quite so appealing to him.

As they flew over the second volcano, Kilauea, he couldn't help but notice how similar it looked to the pit of Hell and the Sea of the Dead.

Maybe it was actually an old portal of some sort. Or maybe he needed to stop thinking about demons so much.

Yeah, it was probably that.

Olivia continued to sneak excited looks his way, and he couldn't help but feel his heart warm ever so slightly.

He was doing a good thing.

Him.

Surely there would be hell to pay for that.

What was that saying? No good deed goes unpunished?

He'd never really been a "carpe diem" sort of guy, but here he was facing a fear and making someone deliriously happy at the same time. All in all, it was oddly appealing.

God, he was glad Deacon wasn't with them. He'd never let him hear the end of it.

As the tour wrapped up, the pilot flew them back to the helipad.

Taking off had been terrifying, but landing was so much worse. He had nearly jumped out of his skin by the time the chopper vibrated against the pad and settled to a stop. He'd never been so happy to be on solid ground in his life.

Although he'd never admit it, his knees were shaky as he made his way around to collect Olivia. They hunched down under the rush of wind created by the blades winding down, and he pulled her toward the car that was waiting to take them back to Shipwreck Beach. From there they would walk.

Kylen was more than ready to return to his element.

"Thank you, Kylen," she said as they walked together toward the cemetery. "Thank you for the sunrise, thank you for the swim and thank you for going on the flight with me. It was amazing."

"We need to get back."

"I know. I just want you to know that I'll never forget this day. Ever." Olivia stretched up and kissed his cheek. Blue sparks like static elicited a startled squeal from her but didn't stop her from giving him another soft kiss.

"Come on. We're running out of time." He pulled her close and wrapped his arms around her slim body, reminded ever so clearly that time was the one thing they didn't have.

CHAPTER TWENTY-THREE

It was nearly 2:30 p.m. by the time they got back to Olivia's apartment. Their trip to Hawaii had only taken a couple of hours, but exhaustion hit him like an anvil. He'd expended a lot of energy, between sharing it with Olivia and traveling so far with a passenger. He needed to refuel or rest or both.

"I need a couple of hours to finish up here. Can I get you anything?"

Kylen eyed the couch longingly. "Ten minutes of shuteye. I'll be right over there."

Heading straight to the couch, he stretched out on his side, resting his head on the overstuffed arm. He closed his eyes, hoping for a quick nap. He didn't really know what Olivia needed or intended to do in her apartment, but she didn't appear to need his help with any of it.

Ten minutes. Maybe twenty and I'll be as good as new.

The sooner this day was over, the better. Then he could get back to his real work.

* * *

Kylen awoke in Olivia's dark apartment. He fumbled for the lamp on the sofa table behind him and turned it on. The light cast the room in a red haze, adding to his unease.

"Olivia?" he called. "Olivia!"

He'd been out for much longer than twenty minutes. The books that had been on shelves earlier were now in boxes stacked three high between the dormers. Other boxes were stacked along the walls of the suite. How had he slept through all of that? He'd only had three beers this morning for God's sake.

"Olivia!" he called louder, turning on lamps as he made his way around the horrible apartment.

She lay sprawled across her bed atop the thick dark floral quilt, her arm slanted across her eyes. For a moment, he feared she was gone. She was still and pale, her face soft and relaxed. Relief flooded through him—dread fast on its heels—when he realized she still exuded an aura: a bright, *white* aura.

He crossed over to the bed and sat, looking down on her. Her hair was fanned across the dark reds of the quilt like a drift of snow. Without thinking, he reached for her and stroked his thumb across her face, blue flames sparking along the line he traced. When he palmed her cheek in his hand, the blue sparks sizzled like lightning, spidering through the veins beneath the surface of her face. Each time he touched her, her body pulled in his energy like drought-stricken ground soaking up an unexpected downpour.

How long could he keep her alive this way? The more time he spent with her, the more he knew it wouldn't be long enough. What god could be cruel enough to send him not one, but two condemned women?

Heaven…Hell? It didn't really matter which side was running the show. They were both heartless masters as far as he could tell. One side was just more overt than the other. Hell didn't bother trying to hide its intentions behind fallacies like free will. He knew better.

Maybe he wouldn't give either side the satisfaction of his death. Maybe he would serve no master but himself.

He was tired of playing their games. Tired of being their puppet. He'd seen what good and evil had to offer and had been unimpressed with either.

But this woman?

Something about her reminded him that living on this Earth had its perks after all, if you took advantage of your opportunities. He'd spent way too many years at the mercy of one side or the other, doing their bidding and little else.

Maybe now was the time to be done with all of that. Let them destroy each other in fiery battles for all he cared. Maybe he could still find a place far from the fight, far from the troubles of yet another Armageddon. A place where he could be invisible.

A place he could take Olivia?

He could do that. *He could.*

His free will was intact; he was still in possession of his soul in spite of both sides' efforts to extinguish him.

Leaning over her, he pressed his lips to Olivia's forehead and a trickle of energy leached out on contact. Her eyes snapped open, electric-blue energy sparkling behind her ice-blue gaze. He was about to pull away, but Olivia clutched his arm, tugging him toward her. When he looked into her eyes, he noticed something new there:

desire.

He hesitated—conflicted—but was unable to resist his own desire. He took her mouth with his, his blue light flooding into her, satiating her parched landscape, seeping down into the long-dying crevasses of her being and filling her empty spaces with his energy—his life. Her lips pressed against his as her hands clutched at his arms, sliding up his shoulders and into his hair, pulling him down to her, demanding more from him than he had to give.

Responding despite his inner turmoil, his body hardened, pulsating against the constricting fabric of his fatigues. As she arched into him, her body pressing against his, it was all he could do to keep from ripping her clothes free and burying himself inside her.

His hand slid beneath the arch of her back and held her to him, blue energy and cloth the only barriers between them.

Blood pounded through his chest and blue light pulsated through both of them with each throb of his long-underutilized heart. He lost himself in the feel of her skin, her lips, her hands on his body. A low, desperate groan escaped from deep inside him.

His own.

He wanted her. *Needed* her.

But while his *flesh* was willing, his mind refused to get with the program. It kept flashing him images of Kara's body on that long-ago battlefield. It didn't take long for his flesh to follow his brain's lead, and after a while he tore himself from her hold.

He wasn't sure who he was protecting, Olivia or himself, but he couldn't take the chance that history would repeat itself. He couldn't open his heart to someone else who might be stolen from him.

As he backed up and away from her, he leaned against the wall, trying to slow his breathing and get his heart rate back under control. Olivia rose up on her elbows, tilting her head quizzically at him, her own chest rising and falling rapidly, her hair wild.

"What's wrong, Kylen? Is there danger?"

Yes.

"No…I'm sorry." He turned toward the living room, not wanting her to see his expression, and closed his eyes.

"What are you sorry for, Kylen? Kissing me or stopping?"

"Yes."

He walked to the window and pulled the blind aside so that he could peer down into the alley. A dozen or more imps were waiting below. The longer he stayed in one place, the more seemed to gather. While he didn't want to encourage them, he couldn't deny that they'd come in handy twice already.

He was playing with fire. He consoled himself with the justification that he was using the resources at hand for the greater good.

Yeah, that's it. He was a freakin' Boy Scout.

Maybe if he kept telling himself that, he'd begin to believe it. Believe that he was somehow redeemable, that this entire situation was.

Not likely.

He heard Olivia padding up behind him, and then her arms encircled his waist from behind, and she pressed her cheek into his back. He stiffened in her hold and suppressed the moan boiling up inside him, demanding that he turn around and finish what he'd started.

"What's out there?" she asked, holding on to him like he was a lifeline.

"Nothing."

"Then come back."

"No. It was a mistake. If you're going to finish

your damn list, we need to go do it. I can't afford to take another night off to babysit you." He pried her hands from his torso and twisted away from her…but not fast enough to miss the look on her face.

He hated that look. Despised himself for being the cause of it. He'd add it to the list of shitty things he'd done in his life.

A list that continued to grow longer.

* * *

Olivia gazed into the mirror in her bathroom and rubbed cover-up over the light blue discoloration that ran along the veins of her throat. She drew apart her robe and looked again at the blue line that tracked through the vertical center of her body from stem to stern. Kylen's kiss had engorged it, and it was even brighter now. The more she touched him, the more he filled her with this remarkable blue light…and the better she felt.

Sliding the red, low-cut dress over her head and down her body, she frowned into the mirror. The bruising on her neck from the other night was still apparent. She tried to lighten it with makeup, but the low cut of the neckline drew attention to it. Between the bruise and her weight loss, this dress just wasn't going to work. Grasping the hem, she pulled it back up over her body, tossing it out of the bathroom and walking naked through her bedroom to her closet.

Flipping through the few dresses she owned, she settled on her one and only little black dress. It wasn't low cut, but these days she didn't have much to show off, anyway. Tonight was about pushing her limits and doing the things on her list that scared her most.

She needed to dress for the occasion. With the right outfit and a few more glasses of wine, she might just finish the damn thing tonight. Except maybe that last one…#59, *give everything away,* would be easy. She'd already boxed most of her personal things and made arrangements for the women's shelter to collect them upon her death. #60, *save a life,* would be a little more difficult. She'd tried to do that in the alley, but obviously that had fallen through. It had been an overly ambitious wish, she realized.

Still, she was so close.

Sliding the sleeveless black dress over her head, she smoothed it down her bony torso and sighed. It would have to do. She slipped on a pair of sparkling silver heels and called it good. She didn't actually know if she could accomplish #54, *dance all night* in the shoes she'd chosen, but they went with the dress, so she'd give it a shot.

Realizing that most of the remaining items on her list involved a bar in some way, she chuckled to herself. They'd all seemed like such a good idea while she was safe in her bed and lost in her daydreams. Olivia had never liked to draw attention to herself.

Walking back into the bathroom, she brushed her hair. The white contrast of her hair against the black dress and her pale skin made her look like a negative image of herself. Peering into the mirror with the hard lens of self-examination, she realized that her chances of completing #58, *have a one-night stand,* seemed more remote than saving a life. Her reflection frightened even her. No wonder Kylen had fled.

She glanced around her apartment. Not knowing if she'd be able to return, she pulled open the drawer of the antique secretary desk in her bedroom and extracted her checkbook. She wrote out a check for her landlord and attached it to the envelope containing her last will and testament, which she'd prepared weeks ago.

With #57, *pay my debts,* now complete, she picked up her borrowed clothes from the bathroom floor and retrieved her list.

She drew a neat line through *#56 learn to use a weapon* and *#57 pay my debts*. Four left. She studied the last fourteen items on the list:

#47 swim in the ocean
#48 fly over a volcano
#49 volunteer at a homeless shelter
#50 have a pet
#51 make the best dessert ever
#52 get drunk
#53 dance all night
#54 sing in a karaoke bar
#55 sleep under the stars on the fall equinox
#56 learn to use a weapon
#57 pay my debts
#58 have a one-night stand
#59 give everything away
#60 save a life

Folding it carefully, she stuffed the list into her tiny, jeweled party purse and draped it over her shoulder.

CHAPTER TWENTY-FOUR

Kylen nursed a Crown and Coke as he sat in a booth across the bar from Olivia, watching her dance. DJ music vibrated against his sternum, threatening to reroute his heart's normal rhythm, replacing it with the pounding beat of the dance music pulsing through the bar.

This might not be the last place in the universe he wanted to be right now, but it was in the top three.

The one redeeming thing about the entire situation was that Olivia looked amazing. If he was going to be stuck watching someone's every move…well, the view wasn't exactly disagreeable.

The sound of her heels clicking across the hardwood floor of her apartment before they left had nearly broken him, torn as he was between guilt and desire. He'd turned and sucked in a hard breath, frozen in place.

She was a vision in black and white. So much so that he fleetingly wondered if the color had drained from his sight again. Her hair hung across her shoulders and down her back, sleek and touchable, and the black dress she was wearing clung to her in a way that left very little to his heated and overactive imagination.

His hands had opened and closed into fists by his sides. How he'd wanted to run those hands down her curves. He'd turned away from her before he could act on the impulse, which, he realized, was becoming a troubling trend.

Now he was watching her dance with idiot after idiot to the relentless beat as his cock pounded along with the music. Each beat was an exclamation point on the stupidity of what he wanted to do.

He wanted her.

He wanted to scoop her up, take her out of here, and have his way with her. Fate be damned. It was an impulsive and stupid idea—one he would *not* act on— but he couldn't banish it.

The urge stewed inside him as yet another man put a hand to her waist and ground himself against her on the dance floor.

Dance all night was not going to be a possibility.

They'd only been there for two hours, and it already seemed like all night. She'd have to call it good enough. Mercifully, a pause in the cacophony brought her eyes up to meet his. She smiled, disengaged herself from the clutches of her current admirer, and walked his way.

The boy trailed after her until he realized where she was heading. Kylen gave him his best "you do not want to fuck with this" look, and the kid veered off toward the bar.

Smarter than he looks.

Kylen's eyes locked with Olivia's, and he watched her every move until she was sitting across from him in the booth, safe from the clutches of stupidity.

Maybe.

She smiled at him. "You don't look like you're having fun."

"I'm not."

"You could dance with me," she cajoled.

"No. I couldn't."

"Are you going to sit here and brood all night?

"No. We're leaving."

"But we can't. Karaoke starts in ten minutes. Besides it's only nine o'clock! That's a far cry from 'all night,'" she pouted, sliding her shoe off to rub her foot.

"You can barely stand in those shoes anymore. Sing your song, and then we're leaving."

She frowned at him before sliding her shoe back into place. "You can't take me against my will."

"Watch me."

She rolled her eyes at him and glided from the booth.

He *did* watch her as she navigated the gyrating crowd to the DJ booth. The DJ bent down to take her request, and then nodded and pulled her up onto the small stage.

A spotlight illuminated her and the music faded into a new song: "Glad You Came" by The Wanted. Olivia began singing the first lines, and as the music swelled and filled the bar, the already-full dance floor exploded into activity.

Three scantily clad young women jumped onto the stage and joined her, singing and dancing with abandon. Olivia continued to sing, her voice surprisingly strong and melodious for such a tiny girl, directing her lyrics toward Kylen like a weapon, using them to pierce his steely heart.

Her backup singers sang the chorus a little less impressively, and the crowd joined them, waving their arms in the air to the music.

Olivia had them all in the palm of her hand. Kylen included.

As the song wound down and morphed into yet another driving beat, the crowd cheered her, parting so she could make her way back to the booth. Flushed and smiling from ear to ear, she was radiant, and he knew exactly what she was thinking—#54 *sing in a karaoke bar,* was complete.

She stopped at the bar and ordered a drink. Kylen watched as a man pushed up against her from behind and leaned in, speaking into her ear. She laughed and took her glass of wine from the bartender.

Kylen's heart was pounding in his ears, and it had nothing to do with the music.

The man slid his hand down her back and rested it on top of her ass. Before he even realized he was moving, Kylen had pushed the man away from Olivia and pinned him to the wall. The admirer's feet hovered several inches above the floor.

Sparks along his shoulder blade whipped Kylen's attention back to Olivia, who was pressing her hand against him, "Please don't hurt him. Let's leave. I'm ready."

Without a word, he allowed his prey to slide to the floor. Fear rolled off the prick as his aura cascaded from him in waves of muddied colors. He was right to be afraid.

Kylen watched the man flee through the crowd, rubbing his neck as he went.

Olivia took Kylen's hand and pulled him toward the exit sign beyond the restrooms. He let her. Together they walked out into the alley behind the bar, the music deadening as the steel door swung shut behind them.

"Well, that was fun. For a while," Olivia said, looking up into the night sky.

"You're finished?" he asked, realizing he was still holding her hand.

"I guess so."

"Good." He pulled her to him and the blue light from his touch glowed around her like fog. She was luminous. He held her tightly against his body and slid his hands up her back and into her hair as his mouth found hers. He was a goner.

All he could feel and hear and taste was Olivia.

She clutched at him, and a soft mewl swelled up from inside her that was damn near his undoing. Somehow, he managed to disengage from her, pulling himself back from the brink of taking her on the pavement in the bleak alley. He dragged her behind him, leading the way to her apartment, desperate to be inside her.

She couldn't keep up—her heels kept getting stuck in the broken sidewalk, threatening to pull her down. In frustration, he scooped her up into his arms. She submitted and tucked her head and face against his neck, sending a shiver down his spine. He carried her the rest of the way home like that.

A herd of imps followed silently behind them, keeping just out of reach of the streetlights. He sensed their presence, but ignored them as he punched her code into the security pad. He lowered her to her feet at the bottom of the stairs and reached down to slip off her high heels. Her hand clutched his shoulder for support as he removed the shoes, and sparks of light spread across his chest, crackling under her touch

"Come." He took her hand and pulled her up the stairs.

CHAPTER TWENTY-FIVE

Olivia's heart drummed in her chest. This was not how she'd expected things to go. Not at all. She'd expected to bring home a stranger to mark this particular item off her list. It had never occurred to her that it might happen with someone she knew. A night in a bar didn't count as knowing.

These past few days, she had come to know enough about Kylen to make her realize he wasn't entirely the bad boy he portrayed himself to be. He was gruff, yes, but kind, too, and he'd gone out of his way to recreate her impossibly ruined list. Taken her to the glorious Shipwreck Beach. Flown in a helicopter despite his discomfort. All for her.

Every moment she spent with him seemed to only make her want more. More moments and more of Kylen.

Not to mention that he'd saved her life. Twice.

And now, as he set her down on her bed, his eyes were twin flames of desire. This wasn't the first time she'd had sex, there had been a few men through the years, but it would be her first one-night stand. She already knew it wouldn't be enough.

His skin was alight with blue energy, and it raced beneath the surface, trailing the caress of her thumb across his face.

He was rough, hard and handsome in that terrifying way of forbidden fruit and bad boys. His blond hair fell forward from his forehead as he lowered himself over her, brushing his lips down the side of her neck, and then up and behind her ear. His rapid breath was a smoldering prayer against her skin.

She shivered, and gooseflesh crawled across her shoulders and up her throat. Her hands tangled into his hair, clutching him for dear life. This time he wouldn't escape her desire, wouldn't have second thoughts or regrets. If she'd learned anything during her illness, it was that life was short.

She wasn't going to miss out on one more day.

Or night.

Kylen groaned and pressed himself against her, and she rose to meet him, intensifying the flow of blue energy between them. Sheer carnal instinct directed her body, and she was its willing slave. When he edged away from her, she panicked and grappled at his shirt to hold him in place.

"Weapons," he explained, brushing his lips against hers before he pulled away.

Olivia watched as he walked over to the mirrored antique dressing table and bent to unlace his boots. He hiked up the right leg of his pants and unstrapped the knife sheathed there, and then repeated the action for the left leg, placing both blades on top of the dresser. He unhooked his belt and jerked it from its loops, snapping it from around his waist. She felt her heart beating in her ears, and her breathing became nearly impossible to control as he peeled his black T-shirt up his torso and over his head. Scars marred his otherwise perfectly defined chest, raised white ridges running like rivulets along his ribs.

He caught her eyes in the mirror, and balled the shirt in his hands, worrying it; his expression threatened danger and passion all at once. Her tongue darted involuntarily across her lips. Dropping the shirt to the floor, he loosened the scythe scabbard and shrugged out of it, carefully placing it on the dresser with his other weapons. He removed a final blade from the back waistband of his pants and kicked off his boots. His muscles rolled as he bent to remove his socks one by one and stuff them into the tops of his boots.

He was only half-naked, but she sensed his vulnerability. His weapons were as important to him as a limb—they were a physical extension of him—and without them he *was* naked. She'd never seen that many weapons on a man.

He was a god.

As Kylen walked back toward the bed, her heart rate picked up its pace even more. She had never wanted a man so much. Reaching up, he grabbed a bedpost high above his head with each hand and stared down at her. Normally, she would have been uncomfortable with his judicial assessment of her, but this was far from normal. Far from *her* normal anyway. She had no idea about Kylen's normal. His eyes fluttered shut, and he hung his head to his chest, pulling in a long breath.

"Are you sure you want this?" he asked, without raising his eyes to her.

"Yes."

Releasing a sigh, he extended his hand to her. She raised herself and crawled over to him, kneeling on the bed before him. Cupping her face in his hands, he ran his thumbs over her cheekbones. The blue energy nearly brought tears to her eyes as it trickled into her.

She searched his eyes for whatever torment he was suffering.

Because he *was* suffering.

What was troubling him? It was hard not to take it personally, but somehow she knew it wasn't her. It was something else. Something she would never live long enough to learn about.

Grasping her around the waist, he pulled her to her feet and pressed his forehead down to hers. He reached behind her, unzipping her dress, and then pushed it from her shoulders as his palms slid across her skin. Blue sparks skipped across her collarbones as he traced them with his feathery touch, and her stomach tightened in anticipation.

"You're sure?" he asked again, this time holding her gaze.

"Yes."

Kylen pulled her little black dress down her arms to her waist, exposing her black bra, and then pushed it over her hips so that it fell to the floor in a puddle. Circling his arms around her waist, he drew her to his chest, skin-to-skin, and she feared they might ignite as the blue energy between them intensified. His body was a wall of heat against hers and tears welled in her eyes at the glory of it. She pressed her cheek against his chest, but he gently nudged her away so that he could look into her eyes.

"Why are you crying?"

"I'm happy," she said, sliding her palm up his throat, weaving her hand through his hair.

He stiffened under her, worry lines creasing his forehead, but then he scooped her up again, setting her down in the center of the bed. Lying beside her, he propped himself up on his elbow and spread his hand across her bruised throat, his fingers aligning perfectly with the purple-and-black bruise.

"Does this hurt?"

"No. The bruise isn't your fault. You didn't hurt me. You saved me." Olivia caressed his cheek, and he closed his eyes.

"Good. I don't want to hurt you."

"You won't."

"Do we need to take any precautions?" he asked, pushing her hair back from her face.

"Under the circumstances, I don't think that's necessary."

He frowned again, understanding the implication. She didn't want to ruin the moment with the reminder of her sickness and impending death, but pregnancy and disease were the least of her worries at this point.

Kylen leaned down and took her mouth, pinning his leg across her and tucking her in against him. His tongue probed hers as his hands explored her body. Spreading his body over hers, he kissed the hollow of her throat and the top of each breast.

He slid his hands across her ribs, and then brought them up to cup her breasts. Olivia arched her back and pressed into him. With reverence, he leaned down to her breast and took her nipple into his warm, wet mouth. She moaned under him as he laved her, first one breast and then the other.

Kissing his way down her torso, he stopped at the top of her black panties and looked up at her. She smiled down at him in what she hoped was reassurance as he grasped the waistband and drew them down her body. Wriggling beneath him, she helped him remove them, and then gasped as he cupped her core, pressing his palm against her hard nub. Energy raced up her spine, warming her from the inside out.

His finger glided into her. "Kylen!"

Encouraged, he worked his thumb over her nub

as his fingers glided through her dampness, deeper and faster.

"So wet."

She closed her eyes, overcome by sensation, and rocked her hips against his hand while her own hands fisted the comforter, pulling her body farther down the bed.

When he stopped, her eyes fluttered open. He was gazing up at her as he unfastened the buttons on his fatigue pants. Backing off the end of the bed, he pushed them down to the floor along with his black underwear.

He was magnificent.

And very, very naked. Olivia followed the curves of his smooth, muscled pecs down his torso, across his scarred ribcage to the vee of his hips and his marvelously hard manhood. He was perfect. Returning to the bed, he pushed her thighs open with his palms and then plunged his thumbs into her core, spreading her open. When he lowered his face to her center and sank his tongue into her, her hips ground against him, pleading for more.

She gasped, and he grabbed her hips, dragging her down the bed to him. She wrapped her legs around him, and he pushed at her entrance with his erection.

Gliding up her body, he took her hands and drew her arms up over her head as he pushed into her. She was nearly too tight to take him, but he eased in and out in a slow rhythm until she stretched around him, accommodating his length and girth. Withdrawing halfway from her, he plunged into her again, and the air huffed out of her body with the pleasure of it.

Kylen held her in place, his forearms on either side of her shoulders, cradling her head in his palms as he thrust in and out of her, his rhythm increasing in intensity with each stroke. His hands tangled in her hair, pulling her head back as he buried his face against her throat and claimed her.

She couldn't think. She could only feel. His skin sizzled against hers, and the blue energy built between them, filling her as much as his body was. When he reached down between them and ran his thumb across her nub, her vision exploded in a shower of brilliant blue stars, her entire body tensed around him, riding the wave of pleasure that consumed her.

His breath, hot and ragged against her throat, seared her skin as he came, throwing his head back and finishing into her in two great thrusts. A blue sphere of light surrounded them, and he leaned back onto his knees, pulling her with him so he could stay inside her. Tiny streaks of blue light leaked from her fingertips as she traced the ridges and valleys of the scars across his chest.

He wrapped his arms around her, and she melted into him as they basked in their pleasure.

CHAPTER TWENTY-SIX

As soon as Kylen drifted off to sleep, he was assailed by a vision that was more nightmare than dream.

From a balcony just inside the palace of Hell, Kylen watched as Camael oversaw the demons as they offloaded cargo into the writhing pit inside the arena below. The grand lobby and viewing deck had been converted to a new depot to accommodate the increased activity. On a normal Tuesday in Hell, this would have all taken place on a lower ring and at a more leisurely pace. Rashnu sorted the souls, and when they arrived in Hell from Purgatory, it was through a different entrance.

In the hundred years Kylen had spent traveling to and from Hell on similar missions, he had never seen it this busy. It was clear that Camael was preparing to open another portal—the biggest yet, judging from the amassed number of demons.

After Kylen willingly offered his body to the demon Orithidon, Lucifer realized reapers were the perfect conduit for gathering the souls he needed to expand his demon army. Souls were the raw material he used to mold his children—the demons. Just as God had molded his offspring from the dust of Earth and light, Lucifer created his from the sludge of Hell and darkness. And the more souls he had stewing in his Sea of the Dead, the more minions he had at his disposal.

Kylen's reaper body accommodated many more souls than the typical human body and wasn't prone to deterioration on Earth. It also didn't need to travel through special portals. Human hosts, on the other hand, were about as enduring as a Kleenex tissue. The added burden and toxicity of carrying a demon inside only hastened the decline. Surviving a week of possession was the absolute maximum for a human shell; one or two days was much more common.

Orithidon was a dazzling example of the benefits of having a reaper host. So when Camael took over as Duke of Hell, he instructed his minions to prospect for other such hosts. After all, the new duke had plans, plans that included having a corporeal body on Earth, something that had been torn from him when he fell from grace. Having a reaper host would catapult Camael's power to new heights. When Orithidon came face-to-face with Deacon, Kylen's life-long friend, and Ruth, a fresh-faced newbie, in Purgatory on a reaper "fishing" excursion, the demon hadn't been able to resist the possibility of procuring two potential hosts for his new boss.

After his minion failed in this quest, Camael took things into his own hands. He opened the portals in Meridian and dragged Deacon to Hell. The problem, of course, was that Camael couldn't force the reaper to be possessed. Deacon would need to invite him in... It was a hard sell, but Camael was confident that with time, it could be accomplished. Kylen was a case in point.

Camael just had to find something to use as an incentive, something that was more important to the reaper than his own life. Something he loved.

Then things went south. Way south. Camael hadn't counted on Kylen surviving after Orithidon was torn from him... And he certainly hadn't thought that Deacon's friends would stage a rescue expedition to Hell. Camael had underestimated Kylen: an act of hubris the fallen angel had come to regret.

Camael turned from the platform and fixed his glare upon Kylen, sensing his presence.

"Welcome, friend."

"We are not friends."

"Join me. This is where you belong. You feel it. Yes?"

Kylen tried to break the tether, tried to wake himself and pull away from the spiral of evil that clutched at him through his subconscious, but the scene before him was mesmerizing...and familiar.

Each arriving demon spewed forth its cargo, which was then sucked down through the swirling whirlpool to disappear into the muck. Once empty, the demon flung its ruined host body off the platform and into the writhing bottomless pit of flesh and bones below before exiting upward to wait for its chance to return to Earth.

The used hosts were still technically alive and they stayed that way, endlessly churning in the pulsating tumble of despair. Clothing, flesh and—over time—limbs were torn and pulverized in Hell's shredder pit. The hosts' memories and personality were attached to their souls. Once the souls were separated from the physical bodies, they were quickly corrupted and all memories faded away. The physical bodies were all but useless except for entertainment purposes.

But the souls! The souls were the true grist for the mill.

"Yes, Kylen. Soon they will take the form their

Father commands and rule the Earth."

"And the humans?" Kylen asked.

"Our demons will burn through them like wildfire, empowering and fortifying their final form."

"Which will be what?"

"A beautiful surprise."

Hundreds of demons gathered around Camael like pets, floating above his head, waiting for their orders. Kylen stood in the shadows, on edge, sweat breaking out along his forehead and neck.

"It won't be long, Kylen. Soon our demons will come and go from Earth as they please," Camael said with a smile. "Come back to where you belong."

It would be so easy to slip back into familiarity. To give in. To give up.

Still, Kylen's stomach turned at the thought of all the things for which he must atone. The draw of the familiar, of evil wasn't strong enough to make him forget that...

When his eyes sprang open, he was wide-awake. Not in Hell, but lying beside Olivia in her ridiculously fluffy bed.

Clearly, evil had the ability to reach him anywhere. He could feel the imps outside—waiting for him, beckoning for him to join them.

He'd never be free of his past. Even in his dreams.

* * *

"It's not safe here."

Olivia rolled in his arms to face him. "Why?"

"We need to go back. I need to talk to Deacon. "

Kylen sensed the growing impatience of the imps. Without looking, he knew there were dozens more than before. With no circle of protection to keep them at bay, it was only a matter of time before they grew bored and sought out other entertainment.

Or a snack.

Or both.

It was a bit after 2:00 a.m., and Olivia's housemates would have returned home. Since he hadn't heard any screaming, he assumed they were okay, but it might only be a matter of time.

The bright moonlight streamed in through the dormered bedroom windows. He pushed off the sheet, disentangling himself from Olivia's hold. Instantly regretting the loss of her warmth, he swung his legs over the side of the bed.

His mind was reeling, both from the horrific nightmare—which he knew was a harbinger of so much more—and regrets about what had happened with Olivia. He didn't know which was worse. After making love with Olivia, he was consumed with what could only be described as...emotions. It made him physically sick, and a lead ball of regret sat cold in his belly. It would end in disaster for him to have feelings for Olivia. It would end in disaster for them *both*.

Her hand softly stroked his back, and he flinched away. He couldn't even look at her. If he did, he'd never leave the bed. God help him if he stayed here all night.

He rose and started to gather his clothes, carrying them to the dressing table. Pulling on his fatigues, he caught a glimpse of Olivia watching him in the mirror. He had no idea what to say to her. There was so much he wanted with her, but he knew he couldn't have any of it...

It was the story of his life.

Sliding his arms into the harness of the scabbard, he took comfort in the feeling of the scythe against his back. He'd been reckless to take it off in the first place, let alone leave it completely beyond his reach. It wouldn't happen again.

He strapped the sheaths to his legs, over his pants this time since he wasn't concerned about scaring innocent bystanders this late at night, and tucked the dagger against the small of his back.

Better.

Now, all he had to do was get Olivia to safety. When he finally turned to look at her, he watched her disappear into the bathroom, closing the door behind her.

* * *

Olivia pressed her hands flat against the cool surface of the bathroom vanity, splaying her fingers to keep herself steady. Her head, too heavy to hold up, hung down and she closed her eyes to avoid her reflection. She considered pressing her face against the marble as well. Anything to give her some relief from her tangled emotions.

She wasn't sure which was more mortifying— the inhibitions she'd abandoned in making love to Kylen or his reaction in the aftermath. Both were causing her face to flush with fire.

He. Was. Amazing.

She couldn't imagine that sex could be any better than what they'd shared tonight.

But what *had* she expected afterward? Proclamations of love? Promises of a future together? They both knew that was impossible. They were adults. It shouldn't be this difficult. Obviously, it wasn't for Kylen. He was already retreating back inside the cold shell he'd constructed around himself. So this was her problem, wasn't it? She didn't have a shell. All of her soft parts were exposed.

She didn't want him to see her emotionally weak and undone. He had already seen her physically weak, so she couldn't help that. But she would die with dignity and strength, not pining away over a one-night stand. She'd accomplished everything on her list. All but the last one, anyway, and it didn't look as though that one could be achieved. It certainly wasn't from lack of trying. She'd have to live with that. Or, in this case, die with it.

Cracking the door open, she peeked into the bedroom. Her clothes were all in a closet on the other side of the bedroom. She wrapped a towel around her body and scurried over there to change.

* * *

Kylen paced in front of the living room window. No matter how many times he glanced into the alleyway, the scene remained the same. The dozens of imps had swelled to at least a hundred as he kept watch. They crouched there, fiery eyes fixed on the third-story window, blinking like malicious fireflies in the darkness. The sheer number of them made his skin crawl.

Sending his senses out into the night, he tapped into the network of darkness.

He could feel the demons gathering beneath the earthly realm. They were nearby, waiting for the portal to open. A growing sense of dread filled him. He couldn't take the chance of walking Olivia the six blocks to the cemetery, not when the portal might open anywhere. He wondered if Deacon, Ruth and Nate were back from the hospital yet. Deacon needed to get Ruth to safety, too. They were running out of time.

Then he felt the surge of power through his tether.

The ground was ripped and rent under Camael's command. In his mind's eye he saw that the new portal was opening in a cemetery. Not Maple Park but another place, outside of town. Using cemeteries and church portals as staging grounds for his demons was Camael's bird flip to the big guy. There was nothing the fallen angel liked better than to desecrate holy places. The demons streamed out by the hundreds descending upon Meridian, but Camael couldn't hold such a big seam open for long. The portal was closed after a few minutes, cutting off the flow, which enraged Camael further. He'd only accomplished part of his plan, thank God. As it was, it would be nearly impossible for the reapers to destroy all these new adversaries.

Kylen snapped back to awareness as the tether snapped. When he heard Olivia's footsteps behind him, he forced himself to turn to face her, an act which felt much more dangerous than facing the imps that awaited below.

She was radiant.

Her pale skin glowed with life, and her white hair cascaded down her back and across one shoulder. It was all he could do to stop himself from rushing over to her and burying his face against her neck. His pulse beat in his ears like a train chugging down a track, and his attempts at coherent thought were worthless.

"I'm ready." Olivia shouldered a backpack and stuffed her hands into her jeans' pockets, looking everywhere but in Kylen's eyes.

Paralyzed, Kylen knew he should respond to her—acknowledge her comment, tell her about the danger—but all he could see when he looked at her was her body spread across the bed, him buried to the hilt inside her. His cock hardened against his will.

Her eyes finally settled on his, and her face flushed a sweet shade of pink. Was she thinking the same thing? Of course not. God, he was going soft. Only not in the right places. He shifted and headed in exactly the direction he didn't want to go—away from her, toward the door.

"Do you have a car?"

"Yes. We're driving now?"

"Only to the cemetery. We have company outside. It's not safe to walk."

She headed to the window and looked down. Frowning, she turned to look at him, "There are at least a hundred cats down there. Are you the Pied Piper of cats or something?"

"Those are imps. Trust me, if you could see them in their true form you wouldn't want to play with them."

She walked to the door, took her purse from the coat hook and fumbled inside until she extracted a ring of keys.

"The car's outside in the garage."

"Good."

* * *

Kylen led the way down the three flights of stairs to the building's back entrance. He hesitated at the door and drew his scythe.

"You really think that's necessary?" Olivia asked, backing away from him.

"Yes."

He cracked open the door, taking a cautious assessment of the distance to the garage—it was open, thank God— before wedging himself through it, scythe first. Reaching back for Olivia, he took her hand and drew her up against him as they made their way to the car.

"Open the locks."

She clicked the remote, and he heard the beep as the doors unlocked. They sprinted the fifty feet to the carport, and he opened the passenger door of the Focus, pushing her inside. He folded himself behind the wheel of the tiny vehicle, and breathed out a sigh. As he backed out of the carport, the headlights illuminated the herd of imps, which had pulled in close, their glowing yellow eyes like a carpet of stars lining the driveway.

As he pulled forward, the imps closed ranks around the car, hemming it in. Rage built inside him as he stared at the beasts.

"Part," he commanded.

When they didn't yield, he hesitated in confusion for only a moment. The imps had been responding to his commands for more than a century. They'd obeyed him just days ago. Surprised, he smashed the accelerator to the floor and ran right over them. The car crunched over a handful of imps, and others careened away and were sent bouncing off the hood of the car.

Olivia screamed.

He knew it must look like he was running over and killing defenseless animals, but that was absolutely not the case. If he couldn't command them, he couldn't keep her safe, either. He had to get her to consecrated ground without delay. The imps wouldn't be able to cross the boundaries of the cemetery unless Camael had desecrated it. Imps could only use the portals leading directly to and from Hell, not the consecrated subway used by reapers. If he got her back to Ruth's, she'd be safe.

Once he got them through the hoard, he drove straight to the cemetery. He didn't stop the car until they were in the center of the small grounds. He leaned his head back against the headrest and closed his eyes, letting his heart break a little as Olivia snuffled softly beside him, her breath hitching. She was crying. For imps.

Holy shit, the world really is going to Hell.

"I'm sorry," she said, wiping her hands down

her face.

"They're not cats, I promise you."

He left the car and walked around to her side. Opening the door for her, he reached for her hand, and when she gave it to him, he pulled her toward a headstone near where they'd entered the cemetery several hours earlier. Imps were lining the perimeter of the cemetery, all the way around the acreage, so the consecration must be secure. This night was completely FUBAR. He couldn't imagine how it could get any worse.

Holding his scythe in one hand, he drew a sobbing Olivia to him with his other arm and concentrated until he felt the familiar swirl and tug that would bring them home.

CHAPTER TWENTY-SEVEN

Ruth's living room was bedlam. The place was wall-to-wall reapers, just like the bar in Purgatory. Huge, badass reapers, all of them talking over one another. Deacon and Ruth were standing just inside the open doorway of their bedroom, having what appeared to be quite an animated conversation. Kylen counted six new reapers, plus a woman who had to be Deacon's replacement reaper, Maeve. Nate stood next to her, a strange expression on his face. The room reeked of testosterone and anticipation.

Deacon spotted him from their bedroom doorway and nodded, making his way over to him. "I am glad you two are back. We have problems."

Olivia stared wide-eyed at the new additions. Kylen wanted to put his arm around her waist and pull her close, but he couldn't summon the courage to do it in front of Deacon, let alone this roomful of strangers. He looked at Ruth, who was still standing in the doorway, and she took pity on him, motioning for Olivia to join her.

Olivia gave him a tense smile. "I'll be back."

"Sure," he said, watching her wind her way through the crowd.

"What was that all about?" Deacon asked. "Is she okay?"

"She's great."

"All righty then. Are *you* okay? You kind of look like hell. And we both know that's saying something."

"It's been a long night."

"It's about to get longer."

Kylen nodded. "I know. A huge portal just opened. And it won't be the last. They're building up to something big."

"How do you know?"

"I had a dream—sort of—then I…felt it open."

"You're still connected? I mean, I knew you had your mojo on for the demon tracking, but has there been more?"

"Nothing specific. Until now. Deacon, I think Camael's trying to open a permanent portal for Lucifer. These small ones have been tremors. He's working up to the big quake."

"I don't know how much bigger we can take. Grim is pissed. We got this one sealed within minutes, but our best guess is that a few hundred demons may have escaped."

"Is that why the Mickey Mouse Club is here?" Kylen asked, nodding towards the crowd.

"Yeah. Grim handpicked them. We have an edict."

"Sounds very official."

"You're about to become a part of it, too. This is big, Kylen." Deacon grabbed Kylen's shoulder, making eye contact with him. "Are you good? Can you handle this? Are *we* good?"

Kylen studied his friend's face. The friend he'd grown up with since childhood. The friend who'd once sworn to kill him before allowing him to be possessed...and then reneged. The friend who'd finally helped save his miserable life. Deacon had risked a lot for him, and if the circumstances had been reversed? Kylen didn't know if the man he had once been would have been able to kill a possessed Deacon, either.

"Yeah. I am. We are." Kylen's bitterness melted from his heart, and for the first time in...forever, he experienced forgiveness. "Do *not* hug me."

"No problem." Deacon slapped his shoulder. "I'm going to need your backup here. You're the only one of us with true inside information. Ready?"

"Best get started."

Deacon smiled, and then turned to address the gathered reapers.

He whistled loudly and the room instantly quieted. "You have each been pulled from your previous positions, which are now being filled by other reapers. You have been handpicked by Grim to join this reactivated order." Deacon walked toward the center of the room, and the reapers parted, making way for him.

"As you know, I am the new Powers, and Grim has ascended to Seraph. For more than four thousand years, there hasn't been a need for the order you are about to join. Demons have stayed in Hell where they belong. But a war has begun once again, and you will be on the front lines. It's the same old story. Good versus evil. But there can no longer be only one Gatekeeper. You've been recruited because of your skills, your strength and your record of success. Your task will be to guard the Earth from evil and eradicate it everywhere you find it."

"We will hunt down and destroy every last demon Camael released today, and we will continue to patrol the borders of Heaven and Hell to protect mankind until our dying day. If you have doubts or misgivings, now is the time to declare them. If you accept this appointment, you will become Authorities in the Order of the Powers, and for your service, you will ascend to The Sixth Choir as an angel upon your death. And I can guarantee no one has seen angels the likes of this motley crew."

Several of the reapers laughed, and Deacon continued. "You are warriors and protectors. This will be your chance to prove yourself. You'll be paired according to your special skills and sent forth to track and dispose of the demons. There are a lot of them. Hundreds. Maybe more. It's not going to be an easy task. You can live here. The accommodations will be uncomfortable for the moment, but we will improve them together. We will be an army and a family, and we *will* succeed."

"If you accept your role, you'll be allowed to return to Purgatory with me, and Grim will install you as members of this elite Reaper Authority Force. It will not be without its perks... For one, you will no longer need to carry a soul to travel to and from Purgatory. You'll be able to travel at will. The downside is that it's a lifelong commitment, and you have to make your choice *now*." Deacon took his measure of each reaper, and then turned his gaze on Nate.

"You might not be a reaper, Nate, but Grim thinks you have special potential, and he has a specific job in mind for you. If you agree, you'll be included as well.

"Ruth is pregnant, so she's not under consideration to join the Authority at this time, but she's agreed to house everyone here. Are there questions?"

"When do we start?" The others were nodding their agreement.

"What is your name, reaper?" Deacon asked, pointing at one of them.

"Raguel. They call me Ragu…'cause I'm saucy." Someone chuckled in the crowd.

"Welcome aboard, Ragu. The rest of you might as well introduce yourselves before we head to Purgatory. You?" Deacon pointed to the reaper farthest left.

"Ouriel."

One by one, he pointed to each reaper, and they stepped forward.

"Dardariel."

"Zachriel."

"Samkiel."

"Leo."

Kylen shot Deacon a look. "Did you know that all the new guys were named after angels?" he asked under his breath.

"Not until now."

"What the hell do you think that means?" Kylen asked, taking a hard look at each of them.

"Means they've got a lot to live up to." Deacon walked back to Ruth and Olivia, who were still lingering in the doorway to the bedroom. He pulled Ruth aside and whispered in her ear before giving her a quick kiss. Kylen's feet were still firmly planted. The flesh was willing, but the withering look Olivia sent him gave him pause.

"Maeve, you're going with us," Deacon said. "Olivia, I'd like for you to stay here if that's okay. I don't like the idea of Ruth being alone."

Ruth rolled her eyes at him, but then gave Olivia a big smile.

Kylen thought he detected a ghost of a smile cross Maeve's face as well, but it was gone before it manifested.

Deacon nodded to Kylen. "You ready?"

Kylen took one last look at Olivia, searching her face for a sign that she was truly all right. She gave him nothing in return. Torn, he answered. "Yes."

Deacon flashed them all to Purgatory, leaving Olivia alone with Ruth, protected only by magic.

* * *

Kylen, Deacon and Nate stood in Rashnu's private chambers in Purgatory while the other reapers waited outside the closed door for their own special instructions. Grim shone resplendent before them, hovering above the floor, his robes trailing like a bridal train, his wings stretched out behind him, spreading from wall to wall. Kylen stared in wonder at the Seraph, a reaper myth come to life. For all the wonders and horrors he'd seen in his two hundred years, this was somehow the most shocking. Grim was the closest creature to the One True Light—to God—he'd ever seen with his own eyes, and was proof positive that for every evil essence there was an equal good to balance it. He'd never really believed that to be true until this moment.

Kylen watched Nate's mouth fall open as he also took in the otherworldly appearance of Grim and the chamber. If this was unlike anything Kylen had ever seen before, he could only imagine how shocked Nate must be. Olivia's apartment had been a Victorian Gothic explosion, but this? This was a gold-plated, bedazzled Hell all its own. Every surface was covered with some sort of gold, fabric or glitter, except for the white-washed walls and the chandelier, which seemed to be composed entirely of diamonds.

It was nauseating. And surprising.

He'd never been past the depot, which was far starker in its decor.

"Welcome." Rashnu worked behind the bar, pouring two dark red drinks into shot glasses before placing them on the countertop.

"It's been a long time since you've poured this particular vintage, old friend." Grim said, folding his wings tightly behind him. He glided across the room to join the men at the bar. He directed his question first toward Deacon.

"You are prepared to lead this force?"

"You know I am," Deacon said.

"And you?" Grim asked Kylen. "Are you ready to forsake your ties to darkness? To accept this high calling?"

Kylen hesitated. Pledging his allegiance would tether him to yet another master. After all that had happened with Deacon, with Olivia and now the portal opening. Was there even really a choice for him anymore?

"Your answer, Kylen?" Grim repeated.

Kylen shook his head to clear his rambling thoughts. "Yes."

Grim bore his gaze down on Kylen, seemingly penetrating through to his very soul. Kylen felt a warmth blossom inside his chest. He took a step back from the Seraph, and then held his ground.

"Yes," he repeated.

Grim nodded and gestured toward the shot glasses. "Very well. This glass contains the blood of Christ. Not the metaphoric blood of Christ, but the *actual* blood of Christ from his time on Earth in human form. By taking this communion, you will be making an oath to serve against the forces of evil for the remainder of your days. It is no guarantee against suffering, only a promise that if you serve to the best of your ability, you will be rewarded. As you work to eliminate the demons, I shall strive to destroy their source. The One True Light has sanctioned this Authority of Powers to restore the balance of good by all means necessary. Each who drinks of Christ's blood shall from this day forth be endowed with the power to destroy evil in its true form, to travel to and from Purgatory without carrying a soul, and to navigate the earthly realm at will without the limitation of consecrated ground. Drink and go forth."

Rashnu pushed the glass toward Kylen. Taking hold of it, he stared down into its mesmerizing red swirl. Finally, he raised it in salute then downed the contents. Kylen expected fireworks or some physical sign of their compact, but all he experienced was the unusual copper taste at the back of his throat.

"That's it?" Kylen asked, a little disappointed with the whole thing.

"Do not be so eager for the dramatic. You will be partnered with Deacon. Drama enough for you both, I'm sure. Each reaper pair will have complementary abilities. Together you will be a force to be reckoned with as time reveals new challenges…and abilities."

Grim turned to Nate. "Nate, the Force will need a tracker other than Kylen to help them find the demons. While it's true that you do not appear to be a reaper, you already possess some special abilities according to Deacon. I'm officially pairing you with Maeve, although you'll each have separate mandates for now. Don't wait for her to get started. I think you can be of great and immediate service to the cause, and I believe this will help you."

A low growl emanated from behind them, causing the men to swivel around. In front of them stood a jet-black dog the size of a small pony. Its ebony coat shimmered in the supernatural light of the chamber and its square head was as high as the men's elbows. Strings of silvery drool dripped from the beast's jowls.

"Nate, meet Bocephus, a hellhound. He's especially adept at finding demons. Eats them for lunch, so to speak. I leave him in your charge." The dog loped over to Nate's side, and then sat obediently at his feet.

Nate reached out tentatively to pat the beast's head, only to receive a sloppy lick that left a string of sticky drool trailing from his hand.

"Wonderful. I knew you two would get along."

"Now we must speak to the rest of the Authority Force. Go. Rashnu will send the others back soon so that we can finish what has been begun."

Grim placed a glowing white hand on top of Nate and Bocephus's heads and Kylen watched as they vanished from the chamber. The Seraph approached Deacon and Kylen next. When he touched them, Kylen felt power surge through him as he was ripped through space and time. He landed back in Ruth's living room with Deacon at his side.

"What happened?" Ruth asked, rushing to Deacon's side. "And where did he come from?" Ruth looked at the dog in amazement as she wrapped her arms around Deacon's waist.

"We were initiated. Grim told us to take the hellhound and get to work."

"A hellhound?"

"Apparently it's more of a demon bloodhound. Nate's got dog duty." Deacon grinned. "And Maeve, too."

"What does that mean, Nate?" Ruth asked.

"It means that I have a pet who's happy to see me." Nate scratched the dog behind the ear and it thumped its tail on the hardwood floor like a drumroll. "And a partner who'll be less so, I'm afraid."

"We need to get going." Deacon said, kissing the top of Ruth's head.

"Already?" Ruth snuggled closer.

"Yes."

Sensing her presence before he saw her, Kylen turned as Olivia emerged from the bathroom, her hair wet from showering. Her cheeks were still pink from the hot water, and his heart contracted inside his chest.

She was a weakness he couldn't afford.

"The others should be back anytime. Kylen, Nate, get your stuff together. We'll meet back here and head out as soon as they arrive."

CHAPTER TWENTY-EIGHT

Kylen could feel Olivia's eyes bore into his back as she followed him to his trailer. His emotions battled within him. He was about to get exactly what he wanted—the chance to kill demons with impunity, but the thought of leaving Olivia alone filled him with a dread that was far worse than anything Camael could do to him.

She was fragile. And dying.

What if she died while he was gone? Somehow his energy had helped sustain her but who knew for how long? He couldn't stand the thought of being responsible for another's life.

He opened the trailer door and stepped inside, knowing she would follow him.

Heading for the top bunk, he rifled through his weapons, obtusely ignoring the unspoken tension between them until it was finally broken.

"What is wrong with you, Kylen?"

Dear God. Wasn't that ever the question of the hour?

"Nothing."

"Then talk to me. Are you going to continue to ignore what happened between us?"

"Yes."

She moved toward him, and he could feel her energy behind him. Still, he was paralyzed; he couldn't turn and face her.

He didn't want the reminder of everything he couldn't have.

When she reached forward and touched his shoulder, he closed his eyes in surrender. If her touch alone could reduce him to a withered shell of angst, what would her imminent death do to him? He couldn't, wouldn't deal with that inescapable reality.

"Please, Kylen. Tell me what's wrong. Is it me?"

His heart tore in two.

Yes. No.

"It's complicated."

"Then explain it to me. I'm a smart girl."

Kylen nodded. He couldn't deny her the truth. She deserved to know that his confusion and indecision was his alone. But when he opened his mouth to speak, the words stuck in his throat.

Olivia slid around him and stood between him and the bunk full of weapons, forcing him to look at her. Her hand grazed the side of his face, brushing down his growing stubble, and his face turned into her touch without his permission. He was like a drowning man clinging to safety.

"Have I done something wrong? Hurt you somehow? Are you repelled because I'm dying?"

"You haven't done anything wrong," he said heatedly.

"Then what? I won't let you leave with this hanging between us. What if this is the last time I ever see you? I don't want it to end like this."

Dread slid through Kylen's stomach. "Don't say

217

that. You have plenty of time."

"I don't, Kylen. That's why it's time for some hard truths. What's tormenting you?"

"Everything."

"What's tormenting you at this moment?"

"I can't lose another lover."

"You've lost others? Who? When?"

Olivia slid her hands up his chest, creating a trail of blue sparks, and wrapped them behind his neck, cradling his head in her hands. He broke under her tenderness. "Kara."

"Tell me about Kara."

The floodgates opened, and before he could stop himself, the words spilled from him in a torrent. He was at once relieved and terrified to unleash his most private pain to her. It was the most he'd spoken in a century.

She would be his undoing.

When he finally ran out of words and stood quietly before her, his soul bared, he closed his eyes against the look of pity he was sure to see on her face. After a moment, her lips pressed to his, and relief and regret spilled from him in equal measure. His body was greedy for her again, but there was no time for that now. There might never be again.

And that was the worst pity of all.

"Thank you, Kylen. I know what it's like to lose the people you love. It's never easy. Even though you know Kara's in Heaven, it doesn't make it any easier. You still never got to properly say goodbye. I've suffered from loss, too. Not a lover, but my parents. Now that I've met you guys, I do believe they're in a better place. A place without suffering, pain or even loss. Have faith, Kylen. Faith that we can all be with our loved ones again one day. I do."

"I'm not worthy of that reward."

Olivia forced his face to his. "Why would you

say that? You are an Authority now, yes? Would they allow you to pledge yourself if you weren't worthy?"

He was silent for a long moment and then finally said, "I don't know."

"Of course not. Somehow you have given me more time, which has been an amazing gift, but you don't have to feel responsible for me. I was dying before we ever met. It's my fate. I'm at peace with it. There is good in you, Kylen. Reach for it. Hold on to it. Cherish it. Keep your faith, and you'll keep your loved ones forever." Olivia stretched up on her tiptoes and kissed his forehead. "And ever." She kissed his lips next.

Kylen crushed her against him, kissing her with a ferocity that scared him to the core.

He needed her.

And it might just kill them both.

* * *

"I'll be back soon," Kylen whispered into Olivia's hair as they walked back into the house. The newest reapers had returned and were gathered in the living area. He knew he would have to leave her soon. It still hurt.

"I know. I'll be here," she promised.

"Let's do this thing. It's time to start killing some demons." Deacon stepped out of Ruth's arms. "If we get separated, we'll all meet back here at dawn. Stay inside the circle, Ruth. No matter what."

Ruth crossed her arms over her chest and narrowed her eyes in defiance. She wasn't the type of woman who liked to give an inch. It was something Kylen admired about her. Deacon gave her a hard look. "Promise me."

"We promise," Olivia offered on her behalf.

"Thank you."

Kylen kissed Olivia one last time and followed a bewildered Deacon to the demon trap in the center of the room where the others waited. Maeve was the only one who still hadn't returned, but Rashnu had made it clear that she was on a different mission at the moment, and they were to continue on without her. Nate held an anxious Bo by the scruff of his neck. Seconds later, the Reaper Authority Force and their hellhound hurtled through the ether to the site of the latest portal to begin their search.

CHAPTER TWENTY-NINE

Maeve couldn't believe she'd just drunk the Authority Kool-Aid. Too bad she'd been officially partnered with Nate rather than one of the new reapers. Nate wasn't even one of them, and now she'd been assigned to "protect the home front." Seriously? No matter how temporary this assignment was supposed to be, she was fuming, and she didn't even bother to hide her disdain from Grim. Nate got a hellhound and a job as a tracker and she got to babysit?

Freakin' Grim!

She was in it way too deep to renege now, but if she had known beforehand that she was going to draw babysitting duty? She shook her head in disbelief. All her hard work and skills were going to be wasted. She ached to kill demons, not do housework and security for a bunch of reaper roomies. If they thought for one second she was going to go all domestic on them, they had another thing coming.

She felt like the last kid picked for dodgeball. Maeve had nothing but a long line of successes on her short reaper resume, so what was with the desk jockey routine?

She twitched with rage, but one look from the Seraph convinced her that her fate had been determined. At least for now.

So much for free will.

She was still steaming when Grim pushed her out of his chamber with a touch of his hand, and she landed back in Ruth's house. When she got there, Ruth and Olivia were scurrying about, strategically arranging bedding for their newest guests throughout the house, and the rest of the Force was MIA. Probably already knee deep in demons. Bastards.

"Maeve! Tell us what happened. The guys didn't give us too many details. They popped in, and then left again to hunt. What happened in Purgatory?" Ruth tossed a pile of blankets onto the middle of the floor.

"Other than meeting the Grim Reaper? Some mumbo jumbo, some Kool-Aid drinking, a sacred oath, blah, blah, blah, and then I got paired up with Nate. Grim told me to stay here and protect the home front." Maeve looked around the room expectantly. "Where is Nate?"

"He left with the others. Have you seen the hellhound?"

Maeve felt her face grow hot. She tried not to curse. Really she did. But a string of unholy expletives escaped in a surge as her hands clenched into fist by her thighs. White-hot rage percolated in her gut and oozed up through her as her rage rekindled anew.

Un. Freakin'. Believable.

A noise outside brought her out of her tantrum, and she raced to the front window to peer into the yard. Imps tested the circle, bouncing off it in a shower of psychedelic sparks like they were on an electric trampoline.

Olivia joined Maeve at the window. "Are those—"

"Demons' minions? Yep." Maeve walked to the couch and flopped down, crossing her legs and winding her arms over her chest in defiance.

"Should we do something about them?" Olivia asked, a worried line between her eyebrows.

"We don't need to do anything. As long as the circle holds—which there's no reason it wouldn't—we get to sit here and wait. Like the good little women we are."

Ruth paced in front of the window for a few moments, her face suddenly as white as the wall. Sweat beaded on her forehead. "No, Maeve. I think something's really wrong here."

A low rumbling began beneath the house, growing in strength until the pictures began to shake off the walls. They stumbled into three different doorways, bracing themselves as the earth trembled beneath them.

"Earthquake?" Olivia asked.

"I don't think so," Ruth said, her voice no more than a whisper.

Suddenly the lamp beside the end table in the living room exploded, sending shards of glass flying, and a cloud of smoke puffed out of the power outlet beside the couch, quickly followed by yellow flames. The old couch caught fire within seconds, igniting the throw blanket hanging over its arm.

"Ruth!" Olivia cried as she left her sheltered doorway, racing toward the couch.

Ruth, who was closest to the blaze, had grabbed the rug off the floor and was attempting to extinguish the growing flames.

Maeve reached her first.

"Ruth, stop!" Maeve shouted as she tried to pull her back from the flames. She was an instant too late.

Ruth's long sleeves had caught fire. Wrestling Ruth to the ground, Maeve rolled her in the smoldering rug until the flames extinguished.

As the house continued to shake, presumably under the extreme pressure of the imps' continued attack, Olivia crouched over Ruth with Maeve, both of them trying to assess the damage.

Ruth's arms were seared from her wrists to her shoulders, and she kept passing into and out of consciousness.

"Oh, Ruth!" Olivia sobbed. Flames raced across the floor rug from the couch and licked up the wall beside them.

Maeve ran from window to window to assess the outside threat. When the floorboards began to crack and splinter, she jumped into action.

"Shit! We have to leave. Now," she said, bending over Ruth. "Grab hold of me, Olivia. We'll flash to the hospital."

Ruth's eyes fluttered open. "Can't flash," she muttered.

"You're kidding me, right?" Ruth shook her head, wincing.

"Deacon told her she couldn't flash while she was pregnant. They don't know how it might affect the baby," Olivia said as she stroked Ruth's hair.

"Baby?"

Maeve wanted to scream. This was quickly becoming a nightmare. She didn't know anything about babies and pregnancy, but she did know that their circle of power seemed to be weakening. It was just a matter of time before the imps penetrated it. And God only knew what else was going on. Those flames certainly didn't seem to have an earthly cause. If she couldn't flash Ruth to the hospital, they'd have to go the conventional way. Only one problem with that…

"I can't drive," Maeve said, her face growing hot with self-disgust.

"I can." Olivia pushed Ruth's hair off her face. "Ruth, where are the keys to the Lincoln?"

"In the car." Ruth groaned, her charred clothes damp with sweat.

Maeve scooped Ruth up into her arms. "We gotta go. Now."

* * *

Olivia was the first out of the house. A ring of flames circled the perimeter of the mown area—the area in which Deacon had asked her to remain inside. Lines of fire burned like spokes on a wheel, extending from the house to the edge of the circle. Just beyond the perimeter of the flames, dozens of black cats paced at the edge of the woods, illuminated by the fire, their eyes glowing in the darkness. She scanned the periphery on both sides of the house. There were a *lot* of black cats. Dread settled into her belly.

She opened the back door to the Lincoln and Maeve eased Ruth inside, setting her across the back seat.

"I need to get something first." Olivia raced up the few steps to Kylen's trailer. Inside, she stood on her tiptoes, sifting through the myriad of blades on the top bunk until she found what she was looking for all the way against the back wall: the scythe Kylen had let her use for pumpkin practice. She slid two other sheathed push blades into one of Kylen's much-too-large belts and tied it into a knot around her waist.

If she had to leave the circle of protection without Kylen, she was at least going to take a weapon…or three. He would expect nothing less from her. As she walked down the steps of the trailer, the first cats penetrated the circle of protection.

"Run, Olivia!" Maeve implored.

Olivia watched in horror as a herd of very determined and clearly unfriendly felines poured toward them from the edge of the woods. She turned and raced to the driver-side door of the car, hoping to beat them there. A white-hot slash down the back of her calves was the first indication she was too late.

The claws tore through her jeans like they were chiffon, shredding four deep cuts from knee to ankle on each leg. She dropped to the ground and immediately flipped onto her back, preparing to defend herself with her already-drawn blades. Their ferocity was terrifying and she kicked at them as they continued their attack.

Before she could gather her wits, Maeve was cutting her way through the beasts like a samurai warrior. Olivia rose to her feet, blood filling her sneakers from the wounds on her legs.

"In the car, Olivia. Now!"

Olivia needed no more invitation than that. She dove into the open door of the driver's seat and slammed the door behind her.

Seconds later, a car door slammed behind her and Maeve was in the backseat.

"Go! And put your foot into it," Maeve called out to her.

Olivia turned the key in the ignition, and the Lincoln fired up. Cats flooded into the yard, the magic barriers powered by Ruth's life force completely shattered. Cats flung themselves onto the hood of the car, the windshield and the metal side panels. Soon there were several dents in the paneling as it was driven inward with each assault. Olivia put the car into drive and floored the gas pedal, spinning gravel behind them until the tires took purchase and the car fishtailed down the driveway, up and over a chunky wave of clamoring creatures.

She wasn't about to cry for the beasts this time.

Fear gripped her gut and shivered up her spine as she struggled to keep the car steady. When the vehicle burst out onto the gravel-packed main road, she spun the wheel to the left and pushed on the gas again as the fiends raced along beside the car.

Since they couldn't flash and there was no way to call for help, the only thing Olivia could hope for was to outrun the beasts. The cats were fast.

She prayed that the Lincoln was faster.

CHAPTER THIRTY

Kylen didn't need a hellhound to know that demons had recently been in the alley. Sulfur lingered in the air and six corpses were flailing against the chain-link gate, blocking the exit to the alley.

The demons were ramping up their activity.

Deacon, Nate and the dog were a block over. The remaining reaper teams had spread out, each team covering a grid, block by block across the city. They'd started from the most recently opened portal on the outskirts of town, but the demons had clearly already made their way into the population.

Unfortunately, from the looks of the poor soulless bastards in the alley, the demons also weren't waiting for their prey to die. They were taking what they wanted with a clear disregard for the previously agreed-upon rules of war.

Virtually brain dead without their souls, these victims maintained only their most primitive bodily functions, with no intention or purpose. They lived, but only on the most animal level.

And they needed to be put down. Nate kept blabbering on about his Pollyanna hopes for soul restoration, but as far as Kylen knew, no soul had ever been successfully reinhabited in its body.

"What we got here, yippee-ki-yay?" Kylen turned to see Raguel approaching behind him. Great, just what he needed—an audience.

"You can see them, same as me."

"Camael's minions haven't been wasting any time, that's for sure. So what's the plan, cowboy?" Raguel glanced back toward the street as Samkiel joined them.

Kylen stepped into Raguel's space. "Do I look like a freakin' cowboy to you?"

"I'm Italian. You all look like cowboys to me."

"I see that you're making friends already, Ragu." Samkiel nodded to Kylen, and Raguel stepped back. "Are those—"

"Wanderers." Kylen said, finishing his question. "They'll have to be dealt with. There's bound to be a whole lot more of them, too."

"When did they start attacking live ones?" Samkiel asked.

"Recently." Kylen offered.

"Isn't that against the supernatural Geneva convention or something?" Ragu asked.

"I don't think they care about the rules anymore." Kylen said.

"So what's the plan?" Samkiel asked.

"That's what Yippee, I mean Kylen, and I were just discussing."

Kylen flicked open his scythe and started down the alley. "We put them down."

"Wait," Deacon called, entering the alley from behind him.

Sweet Jesus, Mary, and Joseph. When were they

going to learn? How many times and how many ways was he going to have to explain this? If these people had a conscious thought in their heads, they'd be begging to be put out of their misery, not debating nonexistent options.

Deacon put a hand on Kylen's shoulder. "Kylen, think about this. Exponentially, we could be talking thousands of these wanderers in a few weeks with this many demons on the loose."

"Exactly. So what are you suggesting?"

"You warned me about this, so I spoke with Grim when we closed the last portal. He's offered a solution. At least a temporary one. Let Samkiel take them to a resting place."

"For what purpose? Perpetual Purgatory? Is that any better than true death?"

"What if Nate's right? What if there's another way?"

"Are you shitting me? Their souls are gone, Deacon."

"But if there's a chance…"

"How?"

Samkiel walked toward the wanderers. He spread his arms wide, and a bright white radiance began to project outward from him like a searchlight. The glow encompassed the wanderers and froze them in place. It increased in intensity until Kylen's retinas began to burn, making him blink. As Samkiel walked toward them, their bodies winked from the corporal plane before Kylen's eyes. The reaper vanished with the wanderers and the alley was plunged into darkness once again.

"What the hell?"

"Our boy has a special gift, newly enhanced with his promotion. Dare and Zak can do it, too." Raguel turned to leave the alley. "We'd better get a move on if we want to take any of these assholes off the street tonight. I'm heading out farther with Dare and Oreo. If the demons are poaching so heavily around here, an exit portal can't be far. The rest of the crew will spread out from here. We've got this. You two do what you need to do."

And with that, Kylen and Deacon found themselves alone in the alley.

"What—exactly—was that?"

Deacon smiled. "One of the many benefits of having a Reaper Authority Force. No more killing innocents or burning bodies. Grim chose these men for their talents, and then…enhanced them."

"And you? Can you do that now?"

"No."

"Interesting. And to what fresh hell are those wanderers headed?"

"Not Hell. A holding place in Purgatory."

"And then what?"

"I don't have all the answers here, Kylen. But it's better than the way we've been working. Burning bodies in our basement? Do you really want to keep doing that? It wouldn't even be possible with the numbers we're dealing with now."

Kylen closed his scythe and slid it back into its scabbard. "Grim's going to need a bigger cell."

"Not if we keep moving."

* * *

As Kylen and Deacon left their alley, Bo galloped onto the sidewalk a block down the street and directed two gruff barks at them before turning back toward the alley. Nate stumbled out after him, his face contorted in pain and terror. Kylen scanned the street for the source of his distress, but there were no attackers in sight.

"What is it?" Deacon asked as Nate crumpled to the sidewalk.

"I don't know. I was fine, and then I started feeling pain. Everywhere... Ahhhhh." Nate folded himself in half and lay on the pavement moaning.

Deacon squatted beside him. "Can you flash? Where do you want to go? Should we take you to the hospital?"

"Ruth..." Nate ground out through shudders.

Deacon grabbed him by the shoulders and shook him lightly, demanding his attention. "What about Ruth? Do we need to go home?"

"Something's wrong with her." Nate moaned on the pavement.

"How do you know?"

"Maybe another of Grim's 'enhancements'?" Kylen offered.

"Holy Hell, could this night get any worse?" Deacon asked.

Kylen nodded an implied *yes*.

"Hospital." Nate groaned.

Kylen looked from Nate to Deacon in frustration. "Better take him. I'll make my way back to the cemetery, and then flash home to check on the women."

"Flash from here, Kylen."

"I can't."

"You can now."

Kylen was sure the man had lost his ever-loving mind. Despite Grim's supposed endowment, the thought of flashing from unconsecrated ground was preposterous to him. Of course, after what he'd just witnessed, maybe it wasn't such a stretch.

"What the hell." As he concentrated on returning home, Kylen started to feel the slow tug to which he'd grown accustomed. Anxiety and dread stirred in his gut as he flashed through the consecrated subway for the first time ever from unconsecrated ground. After all the strange incidents of the night, Kylen couldn't help but wonder what would come next.

Then he landed on the smoldering ash that was once his trailer.

CHAPTER THIRTY-ONE

Olivia careened the car down the road, barely keeping it under control as the cats raced beside the car and gravel sprayed behind them. If she could make it to the part of the road where the pavement kicked in, she knew she could outrun them. She knew she could. But if she put on any more speed over this gravel, she'd T-bone the three of them into a tree. When a handful of cats leapfrogged over one another and onto the windshield obscuring her view, she knew it was game over. She couldn't drive anywhere if she couldn't see.

"The cemetery! Pull into the cemetery!" Maeve yelled from the backseat. It was directly to their left. This she could do.

Olivia wrenched the wheel to the left, taking out two sections of the cemetery's chain-link fence as she slid the Lincoln across the boundary of Good Hope and onto consecrated ground. The cats that were on the car incinerated in little sparks and poofs of smoke as the car skidded through the wet grass, crashing into the side of the concrete Wesley crypt. Maeve and Ruth slammed against the back of the front seats, and Olivia's head collided with the steering wheel before slamming back against the headrest.

Her hands were shaking violently, but she couldn't unpeel them from the steering wheel. Tears sprang to her eyes, but she pushed them back and forced herself to look out the windshield. No more cats. She turned to scan the perimeter of the cemetery. The creatures lined the edges, but none of them had made it through the consecrated barrier.

"Good driving, Olivia."

Ruth lay unconscious on the floorboard of the back seat, her skin a deathly shade of pale except for her injured arms. Panic flooded Olivia, but one look from Maeve set her back on course.

"Don't you even think about coming unglued." Maeve pushed her door open. "We're going to get out of here. And we're going to be fine."

"How? Those monsters have us trapped."

"We're going to flash. You've been able to travel that way before. Surely to God you can do it again."

"And if I can't?"

"Lock yourself in the car, and do not leave it under any circumstances. I'll be back as fast as I can. I know it's dangerous for Ruth to travel that way, but I'm not going to sit here and watch her die."

"Can you give her energy? Can you heal her like Kylen heals me?"

"I don't know what it would do to her in this state. I can't risk it."

"What about the baby?"

"That's out of our hands now." Maeve eased Ruth off the floorboard, cradling her in her arms. "Come around and help me get her out of the car. Let's get to the hospital. It's our best chance right now."

Olivia reached for the car handle just as the driver-side door was ripped from the vehicle. A man stood beside the car. His sleek black hair was streaked with blond highlights, and his eyes glowed yellow in the moonlight. A wave of power washed over her when he reached for her hand. As soon as they touched, Olivia's fear eased immediately. He pulled her from the car, scooped her up and carried her in his arms. She had some sense of Maeve struggling with Ruth and then trying to come around the car to help her, but her surroundings blurred and her mind went fuzzy as an inexplicable feeling of ease settled over her like a warm blanket.

Clearly she hadn't actually survived the crash. She sent a prayer up for Ruth and the baby and another one for Kylen. This was the end. This was her angel, the one who'd come to take her to Heaven. She wished it could have been Kylen, but in a way this was best. Maybe he wouldn't be as tortured since he hadn't experienced her death first-hand.

Her skin sizzled with energy as she was pulled into the consecrated subway. The fine hairs rose across her body, and she pulled in a last breath before they raced through complete blackness and toward the hereafter.

* * *

The acrid smell of burning plastic, shingles, wood and worse things filled his nostrils, but it wasn't the smell that made his eyes well with tears. Ruth's house was gone. No, not just gone. It had disintegrated into a scattered patch of ash and smoldering debris. The only things left standing were the stone walls and fireplace like a sandstone Stonehenge. Red embers glowed everywhere like a carpet of magma covering the front and back yard.

Kylen couldn't muster the strength to move forward to sift through the wreckage. It was all gone. *They* were all gone.

His home. His friend. His lover.

The only reason he knew he stood where his own trailer had once been was the glint of steel that caught his eye in the moonlight. His blades lay in a jumble to his left.

There were no remaining traces of the circle of protection, but the scorched earth followed a perfectly symmetrical ring around the house, which made him wonder if the circle failed before or after Ruth's death…because her death was the only explanation for why the circle would have failed so catastrophically. She was the main energy supply. There hadn't been time to include any of the newbies into the magical power grid. Nate had reinforced it months ago, adding himself, Deacon and, reluctantly, Kylen, but the circle was strongest when Ruth was inside it. Ruth *was* strong, so if she had been here when this happened, the onslaught must have been massive.

Paralyzed with shock and disbelief, he felt himself rocking on his heels, his head shaking side to side of its own accord, a gathering storm building inside him. When he saw two vertical yellow eyes glowing at the edge of the woods, his madness unleashed. Kylen rushed across the smoking ground toward the yellow eyes, already knowing full well what it was, suddenly piecing together the likely cause of this unfathomable destruction. He crashed through the woods in pursuit of the imp. Limbs and thorny vines ripped and tore at him as he raced after the beast. He wouldn't catch it, *couldn't* catch it. But he clawed his way forward, sprinting after the thing until his lungs burned and his heart threatened to seize up and out of his chest.

Then he caught it.

With his bare hands, he tore the arms and legs from the fiend. A wretched odor erupted from the ragged holes left from the severed limbs but he ignored it, grasping the top of the creature's head with inhuman ferocity, and then slowly carving his scythe through its nonexistent neck as its yellow eyes blinked rapidly and its mouth gaped open, exposing row upon row of needle-pointed teeth. The body dropped to the ground, and he stared into the thing's dead eyes before flinging its head up and over the trees toward the house.

Killing the imp had done nothing to satiate his need for vengeance.

Gone. Gone. Gone.

No one could have survived that fire.

He dropped to his knees in the blackness, his heart still pounding an unsustainable tempo against his ribs, and threw back his head, staring up through the canopy of trees at the dark sky. His chest and shoulders heaved with each breath he dragged into his seared lungs. Letting his weapon clatter to the ground, he closed his eyes and pulled in another shuddering breath before exhaling an anguished scream.

He'd failed again.

Failed another woman he...loved. She'd broken the stone walls around his heart, and now she was gone, stolen from him by a death so horrific he couldn't even allow himself to picture it. And Ruth? His own loss was more than he could bear. His friend's loss was beyond comprehension: a lover *and* a child.

"No. No. No. No. NO! NO! NO!" he chanted into the steely darkness like a mantra. The only other sound was the occasional pop of a beam or framing board crackling behind him. There were no signs of life. No rodents or other animals scurried around. Every living thing had vanished around the perimeter of the house and grounds. Even the imps. A spark lit in the back of his mind. If the women were dead, where were their souls? He walked across the still glowing remains of the house to where the living room had once been and placed his palms against the charred debris. Then he did the one thing he'd refused to do for more than a century.

He prayed.

He begged whoever would listen that he could at least take them to Purgatory.

The smell of his flesh burning didn't deter him. He reached into the steaming rubble with his reaper senses as well as his bare hands, searching and grasping for their souls. After several moments with no success, he stood, his palms smoldering.

Nothing.

Of course not.

How had the creatures breached the circle of protection? He'd trusted Nate's magic and this had been his reward: death and destruction. He was a pawn in a game he was beyond sick and tired of playing. For the briefest of moments, he'd allowed himself to think...to hope...

But that didn't matter now.

It was over.

Kylen pushed himself to his feet and collected his weapon.

Olivia had believed faith would save him.

He now knew that *nothing* could save him.

CHAPTER THIRTY-TWO

Maeve landed in the hospital chapel and carried Ruth through the corridors, searching for someone, anyone, to help her. When a staff member finally spotted them, he quickly activated some sort of emergency code that brought an army of personnel down upon them. Maeve was relieved of her burden and pushed to the background as they raced away with Ruth on a gurney. She followed them and was pummeled with questions en route.

She did her best to answer their queries and weave a believable story, but she was less than confident of her fiction. Ruth needed Deacon. Healing energy from him or one of the others was the only thing that would reliably save her.

The seriousness of Ruth's condition came crashing down on her as she watched the staff start a blood transfusion, which was a Band-Aid at best.

"She's pregnant." Maeve blurted.

"How far along is she?" one of the doctors asked.

"Six weeks?" Maeve guessed.

The sight of Ruth's stark-white pallor and lifeless body sent a tremor through Maeve. She prayed for a miracle. She prayed that somehow, someway, both Ruth and the life inside her would be spared.

The alternative was unbearable.

* * *

Maeve slipped out of the room in the bustle of activity as they worked to stabilize Ruth. She made her way back to the chapel so that she could flash away from the eyes of civilians. She needed to find Deacon. Then Kylen.

She'd lost not one, but two people on her watch. So much for home-front duty being easy.

What a FUBAR situation.

For starters, she would flash downtown to the nest where she'd met Nate a few days ago. That area was a hotbed of demon activity, so hopefully the reapers wouldn't be far. Adrenaline coursed through her veins, amping her back into a reaping machine. She was more than ready to slice and dice, and at this point, all she needed was a suitable target. She crossed the threshold back into the chapel, intent on her mission. Her jaw dropped open.

Deacon was just inside the doorway of the chapel, an unconscious Nate in his arms.

"What the hell is going on?" Maeve canvassed the room for danger, cautious as she approached the two men.

"I don't know. He collapsed while he was muttering some nonsense about Ruth."

"Did you juice him?"

"Not yet. No time. I brought him straight here. Are you up to it? We can do it together before we get the normals involved."

Maeve hesitated. She'd only ever shared her energy one time...and it had ended in disaster. It was the real reason why she hadn't tried to juice Ruth. Her energy was poison. Her brother's face still haunted her. He had died during their training. There had been a freak accident, and she should have been able to heal him— quick and easy—instead, her light had somehow consumed his, draining him to the point of no return. It was the first, and last, time she'd tried to share her energy.

"Maeve!" Deacon demanded, pulling her back to the here and now. "You have to help me with him. He's too far gone for me to heal him myself."

"But he's human."

"He's more than human. He can take it. He needs it, Maeve."

She weighed her options. Deny her boss and possibly kill Nate or tell the truth and expose her weakness. It shouldn't be such a difficult decision. She knew the right choice...so why wasn't she making it?

"My light is poisoned," she finally said.

"What?"

"My energy might kill him. It's killed before. Tell me what you want me to do."

Deacon scrutinized her with an intensity that burned through her, yet she couldn't look away. She wouldn't give him the satisfaction. This was on him. She'd admitted to her fault, and he alone would be responsible for the consequences of his decision.

Nate's body grew rigid and began to seize. Deacon lowered him to the floor and the palms of his hands began to glow and radiate green healing energy, which he pushed through Nate's sternum. Nate's seizure grew more violent instead of less, and he thrashed and heaved up from the floor. His body rejected Deacon's light, hurling it into the ether. All that was left was a white aura.

Without warning, Maeve's body responded to the vacuum of energy, humming and itching along her receptors as it searched for an exit. She felt like her body would fly apart into a million little pieces.

Against her will, energy leaked from her fingertips and streaked toward Nate's lifeless body. Upon impact his chest rose, lifting his torso off the ground. Maeve held him there with her tether of energy for several long moments, her power flooding into him without her consent. She was helpless to stop what was happening, helpless to detach from him.

Tears sprang to her eyes. She didn't want to kill him, but she couldn't make it stop.

Once he gathered himself, Deacon sprang to his feet and tackled Maeve to the ground, breaking the link. Maeve lay exhausted and powerless on the floor.

Nate hadn't completely drained her energy, but the inevitable result for him filled her with an unfathomable sadness she couldn't bear. She'd killed before. She was good at it. But only once had she killed an innocent…and so *intimately.*

"Are you okay?" Deacon asked, dislodging himself from her.

"Yes." Maeve sat up, her mouth dropping open with awe as she studied Nate.

His aura had returned to the calm yellow he usually emitted. Even when she came across him in that demon nest, his aura had been that same content yellow. It was a trait she admired in him, even though he was oblivious to it.

Nate's chest was rising and falling in a regular rhythm again, and his body had relaxed into a more sedate position. He looked downright peaceful. His eyelashes fluttered as he came to.

Relief flooded Maeve.

She'd learned long ago to never show weakness—*no matter what*—so she stuffed her emotions into the black hole in her psyche where they belonged and stood.

The look Nate gave her when his eyes locked onto hers just about broke her. Something elemental had changed between them. She had no idea what, but when he smiled up at her, her knees shook, threatening to buckle beneath her.

"Well, I guess you weren't poison after all, Maeve," Deacon said, pulling a seemingly drunk Nate to his unsteady feet.

The goofy grin on Nate's face was so off-putting; Maeve could barely look at him, but she couldn't look away, either. Her heart did a little stutter, and she coughed to try to make it stop.

It didn't.

What. The. Hell?

His smile faded, his forehead crinkling with concern, as he came back to himself and clutched Deacon's steadying arm. "Ruth is still in danger…"

Before he could even explain, Deacon began to dissolve out of the chapel. Now that his friend was apparently on the mend, his mind must have turned inevitably back to Ruth.

"Deacon, no!" Maeve dove toward him, desperate to break his concentration.

He reassembled in front of her, angry and confused, looking like he wanted to tear her limb from limb.

"She's here!"

"What?"

"Ruth is here in the hospital! Come, I'll show you but… Olivia has been taken."

Chapter Thirty-Three

Maeve watched through the glass doors as the others conversed with Ruth's doctor in the E.R. suite. She paced across the hallway, unnerved by her inability to hear what was going on and her itch to find Olivia.

Deacon's obvious agitation and Ruth's continued unconsciousness didn't bode well for a happy ending to the Catastrophe du Jour. Where was Kylen? She hadn't had a chance to ask them in the confusion. It seemed as though wires were crossed everywhere. For the supposed saviors of mankind, they surely had the worst communication system ever.

Maeve felt Nate's gaze and looked up, meeting his eyes. She could almost feel the strange bond that now stretched between them. Something big had happened. Why or how she knew, she had no idea, but there was almost a tangible connection between them now, like she could reach out and pluck it. She turned away, breaking the link. Nate responded immediately, leaving the room to join her.

"How is she?" Maeve asked.

"Bad. The burns, of course, aren't healing yet. The baby is still viable, but she's going to be here for a good long while. Deacon wants her stabilized on both accounts before we take her home. He'll juice her as soon as they leave the room. That should help, but he says he can only give her small doses of energy because of the pregnancy."

Nate took a tentative step toward Maeve, but she backed away.

"What's going on with you?" she asked. "What happened?"

Nate shook his head. "I don't know. It was like I was feeling everything Ruth had experienced, but I couldn't do anything to help her. When she was near the end of her rope, I went down, too. You and Deacon pulled me back from the abyss. You may have saved Ruth in the process."

Maeve shifted from foot to foot, her eyes focused on the floor as if it were a treasure map, and mumbled, "Don't bet on it."

"What are you so afraid of, Maeve? Is it me?"

Maeve looked stricken. "Why would I be afraid of you?"

"I'm just trying to piece together what's changed and why." Nate reached out to comfort her, but she backed away again, reaching for her blade on instinct.

"Not here!" Nate snapped. He raised his hands in submission and backed away from her.

Embarrassed, she blushed and pushed the blade back into its sheath. "I'm sorry. It's been a long day, and I don't want to talk about this anymore. We need to find Olivia. Where is Kylen? Why didn't he come to the hospital with you?"

"He went to the house to make sure Ruth and Olivia were okay."

"Great." Fresh dread coursed through Maeve.

"The house was on fire, and we ran from it when Ruth was injured. The imps breached the circle as soon as Ruth got hurt, and they chased us all the way to the cemetery. I thought they were after us all, but now I'm sure that they were gunning for Olivia. We were trapped at the cemetery. I was about to flash when something showed up and snatched Olivia. I had no choice but to get Ruth out of there."

"Camael?"

"I can only assume. He flashed into and out of the consecrated grounds of the cemetery, and he wasn't a reaper. Know anyone else who could do that?"

"Ah, hell. Let me go tell Deacon. Camael is the only one who is actively playing both sides. His angel essence must allow him to still travel the consecrated subway. Kylen could still travel through consecration even while he was possessed. Camael must be able to do the same. We should see if we can find Kylen before things get worse." He returned to Ruth's room, and she watched through the door as he spoke to Deacon.

Maeve tugged her jacket smooth and tight over her scabbard and pulled her sleeves back down to her wrists, completely covering her sheathed blades. What had she been thinking? She'd practically wielded one of her weapons against Nate in the hospital hallway. And for what, invading her personal bubble? She was losing her mind.

The moment passed, her tension shifted yet again.

She tried to pull herself together as Nate kissed Ruth's forehead, and then snatched up his backpack from the corner of the room before heading her way.

"Let's go get Bo. I left him in the chapel." He nodded toward her and held her stare a little longer than was comfortable. "We'll leave from there and go straight to the house. Deacon needs to stay here with Ruth."

Nate led the way through the sterile maze of hallways to the chapel. The room was dark and empty save for a row of candles that softly illuminated the area around the altar at the front of the small sanctuary. They walked into the room and the doors closed behind them. Bo emerged from behind the altar, his persistent tail wagging like a propeller and swiping the brass accoutrements from the altar. He approached Nate and flopped over for a belly rub.

Maeve's eyebrows inched upward. "That's the hellhound?"

"Yeah. You ready?" Nate gave the dog a pat and Bo rolled over and sat at his side. He gripped the scruff of the dog's neck with one hand and offered his other hand to Maeve.

"I've got it."

"It's not for you. It's for me. I can use the help. No telling where I'll end up on my own."

Maeve smirked and clasped his hand. "Rookie."

They landed in a pile of smoking rubble.

* * *

Maeve immediately flashed them back a hundred or so feet to the edge of the circle, putting them out of harm's way. Nate was in awe. The destruction was total.

Gone was the house, the trailer, the garage…everything. All that remained was the burned out husk of his Honda and the stone walls of the house and the basement. He tried to make sense of it, but it was impossible. What if Ruth or Olivia or…Maeve had perished in the flames?

He shuddered. Bo sniffed at something wet and gelatinous in the smoldering wreckage to his left. Curious, he walked over to investigate. It was a head.

"Imp." Maeve toed at the glob with her boot.

Adrenaline rushed through his veins and his blood thrummed in his ears as he realized that he could now see the imp for what it really was. For the first time he was seeing with the eyes of a reaper.

What does that mean?

Another realization took shape in his mind, gelling into a terrible truth. "Holy hell, Kylen must think Ruth and Olivia are dead."

Maeve turned to him abruptly, her eyes wide. "How do you know?"

Nate pointed to the ruined creature. Not burned, which meant it hadn't been killed by the fire. "Kylen did this."

"Shit." Maeve walked around to the edge of the circle, toeing at various burned flotsam and jetsam. "Where would he have gone?"

"That's the million-dollar question. Considering he's a man who thinks he has nothing left to lose? I'd say he's on a suicide mission and looking for Camael. Alone." Nate kicked at the remains of the trailer and toed out the pile of blades left in the debris. He bent to retrieve the most wicked-looking blade, its steel still hot to the touch.

"We'll have to split up." Maeve drew her scythe from the scabbard on her back. "Purgatory to talk to Rashnu or downtown to roll some demons for intel on Camael? If he's there, he'll be on a tear. Wanna flip a coin?"

He didn't. Both choices were equally bad. He wasn't even sure if he could go to Purgatory by himself since he wasn't a real reaper. Maeve had much more experience fighting demons, but he wasn't willing to admit to his weakness. Still, he didn't relish the thought of going to the other realm alone.

"Meridian."

"Works for me." Maeve took one long last look around the grounds. "We'll meet back at the hospital chapel in two hours. With any luck, one of us will have Kylen."

Nate waited for Maeve to vanish into the consecrated subway. When she disappeared, he and Bo flashed as well.

CHAPTER THIRTY-FOUR

Nate successfully landed in downtown Meridian. At this rate, he should be earning frequent-flier miles for all his supernatural travel. His best chance of stopping Kylen from self-destructing was to find him or Olivia, stat.

The St. Mary's Catholic Church portal they'd used to rescue Deacon had been sealed as soon as they returned from Hell. If Kylen was going after Camael, there was a good chance he was already well on his way to finding an exit portal. Nate had no doubt a motivated Kylen could devise a satisfactory method of finding a way to Hell, even a well-hidden one.

The next problem was how to get Kylen back against his will. The guy was volatile on a good day, and if he was under the impression that Ruth and Olivia were dead? Nate didn't think Kylen would even be capable of *hearing* reason. Besides, the guy wouldn't leave a fight this big without a resolution.

A man with nothing to lose was hard to beat.

This was without a doubt a job Deacon should be doing, but the big guy was fighting for the lives of his

lover and unborn child. No man—reaper or otherwise—
would be able to worry about anything else under those
circumstances.

Tamping down his own feelings about Ruth's
current situation, he marveled at the fact that a few short
months ago he hadn't even known most of these people.
But now his life was intimately entwined with theirs. He
and Ruth had so much in common, right down to being
adopted. She felt like family.

Nate took stock of where he was, and set about
making a more focused search for the portal. He walked
quickly down one alley then another trying to cover a
grid pattern like they had earlier. It wasn't the first time
he'd wished he had the reaper sensory projection Kylen
could sometimes use to sense their quarry. But what he
did have was a hellhound. Bo sniffed the ground beside
a cardboard recycling bin, scaring a rat out from behind
it.

"Bocephus, come."

Nate wasn't privy to the secret Reaper Authority
handshake, let alone the *Hellhound Use and Training
Manual*. He had no idea how this demon-tracking thing
worked. Or even the commands needed to get the dog to
do his thing.

Moments later, Bo hurtled toward Nate,
skidding to a stop before jumping on his chest. The great
dog's forepaws struck him square in the solar plexus,
pushing him down and pinning him to the ground as the
brute panted his hot dog breath all over his face, with a
liberal slathering of dog drizzle.

Nate laughed in spite of his grim mood, rolling
away from the monster's immense bulk. The dog was
the friendliest nightmare creature he had ever met. Better
than the imps by far. Now he knew why he'd never been
a cat person.

Grabbing great tufts of fur behind both of the

dog's ears, Nate gave him a good scratching. He'd never been allowed a pet of his own until his Wiccan guardians had adopted him. Even then, pets had been more like family members than animals. Familiars, some called them. None of the familiars that were attached to the members of his coven had ever been as happy to see him as Bo was now. A glimmer of hope sparked in Nate's chest and bloomed, spreading warmth through him and filling him with a momentary calm. Maybe this would all work out after all.

The spark of hope was extinguished seconds later when Nate smelled the reek of a demon. Bo jumped to his feet, a low growl emanating from him as four demons, using college-aged men as hosts, ambled into view. Hell, they weren't even going to have to track the bastards down at this rate. The demons were so thick they were coming to him.

The group paused at the entrance to the alley. Nate reached over his right shoulder and pulled a short sword from his scabbard. Only reapers rated the "government issued" scythes. He was grateful that he'd heeded Kylen's advice and started to carry a more effective weapon. With the short sword, he didn't have to come as close to make a kill as with the push daggers, but he still didn't like his odds. He'd never faced one demon alone, let alone four.

Adrenaline rushed to his heart, which drummed loudly in his chest and head, blocking out all other sound. He tried to ground himself, retrieving the calm he'd experienced moments earlier, but it was long gone. Fight or flight was his current modus operandi.

Bo made the first move, charging toward the quartet in a flurry of fur and teeth. The demons carried no visible weapons. They had thrown out any notions of subtlety… All they needed to do was get close enough to their victims to jerk out their souls. Nate had no intention of becoming one of their victims.

Bo barreled toward Thing One and Thing Two while the remaining two demons strode toward Nate. Their toxic stench was overwhelming, worse somehow than what he'd experienced while in Hell. As they closed the distance to him, his eyes began to burn and water, blurring his vision.

He blinked rapidly, trying to clear his line of sight, but something was wrong. The stench had surrounded him in a fog, and was mudding his mind as well as his vision. None of the demons he'd helped kill and dispatch had used this sort of weapon before…this was something new.

The demons were evolving.

Nate needed a better defense. He was almost incapacitated, and the first blow hadn't even been struck. Although he'd never knowingly manifested a protective aura alone, he and Ruth had done so together many times in the past. The magical circles he'd cast around his home and Ruth's were mostly static. What he needed now was something more mobile. He imagined a protective circle of energy projecting out from him, pushing away the debilitating poison from the demons. The circle wouldn't stop the demons from attacking him, but he hoped it would reduce or eliminate this new advantage of theirs.

Focusing inward, he drew in a long, deep breath, and then watched in amazement as light began to glow around him. Soon he was enveloped by a bright green radiance.

A screeching noise drew their attention. The demons turned back to see their fallen comrades being ripped and sliced by Bo. The dog's size and ferocity was impressive, and he was more than a match for his two opponents. When one fell to the ground, the dog latched onto its throat, tearing it open like a bloody Christmas gift, all but decapitating the host before he renewed his attack upon the other one. Raking his claws down the demon's fleshy shell, the dog then inflicted a well-placed bite to its neck.

The hosts' heads were still attached by tendons and dangling bits of flesh, but the job was completed—they lay dead and worthless and Bo began to consume the bodies in great fleshy chunks. Two black torrents of smoky mist streamed from the torsos, followed by several lighter gray shadows. Unable to resist the call of the untethered souls, Thing Three and Thing Four retreated from Nate to retrieve the freed souls for their master. They were programmed for one duty: collecting souls. Right now that was working to Nate's advantage.

He watched as they collected the errant souls. The two unhoused demons hovered nearby for a few moments, obviously weighing the possibility of taking Nate's body, and then abandoned the alley in search of easier prey. After gathering the stray souls, the two remaining demons, stuffed and confused, also abandoned the fight, retreating down the alley at a jog.

Nate hoped they would be drawn to the portal to deliver their latest cargo. It was the best plan he had... It was the *only* plan he had.

"Bo, come!" Nate called to the hellhound, who reluctantly obeyed his command this time and retreated from the already-spotless site of his frenzied dinner party. He dropped one remaining bloody femur at Nate's feet, wagging his tail. "No time for fetch now, boy. Let's follow those demons to the portal."

Careful to stay far enough behind them not to draw their interest, Nate and Bo followed the quickly deteriorating hosts to the edge of town. The demons were slow and lethargic, but they seemed determined. Nate was becoming increasingly certain that they'd lead him to exactly what he was looking for.

They were heading into the industrial part of town near the old railroad hub, an unfamiliar area for Nate. The train yard had long since closed and only the daily coal trains passed through the area on their way to the power plant. No cargo loaded or offloaded here anymore, and auto traffic was virtually nonexistent. It was the perfect place for nefarious activities...and a portal to Hell.

The most-used train track was still well maintained, but one abandoned line veered off into the woods before vanishing into the undergrowth. The demons followed the path less traveled into the darkness of the woods. Nate and Bo stayed as close behind as they dared until the tracks ended at an abandoned railcar.

Thing Three and Thing Four entered the railcar, and seconds later a flash of light filled the container, pouring from the dilapidated sides for a split second before vanishing. Nate hesitated, considering his options. Should he continue his search for Kylen, or find the others and lead them to the portal?

He decided to flash himself back to the hospital chapel to rendezvous with Maeve. Surely she would know what to do. He was all out of ideas.

Chapter Thirty-Five

Kylen landed in Purgatory and stalked through the steam leaching up through the cracks in the stone floor, pushing aside anyone or anything that had the misfortune of stepping into his path. He was walking a fine line by being physical with the other reapers, but he didn't care.

His needed answers.

Purgatory was a no man's land where reapers of all races and species brought the souls of their dead for sorting. The Grand Central Station of death. Everything except for demons and imps, both of which were *born* of Hell, had a soul. And all those souls required reaping.

The angel Rashnu spotted him as the other reapers made way for him. When the angel raised an arm over his head, Kylen was certain for a moment that he was about to be struck down for insubordination, but instead Rashnu pointed to a tunnel at the end of the station, which illuminated of its own accord.

Kylen walked toward the tunnel, the other reapers parting before him like the Red Sea before the

Israelites.

As he stalked his way into the tunnel, he was blinded by the searing light that seemed to emanate from the walls. A heavy wooden door sealed off an arched doorway to his left. He recognized it as the door to Rashnu's quarters. Turning, he put his back to the wall and waited, his scythe still drawn.

After a moment, Rashnu joined him. "I thought you were going to incite a war out there. It would have been a shame to have to smite you after all you've survived."

Kylen scoffed, unconvinced by his forced concern. With a wave of his hand, Rashnu opened the door. "Please," he said, motioning toward the bar. He pulled out a chair for him before walking behind the counter and setting down three glasses.

Kylen frowned. *Three?*

Rashnu muttered and mumbled beneath the bar, his long dark hair a wild mass bobbing up and down like a buoy on the sea. Finally he rose to his full height, a bottle in each hand. He carefully measured out a shot from each of the bottles into one of the glasses before returning the bottles behind the bar. He topped off his own glass from a dark decanter, and then filled the third glass from yet another bottle.

"You are a drinking man, yes?" Rashnu slid a glass toward him.

Kylen picked up the tumbler and sniffed its contents. It smelled like whiskey and something sweet he couldn't quite place. Not entirely unpleasant, but something held him back. "Why aren't you drinking the same thing?" Kylen asked.

"Because I'm not taking the same journey as you."

The only thing Kylen hated more than riddles and evasions was...yeah, nothing. He had come here for answers, and he wanted them yesterday.

"Talk sense."

"Why did you come here tonight, Kylen?" Rashnu tipped his glass to his lips and sipped. "I can sense the rage in your heart."

"Where is Grim?"

"If you've come to see Grim, he's unavailable. But rest assured that I can help you with anything you need. So, again, I ask you, why did you come here tonight?"

"I want their souls returned."

"Whose souls?"

"Ruth's and…Olivia's."

Rashnu tipped back his glass and let the remaining liquid slide down his throat. "I'm afraid that's impossible considering the current state of affairs."

"Where are they? I know you know. Tell me, and I'll retrieve them myself!" Kylen slammed his fist and his scythe into the top of the bar.

"That would be difficult considering the fact that they both still hold their souls."

Kylen blinked. First he was unsure of what he'd heard, and then he was positive it was a trick. "They are alive? Both of them?"

"Yes. Both are alive. Although, Ruth is gravely injured. And Olivia…"

"Where are they?"

"Ruth is under Deacon's care. And Olivia is with another. I do not know where. I only know that she is alive. For now."

Kylen's blood sizzled in his veins. He wanted to reach across the bar and tear the angel's head from his shoulders. Rashnu was purposely messing with him, and he was in no mood for games.

"Who is she with?"

"I think you know. Haven't you been wondering

why those imps have been following you?" Rashnu downed the rest of the drink with one gulp and held the glass up to the light, admiring it.

"How do you know about that?"

"It's my job to know about lost souls, Kylen. It's your job to make the right decisions so that yours can be found. Even more so now that you have committed yourself to the Authority. Or has your resolve already waned?"

"I'm sick of your bullshit, angel. Who has her? And how can I get her back?"

"Who do you serve, Kylen?"

Kylen blinked and sat back in the bar stool like he'd been struck.

Who did he serve?

Himself, that's who.

"You prayed earlier and asked for help, no? You arrived here unharmed and now have private audience with me, answers at your fingertips and a stiff drink before you. All you have to do is choose. Who do you serve? Sure you've been installed as an Authority, but you and I both know your heart is not yet in it. You've seen the best and worst both sides have to offer, no? Very few ever get to have that experience, Kylen. They choose without nearly as much information as you have at your fingertips, damning or saving themselves in the process. So what will it be? Who do you truly serve? There are really just two choices. Good or evil? Light or dark? Pick one and choose your path. Once and for all."

Kylen's head reeled. Why should he have to choose? His earlier plan of disappearing was looking better and better, but he was well beyond that option now. He was sitting with an angel in Purgatory while Olivia was... somewhere with Camael. Yes, he knew there was only one who could have taken her. He was the one creature vile enough to use a dying woman as bait, to take the woman Kylen...loved. Even now he could barely think the word.

He should have known the imps weren't there for him to command. The whole time, they'd been there to keep an eye on him. Camael had known all along that he could still tune in to Hell. The bastard had kept the channels open to him hoping he could use the connection to entice him to return. Hadn't that been the reason for all his nightmares? Now that he was being honest with himself, he'd known that all along. Had known and let that knowledge fester inside him because he thought he deserved to be damned.

Could he ever clear his memories of the time he'd spent controlled by Orithicon? No, he knew his destiny. He would always remember. The question was whether or not he would let himself be ruled by those memories.

"Who do you serve, Kylen? Your answer will make all the difference in how we go forward."

Kylen swallowed hard. His hands shook as he wrapped them around the glass in front of him. He realized he wasn't just choosing for himself. He was choosing for Olivia, too. If he chose wrong, she'd be damned as well, and that he couldn't allow. He'd carried Kara's soul to Purgatory so that she could ascend. When the time came, he'd do no less for Olivia, no matter how painful it was for him.

"The One True Light," Kylen said, his voice sounding weak even to himself.

"Well, thank God for that." Rashnu tossed back the last half inch of his drink and slammed the glass down on the bar with a hearty whack. "Now drink up. You're about to have a visitor."

Kylen snapped up his gaze to meet Rashnu's glittering, green eyes. "Who? Olivia?"

"No, you're going to have to save Olivia on your

own. Drink if you want to find out." Rashnu walked out from behind the bar, heading for the door.

Kylen picked up the glass with both hands and pressed it to his lips. It trembled there for a moment, and then he tipped his head back, letting the amber liquid slide down his throat, feeling more like a death sentence than a rescue. A purple mist emanated from his throat and chest as the drink made its way through his insides like a stream of molten lava. He slammed the glass down onto the bar and tried to curse, but he couldn't pull in enough breath to force out the words. Panic rose up from his gut, and he was sure he would suffocate from it when he heard the door open and shut behind him.

When he turned, Kara stood before him.

CHAPTER THIRTY-SIX

Kylen closed his eyes and rubbed them hard with the heels of both hands. What had that damn angel given him? He needed to lie down…for a month. This entire debacle was exhausting. But when he opened his eyes again, she still stood before him, wearing a flowing white robe, her green eyes luminous.

He stared at her, unable to believe she was anything other than an illusion.

When she took a step toward him, he startled and nearly fell from his bar stool.

What the hell?

"Kylen. It's me. It's not a trick." Kara held out a hand in a placating gesture like he was a frightened child or a wild animal to be tamed.

Her eyes sparkled as she approached him, but her smile was what shattered him.

Planting his feet on the stone floor, he took a tentative step toward her. His legs crumpled beneath him, leaving him on his knees before her. He hung his head and gasped in ever-more labored breaths, trying to keep himself from passing out. When her hands tangled in his hair and pulled his face up to meet hers, he couldn't hold back the groan that choked from his heaving body.

He was ruined.

If this *was* a trick, he was lost.

She stroked his hair and pulled his face against her thighs as his arms wrapped around her of their own accord. He wanted to stand but couldn't make his legs work.

Mercifully, she knelt in front of him, and he raised his trembling hands to the sides of her head. Cradling her face between his palms, he studied her against his memories. Her green eyes and straight white-blond hair were the same. He smoothed a hand down her cheek, letting it linger there. She pressed her face against his palm, and he broke.

"How?" he asked, not wanting the answer but desperate for it, too. He'd dreamed of seeing her again, yet he'd never believed it was truly possible.

"I came back to bring you a gift, Kylen. A gift of life."

"Return to me."

"I can't. Purgatory is as far as I can come and only this once. Rashnu broke all the rules to get me here. He wasn't supposed to let me return to the fourth Heaven if I chose this, but he figured out a way…if you made the right choice first." Kara stroked his face and pushed the hair from his eyes. "I'm so glad you did."

"I'm sorry," Kylen said, his voice cracking.

"Why are you sorry? You saved my soul. You gave me everything."

"I betrayed you."

"With Olivia? Kylen, you still have a life to live. Live it. You betrayed nothing. I know you love me. You proved it when you saved me and Deacon and a thousand times before that. You deserve to be loved by someone who's alive. Let her love you." She leaned in and kissed his lips. He was paralyzed by the fear that she'd vanish.

"How?"

"The same way you loved me, Kylen. Utterly." She kissed his forehead. "Fiercely." She kissed his closed eyes. "Completely." She kissed his lips once again, and then drew a vial from her robe and offered it to him. Its pink contents shimmered and swirled in the light.

"What is that?"

"It's the essence of the Valkyrie. My essence. My strength. I don't need it where I am now, but if you give it to Olivia before it's too late, you can save her. If you take a sip here and give the rest to her when you find her, it will bind her to you. It's been blessed, Kylen. Olivia will be healed. So no more thoughts about giving up. Keep your light and your head, and you'll keep your woman. You have a job to do and a life to live out to its end, however long that may be. Live it well, love."

Kara unplugged the vial and held it to his lips. His lips parted, and she poured the liquid into his mouth. The room before him fractured as his vision exploded, shattering everything into a million disjointed images. Memories unraveled from his mind, the worst of them, the demon's, torn out like weeds, streaming away from him in a visible line, much like the souls he'd purged thousands of times.

He fell to the floor prostrate and laid his forehead against the cool stone as Kara caressed his back. Nausea came in wave after wave as the demon's memories were purged from him. When the pain finally ceased, he lay weak and helpless on the floor.

Kara wiped the sweat from his brow with the hem of her robe, and then plugged the vial with the stopper, tucking it into his pants pocket. "Find her, Kylen. Save her. Save yourself."

She leaned down to kiss him, and he struggled to hold on to her for a moment longer. Gaze upon her for one more second.

"I love you," he pleaded, tears searing down his face.

"I know." She pulled away and walked to the bar. Raising the glass, she tipped it toward him. "To your health, Kylen. I'll love you always, too. Be well. Be loved."

As soon as the liquid disappeared down her throat, she began to shimmer. In a blink of his eye, she was gone. Again.

Forever.

He closed his eyes and tried to believe it was all another dream. A crazy, cruel dream, but the vial in his pocket proved otherwise. And now that the worst of his demon's memories were gone, a glimmer of hope ignited in him.

He had a chance.

A chance to say goodbye and a chance to save Olivia.

He'd made his choice.

Now all he had to do was find her.

CHAPTER THIRTY-SEVEN

Kylen had no idea how much time had passed when he finally managed to pull himself together. He scrubbed a hand down his face, wiping away the evidence of his emotion. With renewed purpose and much steadier legs, he stalked across the room to the only door, scythe in hand. As he reached for the handle, Rashnu pulled it open from the other side and stood in the doorway.

"Now what?" Kylen asked.

Rashnu laid his hand on Kylen's shoulder and squeezed. "Welcome back…for real this time."

"Let's not get all Dr. Phil just yet. I still have to find Olivia. Now." Kylen shrugged from his hold.

"Yes, I have work to do, and you have a woman to save. Good luck, Kylen."

Kylen pushed past him, but then stopped just outside the doorway. He stared down the long tunnel, unable to look the angel in the eye. "Thank you, Rashnu."

"You are most welcome. I'm happy you chose well."

"Thank you for...all of it."

"Yes."

As he turned, Rashnu touched his shoulder and flashed him out of Purgatory.

* * *

Kylen landed in Ruth's hospital room. "So it's true. They're alive?" He looked at Ruth's burned and bandaged body, so frail in the cold room.

"Kylen?" Deacon offered him an awkward embrace. "What happened to you?"

"Kara. I got to say goodbye."

Deacon nodded.

"You asked Rashnu to do that for me, didn't you?"

"I planted the seeds, but I didn't know what the outcome would be."

Nate and Maeve appeared in the doorway, disheveled and out of breath.

After stepping into the room in front of her partner, Maeve gave Kylen an appraising once over, her forehead wrinkled with a question. "You're back? We thought you'd gone postal."

"Not yet." Kylen said.

As Maeve told them the story of Olivia's kidnapping, Kylen grew increasingly agitated. "We're running out of time."

Deacon turned to look at Maeve. "I need you to stay with Ruth. Promise me you won't leave her side."

"I promise."

"Where do you want to start?" Deacon asked, stroking his hand through Ruth's hair.

"I found an exit portal. I followed two demons to it. Do you think he would have taken her to Hell?" Nate said.

Kylen shook his head. "No. I think he's holding her as bait. We should start at Good Hope, where Olivia was taken."

"Maybe Bo can pick up her scent," Nate said. "He's in the chapel."

* * *

Olivia awoke on a hard wooden pew. She was afraid, and had no idea where she was other than in an empty church. Two of the windows to her right were broken and boarded over with plywood. Moonlight illuminated the room with slants of light, enough for her to make out the typical accoutrements of a church, but from this vantage point she couldn't get a true sense of the size of things…or a possible escape route.

Her rapid breaths reverberated through the otherwise silent room. Exhaustion coursed through her body, making her limbs heavy and her bones hurt. Pressing the little button on the side of her watch, she saw that it was 3:00 a.m. Three hours since she'd died.

Clearly this was not Heaven. Or at least no version she'd ever imagined. Bits and pieces of the night floated back to her. The cats, yowling and hissing. The fire. The terrifying car ride. The cemetery. She drew her knees up to her chest, curling into a ball on the bench. The small movement reignited the pain from the wounds in her calves. Images of the handsome man with sleek black hair and the yellow eyes of a beast returned to her.

He'd bewitched her somehow. He was no angel.

And she was not dead after all. Not just yet, anyway.

She sat up carefully to examine her wounds. Deep angry red gouges festered beneath her shredded jeans. Rising from the bench, she looked around the sanctuary, searching for any sign of her kidnapper.

Determining she was alone, she crossed over to the door and tried to budge its heavy wood. It was locked and much too solid to break open, at least in her weakened state, so she walked over to the remaining stained-glass windows and tried to peer through them. The images outside were distorted by the colored glass, and the small amount of moonlight wasn't enough to provide illumination. Still, blurred movement caught her eye, and a shiver skipped down her spine, raising gooseflesh on her arms and legs. She wasn't alone after all. Something *was* out there, stalking around the church. Something small. A *lot* of somethings.

Like cats.

Olivia searched the sanctuary for anything she could use to break through the window. Surely it would be safer to go outside and face the cats, or whatever they were, than to stay here waiting for her captor to return.

Camael.

The name whispered in the back of her mind. Had he told her his name? She couldn't remember. Picking up the wooden lectern, she carried it to the window. Closing her eyes, she pulled it back and rammed it into the stained-glass depiction of the Fall of Man. It bounced off the window without leaving so much as a crack in the glass, but sparks exploded upon impact, crackling through the wood. She released the lectern in surprise and it crashed to the ground, splintering into dust.

So much for breaking out the windows.

A sudden wave of fatigue overtook her, almost crumpling her to the floor. Her surge of adrenaline had been spent. She made her way back to the pew and laid down, curling herself back into a ball, tucking her hands under her head for a pillow.

Closing her eyes, she prayed that Kylen would find her before the man returned. She pulled the front of her T-shirt out enough to peer down between her breasts. The electric-blue blaze, the strange aftereffect of their lovemaking, had all but vanished. She couldn't help but think that she was fading, too. Her old pains had crept back into her bones and joints.

Time was short.

Would she pass away here in an abandoned church, all alone? A twinge of fear stabbed at her heart.... She had thought she was ready, but she didn't want to die. Not yet. Not without telling Kylen goodbye. Despite her best efforts and intentions, she did love him. Already. She wanted a future with him.

As unfair as it was and as much as it would hurt both of them, she wanted the opportunity to tell him that.

She resolved that whatever happened to her here in this church, she wouldn't die. Not until she saw Kylen again. Peace washed over her with that resolution. She couldn't escape. But she could wait.

Closing her eyes, she listened. Somewhere in the night she could swear she heard a cat mewl.

CHAPTER THIRTY-EIGHT

Kylen stood in Good Hope Cemetery and sent his senses out into the night, desperate to find some sign of Olivia. If they found an imp or a demon, he would get his answers, one way or another, but nothing returned to him. He was blind to the dark side; his tether to it had been severed for good.

Nate encouraged the hellhound to pick up Olivia's scent from the front seat of the car. Deacon watched while the beast sniffed the Lincoln and then the ground around it. "That's one huge-ass mutt," he said.

The beast's tail started to whip back and forth. He lifted his head, letting loose an unearthly howl that was promptly answered by dogs and coyotes from miles around.

The dog sniffed excitedly along the ground, weaving in a line toward the wrought-iron fence. He jumped up, setting his paws down on the grates on the small side-entry gate, and howled again.

"Shut that damn thing up."

Nate jogged up to the dog and patted its head. "What did you find there, Bo? Good boy!"

Deacon pulled Bo back by his collar and unlatched the small side gate, swinging it open. "He's on to something."

Bo sniffed circles around the grass, moving up and down several feet along the street before sitting down and waiting.

"That's it?" Kylen asked, disgusted.

"She must have left the cemetery from here but not on foot. I guess he flashed with her like Maeve thought.

"Now what? At least he has both their scents." Nate said, scratching the dog's ears.

"Now we hunt. That dog better show more of an ability to find demons than he does humans, or he's going back to the Purgatory pound. One demon is all I need. I'll make it tell us where she is. Trust me."

"Okay," Deacon said. "Let's try your portal, Nate."

* * *

They flashed back to the exit portal and waited. A stakeout was the last thing Kylen had the patience for, but under the circumstances it was their best bet to catch a demon before the creatures bedded down for the night. They'd probably rest somewhere near the portal or, if they'd had their fill, head back to Hell. Either way was fine by him.

The boxcar was dark as they approached the closed steel door.

"Sure would be nice to know what's waiting for us behind this door," Deacon said, smiling at Kylen. "But then again, I've always liked surprises." Deacon and Kylen drew their scythes.

"Here we go," Nate said, straightening to his full height and pulling his short sword from the scabbard under his shirt.

Kylen gave him a questioning look.

"What?" Nate asked. "If you can't beat 'em, join 'em, right?"

Kylen shook his head and pointed to the door, a twinge of a smile curling his lips. "Do it."

Deacon slid the door back in one swift motion and they poured into the dark rail car.

It was déjà vu all over again, this time the darkness was nearly complete until Deacon manifested a soft glow, illuminating the car enough for them to see the silhouettes of the demons. All males again.

Good.

Kylen slashed and tore his way through three of the eight demon hosts while Deacon and Nate worked on a couple of their own.

Kylen picked up a fourth demon and pressed it into the wall, his knee imbedded into the demon host's groin, holding him several inches off the ground. His scythe curved neatly around the creature's throat, securing it in place. If it surged forward, it would be beheaded. If it tried to slink below his blade, it would be beheaded. If it tried to crawl up the wall, it would be beheaded.

It was a nice place to be. If you were a reaper, that was.

Kylen forced his knee deeper into the host's soft groin. The desire to hack the abomination to bits was so strong he could barely contain himself. His arms shook with anticipation.

The fighting came to an end behind him, and Nate and Deacon flanked him as he held the prick in place.

"Where is Camael?" Kylen asked. Once. Nicely.

The demon laughed. "You're going to kill me, anyway. Why would I help you?"

Kylen glanced at Deacon, making a choice without asking him. "I *am* going to kill you. But the question you have to ask yourself is do you want to live to fight another day? When I kill your host, you can either slink out of here to find a new one or we'll hoover you up like the scum you are and it's lights out. See... you *do* have a choice. Now, choose."

Nate shook his head and stepped back, but Deacon pulled in closer and pressed a push blade against the demon's rib. "You heard him. Choose."

The demon's eyes darted nervously between the two men as sweat broke across his brow. "He's at an abandoned church. Pharr Cemetery."

Kylen dragged the blade across the demon's throat, and its head tilted to the side before tumbling off. He stepped back from the wall and let the body slide to the floor. The demon streamed out of the host's neck and was through the door in a heartbeat.

"Great. More bodies." Nate slid his backpack off his shoulder.

Deacon turned his gaze on Kylen. "So we're freeing demons, now?"

"Temporarily. I'll find him again. Soon."

The sound of bones crunching spun their heads around to the far corner where the hellhound was happily tearing the flesh from the leg of one of the hosts.

"Still think he's cute?" Kylen asked Nate as he walked to the door.

Nate shrugged. "He's efficient. And it'll cut down on dog food."

"Nate, will you stay and take care of this, and then go join Maeve and Ruth?" Deacon said. "I don't like the feel of things."

"You got it."

Kylen and Deacon shimmered and flashed to
Pharr   Cemetery.

CHAPTER THIRTY-NINE

Olivia was fading fast. Her heart was beating more slowly now. She could count the labored beating of the betraying muscle in her chest each time it filled and released. She concentrated on it, willing it to continue its work. Her head grew heavy, and her eyes wouldn't open any longer. Dawn had to be near. Something inside her told her she wouldn't see the sunrise. A tear rolled down her face. She'd accomplished so much in the past year, but it wasn't enough. The one thing she hadn't dared to put on her list, *to be in love,* was the only thing that was currently keeping her heart beating.

She knew it was selfish to want it. Cruel to solicit it. And yet, there it was, wrapped around her heart like a crushing fist, forcing the broken organ to continue doing its job.

She clutched her crumpled list in her damp hand, struggling through the excruciating pain that shot through her body. She couldn't escape it. There was no way around it. The pain had trapped her as surely as this church did, and it was consuming her. The only thing that distracted her from the sensation was counting the items on her list and reliving her accomplishments. Time passed, and she began a new prayer: a prayer for the pain to end. She couldn't take it much longer. The burden was too great.

Drawing in a shuddering gasp, she held it inside, feeling the slow, thick thud of her heart stop as it finally gave up the fight. Her hand fell open and the list rolled to the floor as her last breath escaped in a long, slow sigh.

* * *

Kylen and Deacon flashed into the Pharr Cemetery. Eleven headstones gleamed up at them in the moonlight of the disheveled, unfenced graveyard deep in the Arkansas wilderness. A small white church stood nearly a hundred feet in front of the cemetery. The entire grounds were surrounded by trees. The place hummed with power and was lousy with imps.

"Do you feel that?" Deacon asked, scanning the grounds and taking inventory.

"Yes."

"This place is a ticking time bomb. We can't do this alone."

"I'm not leaving without Olivia." Kylen took a step forward.

Deacon grabbed his arm. "You won't do her any good if you're dead."

Kylen tore from his hold. "Stay, if you're afraid."

"Fuck you." Deacon stalked ahead of him, leading the charge toward the church's door. Imps scattered out of his path and peered around the edges of the building. The grounds were losing their consecration if the imps were this close, which could only mean that an overwhelming force of evil was amassing nearby. As he reached the front steps, head down and determined, Deacon careened into an invisible force field that shot him back across the disheveled front lawn, landing square on his ass.

Kylen swore the imps were laughing at them.

"Dumbass." Kylen helped his friend to his feet and stepped forward.

"Who's the dumbass? You're planning to do the exact same thing I just did."

"He doesn't want you, Deacon, or he would have taken Ruth. I'm the one he's expecting. The door will open for me."

Deacon didn't argue as Kylen took another tentative step forward. Kylen was positive that Olivia was inside. His heart ached for her. When he got her back, he was never letting her go again. Ever.

He passed over the unseen threshold and ran up the stairs without resistance. When he reached the doorway, it swung open for him. He looked back at Deacon and shrugged. Tightening his grip around the handle of his scythe, he stepped inside the church.

* * *

Moonlight streamed through the west windows of the chapel as the bright orb hovered over the pine trees, and the sky to the east began to lighten at the horizon with dawn's approach. Both sides of the chapel windows glowed dissonantly—one with moonlight, the other with sunlight. The light was tinged with color from the stained-glass windows.

The chapel was silent as a grave. He took long strides down the center aisle, his eyes trying to adjust to the awkward lighting, searching for Olivia. When he got to the front of the chapel, his breath caught and his throat closed off. Olivia lay motionless on the pew, curled into a ball. She looked deathly pale even in the low light, and a dim white aura glowed around her.

"Olivia," he choked out, rushing to her side.

"Olivia!"

He shook her and dragged her still-warm body into his arms, pushing his electric-blue energy into her when she didn't automatically draw it from him. It coursed through him, flowing into her body. He covered her mouth with his and filled her with his light until she practically radiated with his energy.

She still didn't move.

He fumbled for the vial, retrieving it from his pocket with trembling hands. It *couldn't* be too late. This had to work. Ignoring the quickly fading glow of his energy as it leaked from her, he opened her mouth and poured the pink contents from the vial down her throat. Crushing her more tightly against him, he pressed his mouth to hers again, pushing the liquid into her with his breath and energy.

Holding her in his arms, his heart fractured as the seconds ticked by. Nothing. No sign of life. He was too late.

Again.

"It seems like you're a little late to the party." Camael strode from the shadows at the far corner of the sanctuary, his host's body deteriorating around him.

Kylen closed his eyes and prayed for the strength to destroy the bastard once and for all. As he gently settled Olivia back onto the bench, her aura vanished. He'd carry her soul to Purgatory himself as soon as he kicked this asshole back to Hell. For good.

Or died trying.

His hand anxiously opened and closed around his scythe. Rage filled his body, nearly blinding him until he tamped it down. He leveled his stare at Camael.

"You killed her."

"No, Kylen. You killed her by taking so long to come to me. You know where you truly belong."

"You don't own me anymore."

"Own. Rent. Is there really a difference? The point is, that rage in you won't go away, no matter what balm you apply to it. Why not use it as it's meant to be used? I thought Deacon could do the job, but he was found...lacking. You've had imps at your beck and call before. Why not demons? Give me your body, and together we can change the world. We can have legions of demons at our bidding to command right here on Earth. We can take back what was meant to be ours."

"Seems to me your efforts aren't nearly as effective as you'd hoped. A few hundred demons won't win you world domination. You can't even hold a portal open for more than a few moments."

"A temporary setback, my friend. You'd be amazed by what can be accomplished when the conditions are right."

Kylen stretched his neck to the side until he heard the familiar pop, and then tilted it to the other side until it popped again.

"You know, Camael, a week ago, that might have sounded like a better offer But now? I don't think so. I'm a changed reaper." He drew his scythe back and charged toward the fallen angel. He wondered briefly if hacking the angel to bits would leave a mark on his newly cleansed soul, and then decided he didn't give a shit.

Camael flashed away just as Kylen reached him,

but his blade sliced through the angel's clothing before he disappeared. Surprised by the angel's agility, Kylen turned, waiting for him to reappear. When he drew the blade closer, Kylen was taken aback by the bright red blood covering the steel. *Red?* He didn't know what he'd expected from the angel, but this wasn't it. Red seemed so…mortal. He knew Camael needed to use a host here on Earth, but the flashing and the blood?

At least he'd hit him. Somewhere. It was a start.

When Camael reappeared seconds later, his host was noticeably worse for wear. The body looked like it was rotting, and a fresh red gash sliced across its chest. Kylen swung his scythe and Camael deflected the blade with the force of his energy alone. The scythe flew from Kylen's hand and skittered across the floor toward the front row of pews. Kylen drew both push blades from his thighs and stayed low, waiting for Camael to advance. Blood leaked through the white fabric of the angel's shirt like a blooming flower, and Kylen felt a smile of gratification stretch across his face.

His heart thundered behind his ribs as adrenaline flooded him. This was it. He wouldn't walk out of here, but he'd be damned if he was going down without a fight. Deacon might have to take both his soul and Olivia's to Purgatory this morning. At least they'd be together, but this was certainly not the reunion he'd had in mind. Still, he would need to injure Camael badly enough for Deacon to at least get to them. And Camael was not invincible here. He was in a host body just like his demons. He was still stronger than any demon or reaper, but he was not invincible.

With renewed vigor, he gathered himself and rushed at Camael, burying both blades into the angel, one in his neck, the other in the soft hollow of his side. With any luck, he might have skewered at least one vital organ.

Camael laughed and pushed Kylen back with a flick of his wrist, bowling him into the east wall of the chapel like a cannonball. The angel was too strong, and the damage Kylen was inflicting wasn't nearly enough to end him.

He raised his eyes to the angel, both blades still gripped tightly in his hands, as his body slid down the wall. His arms refused to rise. He couldn't even protect himself anymore. All the fight drained out of him, and a strange and foreign sense of peace settled over him as he accepted his fate. Someone else would have to fight the fight after all, Deacon or Nate or anyone other than him. He'd done his part. He'd earned his rest.

The familiar phrase "no rest for the weary" played on repeat at the edges of his consciousness, but his head hung to his chest and he let his blades fall from his hands in defeat.

* * *

Olivia opened her eyes with a start, momentarily discombobulated, as if she were waking from a strange dream. Desperate to make sense of what she was seeing, she tried to remember where she was and why, but she came up completely blank. Lying perfectly still, she watched in surreal awe as two men fought in front of her.

Kylen! She wanted to call out to him, but she was terrified she'd distract him.

She watched in horror as the man batted Kylen about the room, toying with him. Her captor was the only one bleeding—yet—but when Kylen's scythe was knocked from his hand, she sensed that he was giving up.

"No!" she wanted to scream at him, but she couldn't find her voice. That was when she noticed

something unexpected and spectacular—her body was coming back to life.

Yes, back to life!

Her heartbeat was so strong and loud it was a wonder they didn't both hear it. She followed them with her eyes, staying motionless until she saw Kylen slump down the wall in defeat. Camael crossed the room and loomed over him. Then he threw back his head and laughed.

Laughed at the man she loved.

It was enough to spur her into action. She grabbed the scythe, which had landed just a foot away from her pew, and gripped the handle in both hands, like Kylen had shown her. Drawing it behind her head, nearly to the center of her back, as she approached them, she put as much power as she could into her swing, aiming for the base of the angel's head like it was a fall pumpkin. She followed through on her swing and sliced through his neck—bones, tendons and all. For a second, she thought she'd missed, and then in slow motion, Camael's body tilted to the side, his head following separately. Blood pumped from his neck in pulsating torrents, flowing through the cracks in the hardwood floor of the chapel like it was a drain.

Kylen looked up at her in awe and utter adoration. Then a black ooze and a cloud of thick smoke exuded from the body, filling the chapel with its sulfurous poison. Olivia choked and coughed, falling to her knees in front of Kylen as she cradled his head in her hands. Blue light sparked between them, circling them in a protective glow that pushed the black fog away. Pressure built inside the chapel and pressed against them, threatening to crush them. The stained-glass windows gave under the strain and exploded outward, shattering marblelike fragments onto the ground outside. Sunlight blazed through the eastern windows in three blinding shafts of light, chasing the last of the fog and darkness from the chapel.

Kylen held Olivia in his arms and gazed at her face, her white hair incandescent in the morning sunlight. "You look like an angel."

"You look like hell. And I love you." She smiled down at him, and then pressed her mouth to his as she melted into his arms. He crushed her to him, pummeling her mouth in desperation. Pulling away from her slightly, he buried his face in her neck and hair, his hands still clutching her to him.

"I love you, too. I thought I'd lost you," he said, his breath scorching her skin as desire bloomed low inside her.

Deacon barreled through the doorway, eyes wild and scythe drawn, interrupting their reunion.

Kylen laughed. "Show up when the work is done, why don't you?" He tightened his embrace, pulling Olivia closer.

"Oh, I don't think it's done. You'd better come outside."

Deacon reached down to help them up, and they followed him outside.

* * *

As they left the chapel and headed down the stairs, Kylen felt the ground vibrating under them. They rounded the corner of the chapel. Dozens of imps lay dead outside the windows, impaled by the glass from the explosion. Several more scurried into the safety of the woods and disappeared into its dark undergrowth.

"Kylen! What are those things?" Olivia cried out, horrified.

Kylen spun her toward him. "You can see them? What do they look like?"

"They're horrible. They look like exploded toads with...fangs."

Kylen snorted and pulled her close protectively. "Those are your precious cats, my dear."

"No!" Olivia shuddered.

Maybe now she'd leave the damn things alone.

"Do you feel that?" Deacon asked, walking toward the cemetery.

"Yeah. What the hell is it?" he asked, clutching Olivia's hand.

"Nothing good."

The ground trembled and cracked across the topsoil of the cemetery, sending the tombstones toppling over. The earth heaved near the center of the small grounds and pushed open like a mouth. Camael's swirling torrent of black smoke screamed from the forest canopy like an errant bottle rocket, disappearing into the void. The ground sank down behind it, leaving a tremendous sinkhole.

"Holy shit," Deacon said, backing away from the cemetery.

"Do you think he's gone? For good?" Olivia asked.

Deacon and Kylen exchanged a look. "I'd better go tell Grim what's going on. That portal might need some reinforcing. Take her home, Kylen."

Without hesitation, Kylen embraced Olivia and flashed her home.

CHAPTER FORTY

Kylen had never been so happy to see Victorian wallpaper in all his life. He did a quick survey of Olivia's apartment to ensure it was safe, and then peeked out the window. At least there were no imps in the alley. He tightened his hold on her, reassuring himself she was real. She was alive.

"That's a little too tight." Olivia smiled.

"Get used to it. I'm never letting you go again. Come, sit down." He noticed her injuries as she walked in front of him, her jeans streaming like shredded banners behind her legs. "What's wrong with your legs?"

"I'm fine, Kylen. I feel…amazing. I can't explain it." The words tumbled out of her. "I don't know what could have happened to me. I'm pretty sure I was dead. I tried to hang on for you. I really did, but I felt the life draining out of me. The longer I was trapped in that church, the worse I felt, until I couldn't hold on anymore, and I…" Her voice faltered and a tear rolled down her cheek. "Let go."

Kylen closed his eyes, pained by her admission. Her suffering was on his shoulders. He should have found her sooner or, better yet, not lost her at all. It wouldn't happen again. She was never leaving his side, and if he did have to go away from her, she would be protected. End of story. Final. No discussion.

"What are these injuries? Did Camael do this to you?"

"No." She looked up at him through her lashes, her cheeks pinking in embarrassment. "It was the imps. You were right. I'm glad I couldn't see them before. It would have been much worse."

He knelt in front of her to more closely inspect her injuries. They had healed. Only dried blood remained. She took his face in her hands. "Kylen, you saved me. I don't know how, but you brought me back."

"It wasn't me. It was Kara. She gave me a gift for you, Olivia. For both of us. The essence of the Valkyrie."

"I don't understand, Kylen. You told me that Kara's dead." Olivia stroked her hand down his face and cupped his cheek.

"She is, but I got to see her. I got to say goodbye, and she gave me the gift that saved you. That saved us both. You're healed. No more cancer. No more sickness. No more death. You're as strong as a Valkyrie. You're human, but...more. As long as you keep your energy and your head, you'll live indefinitely."

"Like you." Another fat tear rolled down Olivia's cheek, and Kylen thumbed it away. She caught his hand in hers and turned it to kiss his palm.

"Thank you, Kylen. I love you so much." Kylen's face burned, and he felt his own eyes filling with tears.

"I love you more."

He rose and reached for Olivia. "Come. Let me

show you."

* * *

Emotion blocked his throat, and he couldn't speak as he led her to the bed. His own heart seemed determined to escape from his chest. Kylen felt his energy wrenched from him as it reached out to her and watched as it combined with Olivia's aura in an electric-blue shroud that surrounded them both. She circled her arms around him and curled into him.

His hands found her hair and wove through it, and he pulled her face back from where she'd burrowed it against his chest, her tears dampening his shirt. He studied her, searching for signs of illness, desperate to reassure himself that she was his, that she was here and healthy and whole.

"Kylen," she said, her voice filled with need.

"I know."

"Weapons?" Olivia smiled and Kylen dropped every piece of steel he was carrying to the floor.

He reached for her and scooped her into his arms, laying her across the bed with reverence. He couldn't take his eyes off hers.

Stroking her face, a tumble of questions beat against his lips, but he suppressed them. There would be time for that later. He'd make sure of it. He wanted her far from the troubles that plagued him, plagued them all, but he couldn't seal her up in a doorless tower somewhere protected by magic. Magic had failed him before. What he needed was stronger than magic, and he finally realized he'd possessed it all along. He'd only forgotten how to trust in it. One prayer had been answered, and now…another.

Faith.

He'd been given everything he didn't even know

he needed, and he was doubly blessed now that he finally realized that. He leaned over Olivia and closed his eyes as he brushed his cheek against hers. She sighed under him and that small sound filled him with a flood of warmth almost too strong to bear. Pulling her tight against him, he held her in silence for what may have been minutes or hours.

He was lost in her.

Kylen slid his hand along her cheek, glorying in the glow of her skin. She was healthy and alive. He couldn't imagine anything more lovely. He moved his hand up and under her T-shirt to touch her skin, and his need grew so intense he couldn't hold back any longer. Falling upon her, he buried his face against the hollow of her neck and breathed in her scent as he unfastened the buttons on her jeans.

"God, Olivia. I'm so thankful for you."

Her hands slid along his lower back, pulling his T-shirt over his head. When she traced her fingers along the scars on his chest, he shivered under her touch and a moan escaped him.

"I'm not going to last very long."

"You won't have to."

Olivia pushed at his chest and rolled him onto his back, straddling his waist. Her rough jeans rubbed against him and his balls tightened at the sensation. Reaching across him and over his head, her breasts brushed his face as she pulled the ties holding the velvet drapes to the headboard posts. They fell free, and she drew them along the sides of the bed. When she loosed the footboard ties too, they were completely cocooned in her bed—the only place he ever wanted to be.

She rolled off him and skimmed her jeans down, taking her panties with them, and then crawled back to him. She unbuttoned his jeans so slowly it was torture, and he lifted his hips so she could peel them off him.

Her hands slid along the sides of his hips, and she lowered her face to his throbbing erection. He held his breath as she brushed her feather-soft cheek against his shaft. Moisture pearled as she sighed against him.

"Olivia, don't tease."

"I'm not teasing."

Her tongue glided from base to tip along one side of his erection, and he slammed his shoulders and head back into the mattress as his hands balled great clumps of the bedspread into his fists.

When she administered the same attention to the other side of his shaft, he lost the last vestiges of control.

"Please, Olivia."

Trailing her tongue from his base along the fine line of blond hair that trailed to his belly button, she pushed her hands across his torso to his chest and straddled him once more; this time her heat covered him. She braced her hands on his pectorals, raising her hips until she was aligned just right, and then lowered herself onto him. He pushed up to meet her, and she was like liquid fire around him. Olivia raised her hips and plunged back down, impaling her frail body on him, once…twice, and he was gone.

He cried out and gripped her hips, holding her in place as his body pulsated, releasing into her, and then collapsed boneless into the mattress, too weak to even keep his hold. She stretched out across his chest, her body warm from exertion, and rested her head under his chin. Her heart pulsated against his, quickly learning his rhythm, then matching it.

"Thank you, Olivia."

"My pleasure," she said, her breath brushing across his chest.

"Mmm, not yet, but it will be." He rolled her onto her back and hovered over her on shaky arms as he worshiped her body with kisses, wanting to taste every sweet and salty inch of her. He laved her body, savoring her until he grew hard again. Still desperate for her, he drew a pearled nipple into his mouth and rolled his tongue around it until she squirmed beneath him and mewled soft sounds of pleasure. He would never tire of those sounds.

He pushed into her and she clutched his head in her hands, drawing her hips against him, demanding more. His thumb worked at her nub as he stroked into her, driving her hips down into the bed. The harder he pushed inside her, the louder and more demanding she became. Feeling her tighten around him, he drove into her hard and fast until they both shattered and he collapsed beside her.

Time didn't seem to pass as they lay together out of the fray for whatever precious few moments they could enjoy together. He needed her. Needed to know her and feel her flesh against his if only for the briefest respite from the horrors around them.

Olivia's palm pushed the hair from his forehead, and she pulled his face to hers.

When their lips met, the blue sparks sizzled between them again.

He'd nearly thrown everything away. But Olivia calmed his inner beast, his demon side. While his demon's memories had been erased, his own memories of his time with the demon remained. Perhaps that was what made him who and what he was now: for good and for evil. Mercifully, Olivia seemed to be fine with him despite his many faults.

* * *

His chest heaved as he came up for air. "God, I love you."

"I don't think I'm ever going to get tired of

hearing that."

"Good, because you're going to live a long, long time now. You're going to have to make a new list."

She pushed up on her elbows. "My list! I must have left it at the chapel."

"Nah, I picked it up. It's in my pocket."

"You saved it?"

"Yes."

"How is it you keep saving it? And me? I would have never finished that list without you. Or almost finished it, anyway."

"You did finish it." He smoothed her hair off her face and framed her head with his palms.

"No. I had one left. The last one."

"Number 60, *save a life?* What do you think you did when you sliced off Camael's head like a pumpkin? You saved *my* life. Not once but twice. You saved me the first time we met. I was dead inside, Olivia. If not for you, I still would be. I can't lose you again." He pressed his forehead to hers.

"You won't. I promise." She pulled his hips down and arched up against him, pressing her core against his hard heat. "We'll make a new list together. Let's start with this."

Kylen groaned against her breast and nipped at her with his teeth. He pressed against her slick core and pushed into her like a blade into a sheath. She was exquisite. Her heat wrapped around him, and her walls tightened against him, holding him inside. When she released, he drew back out, and then plunged into her again. She arched against him and pushed herself down the bed, driving him deeper into her.

Clutching her shoulders, he pinned her into place and held her as he found a rhythm and drove into her again and again. She clawed for purchase at his back and held onto him as he slid one big hand under the small of her back to press her full body against his. Blue light sizzled between them, and Kylen was sure the dormers must be glowing like fire from the outside.

He couldn't believe that Olivia wanted him as he was: broken and raw and ruined. Hope flared like a beacon in his chest, but its nemesis, doubt, wasn't far behind. How could he ever keep her safe enough?

With her new lease on life, he knew she'd be more than ready to live again. Even though she was strong and nearly invincible, she wasn't *completely* invincible. How long before Camael or something or somebody else came after her again? He pushed those thoughts away.

All they could count on was the here and now. He was going to have to learn to live in it, one way or another. Shattering beneath him, she compressed her muscles around his shaft and squeezed his own release from him. He came inside her again and filled her with blue light, his essence, and a prayer for her long, long life.

CHAPTER FORTY-ONE

When Maeve felt the pull of newly dead souls from her watch station by Ruth's bedside, she knew they were in trouble.

"Whoa, do you feel that?" Ruth asked, struggling to sit upright in the bed.

"Yeah."

"What does it mean?"

"This many souls simultaneously in need of reaping? Disease. War. Disaster. In light of the current demon problem, I'm betting on disaster. The demon variety."

"God help us."

"That would be nice for a change." Maeve moved to the doorway and pulled it open a crack, the bright light of the hallway filling the gap.

Outside Ruth's room, orderlies and nurses continued with their normal busy hustle and bustle, oblivious to the coming threat, until the overhead intercom system sounded a series of sirens.

"This is a Code Black: Dangerous Intruder Alert. Repeat, a Code Black: Dangerous Intruder Alert. Please find a room and barricade all doors until the All Clear is sounded."

Maeve watched for a moment as the staff spurred into action, and then closed their door. Dragging all the furniture she could move over to the doorway, she stacked it into a pile against the entrance. It was a ridiculous defense. One that would stop only the laziest of humans. Certainly not a determined demon.

What better target for a freshly minted horde of demons to cut their teeth on than a hospital? St. Mary's Hospital held the population of a small city even when it *wasn't* crowded. Lately, it was packed to the gills. Deacon had used his reaper powers of persuasion to ensure that Ruth got a private room, but most of the patients were packed like sardines in a can. Now that the demons weren't following the rules, so to speak, and were tearing the souls from still-living victims, what was easier than attacking a patient? Weak, defenseless, easy pickings. It was a miracle it hadn't happened sooner.

The question was fight or flight? If the horde was moving through the hospital, there was a chance they wouldn't even make it to Ruth's fourth-floor room on the first round, but it was a chance Maeve wasn't genetically wired to take.

"What are we going to do?" Ruth said weakly as she flipped back the blanket covering her and tried to get out of bed. She managed to get her feet swung over the side before the pain of her wounds laid her back flat, sweat beading on her forehead and chest.

"Something that doesn't make you pass out." Maeve wracked her brain to figure out their best option. Flashing with Ruth again was absolutely out of the question. Flashing without her to find Deacon was equally impossible. That left staying and fighting.

She was good with a scythe, and she knew she could hold a demon attack at bay, but for how long? She could dispatch one or two easily enough, but more? She didn't like her odds or her options.

Maeve hiked up her pant leg and drew out the push blade sheathed there, handing it to Ruth. "Here. It's only good up close. Let's hope you don't have to use it."

"We should just flash."

"Absolutely. Not. Deacon will have my head if I flash you again. We'll do this together. The cavalry will show up anytime. They will have felt the pull of souls as well, and they won't be able to ignore it. Not when it's this strong."

"Thank you, Maeve."

"Thank me when it's over."

Closing her eyes, Maeve listened hard to the sounds outside the doorway, trying to gauge the level of panic to determine how the horde was progressing. If the rumble from the floor below them was any indication, it felt like a one-way exit portal was being opened beneath the foundation of the hospital—Camael's version of a Slip 'n Slide to Hell.

The evil was almost palpable as adrenaline flooded her heart. She wasn't much for prayer, but she prayed now. She prayed for a way to protect Ruth from whatever was coming for them. It didn't take long to discover who led the charge.

"Little reaper, little reaper, let me come in." He taunted from the other side of Ruth's door.

Camael.

Even without seeing him, she sensed the same power she'd felt in the cemetery when he'd taken Olivia. His essence was recognizable.

Goose bumps rose up across Maeve's arms, and her heart hammered in her chest Stepping to the side of the door, her back against the wall, she made eye contact with Ruth and raised one finger to her lips, indicating that Ruth should stay silent. Gripping her scythe in both hands for maximum force, she drew it back behind her head, ready to strike the first blow against whatever burst through the door.

Until this Meridian gig, Maeve had been a vanilla reaper. She'd only experienced demon hunting in books and training drills. Now she was a seasoned expert. Still, nothing she'd experienced or learned had prepared her to deal with a fallen angel.

"Let's not make this more difficult than it has to be. I know you're in there. You know I'm out here. How about we just get this all over with so we move forward?"

There was no way in hell that Maeve was going to make things easier for the bastard. If she stalled, maybe the Authority would make it here in time to help protect Ruth. Until then, Maeve was all that stood between the two of them and Camael's diabolical plan.

"I see you've chosen the hard way. Of course."

A discharge of light blasted open the door, pushing the furniture across the room in an avalanche. Camael stood just outside the doorway in another host body. He sent in two of his demon minions like lambs to the slaughter.

Maeve separated the head of the first with one blow of her scythe, and then sliced through the midsection of the second on the backswing. The demons streamed forth immediately, retreating to the hallway to search for another host. She should have tried to retrieve the demons, but there was no time to test her supposed new skills with Camael waiting in the wings. Seconds later, the host souls streamed forth, handicapping her efforts further. Maeve, her new reaper senses now heightened, was helpless to resist the pull of the souls despite the danger before her.

Before she could think about what she was doing, the souls streamed toward her like magnets and she consumed them. In the melee, Camael had entered the room and was nearly at Ruth's bedside.

Helpless to defend herself, Ruth was visibly steeling herself for an attack.

As she snapped out of her trance, Maeve leaped across the room toward Ruth. When Camael turned to defend himself, Maeve saw that the flesh on his host's face didn't completely cover the skeleton beneath any longer. While his host was ever-changing, Camael couldn't hide his true nature. She would recognize him in any form now.

Maeve stepped in front of Ruth in a protective gesture, pushing him away. Amused, Camael walked toward them with stiff, jerky movements and an odd cant to his head. He stopped to peel a dangly bit of flesh from his neck, flicked it across the room, and then smiled at them grotesquely. A hairline fracture appeared in his face, spidering across his cheek and down his neck.

"That's enough, Camael." Maeve backed up against Ruth, using her body to push the hospital bed closer to the wall.

"Easy now, reaper. As you can see, my host is…not up to par. I'm afraid I'll need a new ride for my work on Earth. God knows I'd love a good reaper." He smiled again and his left ear slid along the side of his face like a slug before falling to the ground. "Sooner would be better than later."

"I don't think so." Maeve drew back her scythe, ready to administer what she hoped would be a fatal blow.

"Again with the hard way? You can make this all go away, my friend. I came here with the idea of inhabiting the new reaper. Considering her current state, it would be a matter of mercy. But if you want to make a deal with me, I could be persuaded to settle for you instead."

Maeve laughed. "What makes you think either of us would agree to that? Besides, if you're some mighty angel, why do you even need to inhabit a body?"

"Fallen angel. While the rewards are many, there have been a few… drawbacks."

"Like spending your immortal life in Hell?"

"Actually, Hell is quite pleasing to me most days."

The lights went out, leaving only the eerie illumination of the emergency backup lights and exit lights in the interior hospital room. Maeve was preparing to attack when the floor and walls bulged and began to tremor.

"You have two choices, dear Maeve. Allow me entry, or I'll bring this entire hospital down upon you and your friend. I swear to Lucifer, I'll open a portal right here in this room so large that it will swallow this place whole. I'm certain the thousand or so guests in this hospital would not survive. Such a pity. Even your reaper friend's survival would be questionable from the looks of her. It will be a soul buffet!" Camael spread his arms wide and his fingernails fell to the tile floor like ice chips.

"From the looks of your host, it will be the last thing you do in that body."

"We shall see."

"Why are you doing this? You're an angel."

"When everything you love has been destroyed, perhaps you'll understand."

A shudder shimmied up Maeve's spine and electricity crackled all around her, emanating from Camael in waves. She shuffled backward as a ragged fissure appeared along the floor between her and Ruth and began to open into a slivered chasm. Noxious fumes poured from the split as it grew wider and filled the room blurring Maeve's vision.

Camael's body vibrated with power.

"Stop!" Maeve cried out in desperation. "I'll do it. Stop now."

* * *

"No, Maeve!" Ruth pulled herself up and against the wall, but Maeve had already leaped across the growing chasm in the floor, willingly offering herself as a living sacrifice.

"Maeve! Maeve!"

Unable or unwilling to respond, Maeve made her way to Camael and stood before him. The chasm separated the women, its distance too great for Ruth to span in her weakened state even if she could get out of the bed.

Ruth gazed down into the abyss through the wreckage of the floors below her. Dizzied by vertigo, she tried to make sense of the tumult. Instead of being able to help Maeve, she was being forced to bear witness to this, this horror. All the humor vanished from Camael's face, but what still remained of his host's visage held a smug satisfaction. Ruth wanted to render that face in two with her blade, but she was powerless.

Please, God. Help us now!

Maeve dropped to her knees before Camael, her head hanging like a ragdoll in defeat. Her hand uncurled from her scythe's handle, letting the blade clang to the floor—useless. Camael casually kicked the weapon into the chasm behind her.

"If I do this, you'll stop this madness. You'll close the portal and you won't harm Ruth. If you don't promise me that, you'll never have me."

Camael sneered. "I think we're beyond

negotiation."

"You can't take my body if I resist, and I can make things very difficult for you. I want your assurance. Ruth lives and the portal closes. Say it."

Fueled by Camael's rage, the tremors increased in intensity—hanging pictures vibrated off their nails from the hospital's walls and fell to the floor, and Ruth's dinner tray and water crashed off the bed cart. Screams rang up from the floors below as concrete and steel shifted and bodies and equipment plunged toward the split.

Camael's fury was clear but so was his need. "Agreed."

He spanned the distance between them and grasped the sides of Maeve's head, pulling her body up long and straight, her toes hovering inches above the floor.

"Do you freely accept Camael into your body, forsaking control and command of your form from this day forward?"

Ruth watched as Maeve's body became seemingly boneless. A soft whimper nearly escaped her own throat on Maeve's behalf. She stuffed it down and deliberated on the distance of the chasm once again. Maybe...

"Yes."

"No!" Ruth screamed.

Camael pulled Maeve farther up, placing his mouth against hers in a grotesque kiss. Ruth wretched as Maeve's body began to tremble and shudder. Camael's host body crackled and desiccated even more as he forced his essence into Maeve's body. Soon all that was left of his former host was dust, and Maeve tumbled to the ground.

Everything stilled. The chasm remained, but the screams had been silenced, replaced with low keening.

The sound of Ruth's pulsating heart filled her ears as her vision coned to a pinpoint. She fought for consciousness while Maeve hunched on the floor silently for several long moments. Maeve reached back and pulled out her hair tie, letting her glistening black hair fall loose to the middle of her back. She rolled onto her heels and drew herself up from the floor.

But of course she wasn't Maeve any longer.

Her hair swung over her shoulder and across her chest as she switched around to look at Ruth. A mocking smile broke out across her face, and her head cocked jerkily to the side as Camael adjusted to his new home.

The temperature plummeted in the room, and Maeve shimmered in front of Ruth, stepping into the void and dissolving into the ether. The chasm began to suck all the power and energy from the room behind her like a great vacuum. The door tore from its hinges and was pulled into the gorge, as were the remaining furniture and other accoutrements in the room. Ruth's bed began to roll toward the abyss as well, and she scrambled to untangle herself from the coverings. She still wasn't strong enough.

A brilliant white light filled the room, blinding her.

Her eyes shut tight against the glare, Ruth felt the bed roll to a stop and waited for the sickening, stomach- dropping fall into the abyss. When it didn't happen, she opened her eyes to find an angel hovering over the chasm, blazing with light and dressed in full regalia, wings spread across the length of the room.

With a touch of the angel's spear to the edge of the split, the chasm began to mend itself deep within the Earth, sealing the bottom of the crevasse but leaving five floors below them exposed. Chaos shook the hospital corridors as hospital staff raced to evacuate the surviving patients.

Alarms rang throughout the building and an automated voice over the intercom directed a new message for the swift and orderly evacuation of the building along marked disaster routes.

"Who are you?" Ruth asked, pain overcoming her.

"Temperance."

Ruth's vision pinpricked to black.

CHAPTER FORTY-TWO

Nate and Bo flashed into a war zone. The hospital was bedlam. Not only was the floor where Ruth had been staying all but destroyed, but the hallway to her room was blocked by mangled concrete and steel. A twelve-foot fissure traversed the floor beneath them. Bocephus crouched near the edge of the crack and growled into the void.

Unease struck him like a sledgehammer. What if something horrible had happened to Ruth? Not only that, but Maeve was just...gone. His fragile connection to her from their energy share had been severed. Trying to make sense of the destruction, he searched for Ruth's room number along the now-crooked wall. A white glow pulsated from the doorless entryway as he picked his path through the rubble.

Even though he was staring right at it, he couldn't make sense of what he was looking at. At first he thought Grim had deigned to visit them, but then he realized that the angel before him was female. Scary as hell, but definitely female.

When he approached the doorway, the angel raised her spear and pointed it at his chest. Nate couldn't see past her wings to determine if Ruth was still in the room.

"Whoa, there. I'm a friend."

"Temperance, no. Let him pass."

"Ruth?"

The angel lowered her spear, although she didn't seem too happy about it. Her wings stayed extended, flames licking from their feathery tips. Her wings were perhaps a bigger threat than the spear had been.

Slowly, hoping not to rile the angel, he entered the room, keeping to the edge, well away from her wings. The chasm still gaped open in the floor, but it was covered by a shimmering light. Nate took a tentative step onto the clear platform, and then crossed it to join Ruth.

"Nate," Ruth whispered weakly from her bed.

"What happened, Ruth. Where's Maeve? And who…or what is your new friend here?"

Ruth tried to sit up to talk to him, but the effort made her grimace in pain at the effort. Temperance growled a warning.

"No. Ruth. Stay put. Just tell me what happened."

"Nate it was awful. Demons were everywhere. So many souls were torn free in the hospital."

"And now? Can you still feel the departing souls? Are they gone?"

"They're gone. They were taken after Camael…"

"Camael was here, too?"

"Nate, he took Maeve. No, not took her. *Possessed* her."

Nate's heart dropped into his stomach. Not.

Possible. Maeve was the strongest woman he'd ever met. There was no way she'd fall prey to Camael. But the broken tether said otherwise.

"How is that possible, Ruth? He's an angel, not a demon."

"He's an angel no longer." Temperance offered. "When he fell, he lost his ability to maintain his angel form here on Earth. He requires a host, just as demons do."

"It's true," Ruth said, "His host was disintegrating before our eyes, and he wanted a reaper. He wanted me, Nate. He thought I would acquiesce because I'm so injured, but Maeve…"

"Maeve saved you."

"Yes. Camael threatened to open the portal and drop the entire hospital into the chasm. He was determined to leave with one of us. Maeve offered herself. But now? Oh, Nate. She's not Maeve anymore."

Ruth sobbed into the pillow and Nate took her hand in his own, trying to make sense of how this could have happened and what it meant for them all. Now that Camael had a reaper's body, he'd have free reign on Earth. Nate couldn't even imagine how much worse things could get in the coming days. If Camael had been limited to a quickly deteriorating host previously, he would be unstoppable as long as he possessed Maeve.

Temperance's wings ignited in yellow and red flames. She spread them around Ruth's bed as a commotion in the doorway drew her attention.

"What the hell is this?" Deacon's voice bellowed from the hallway.

"That's new." Kylen offered.

"And it's a chick." Raguel chimed in.

Other familiar voices joined in the general melee.

"Temperance! Let them pass." Ruth said.

Temperance extinguished the flames to a slow burn and tucked her wings in just enough to let the group of men pass. Nate had never been so glad to see a bunch of reapers as he was at that moment.

"We felt the pull. It was so strong we couldn't ignore it. What happened? Are you okay, Ruth?" Deacon rushed over to her and carefully pulled her into his arms. Nate watched as he clutched her hands in his and pushed his green healing light into her. The energy flowed up both of her arms until it reached her shoulders, and then he stopped the flow. With time, she would heal completely, but it would take longer than usual because she could only be given small amounts of energy at a time.

Ruth's face smoothed, the lines of pain temporarily erased.

"Deacon, Camael has possessed Maeve. We need to find her. Now." Nate turned to look at the Authority reapers. They were all present. Even Olivia. Tears were welling in her eyes, but she was trying to stay stoic.

"Unbelievable." Kylen pulled Olivia closer. "And this?" He nodded toward Temperance.

"She's my guardian angel. No. Not mine." Ruth squeezed Deacon's hand. "The baby's guardian angel. She's been sent to protect us."

A great groan rose from the floor below them as the building's supports began to give way under the strain. The floor shifted, pitching the reapers against the wall.

"We need to get Ruth out of here before this entire building collapses around us." Deacon said.

"Agreed. Where do you want to take her?" Kylen asked.

"Home. I want to go home," she said, her voice small.

"That's going to be a problem, baby. The house is gone, Ruth. Camael burned it to the ground. It's a long story. I'll tell you all about it on the way to Oakland Hospital."

"What do you want us to co, boss?" Ragu asked. "We dispatched a couple dozen demons between the six of us and cleaned up the mess. It was a busy night. When we got to the house, we didn't know what to do. Everyone was gone, but since there weren't any bodies or detached souls, we assumed you'd all turn up eventually. We were waiting there when we felt the pull and came right here. Say the word, and we're on it."

* * *

Kylen knew Deacon was itching to get Ruth to Oakland, and there was no reason he should bear the burden of their familiar details.

"Deacon, take Ruth. We'll get things sorted out at home, and we'll start fresh with our search tomorrow night. It's dawn and the demons will be down for a while."

Deacon nodded to him. "Thank you."

"Bring Nate with you, too. He's dead on his feet, and he could use the rest. And for God's sake, take the mutt with you." Kylen said.

Deacon turned to Nate. "Let's go. We'll find Maeve...soon. In fact, the way things have been going, I'm pretty sure she'll find us. All we have to do is figure out how to free her. You and Ruth did it once, Nate. We'll do it again."

"We got this, boss. No worries," Ragu said, and the reapers murmured assurances, too.

"Come, Bo." Nate grabbed the scruff of the dog's neck.

Deacon scooped Ruth into his arms and the three

of them picked their way through the rubble and out of the hospital, Temperance following close behind.

* * *

The remaining reapers flashed back to Ruth's property. Kylen debated whether he should have sent Olivia with the others, but there was no way he could willingly part from her again so soon... or maybe ever.

"Ragu, Samkiel, we need housing here. When Ruth comes back from the hospital, there needs to be a place for her to live. For all of us to live. I want six thirty-foot trailers circled end-to-end there before dark. Leo and Zak, you salt the ground within the circle of protection, and when Nate gets back, he'll cast it again to include all of us. Dare and Oreo, you're responsible for filling the trailers with all the household necessities." Kylen turned to Olivia. "Can you help set up Deacon and Ruth's trailer?"

"Of course."

"The rest of you jokers are on your own. Outfit your trailers how you like, but keep the center of the circle clear. Any questions?"

"I have some clothes already packed up in my apartment that Ruth can probably wear. I was planning to give them away when I was...dying." Olivia swallowed hard but then smiled up at Kylen, and he couldn't help but kiss her.

So much for his tough-guy persona. One of the reapers whistled, and he broke free to pinpoint the culprit, but by then they were all whistling different tunes to protect the perpetrator. It was clearly an us-versus-them sort of thing. The new guys against the old. But the mood was lighter, and Kylen actually felt good to have a plan that didn't involve fighting demons. Yet.

"Everyone have their marching orders?"

"Just sayin', it would be nice to be able to communicate with each other directly rather than relying on dumb luck or random summons," Oreo offered.

"Done. I'll take care of communication while we're in town today. You'll all have a place to lay your head tonight. Let's go."

They flashed off to complete their various missions, leaving Kylen and Olivia alone in the ruin.

"Are you afraid?" Olivia asked.

"Only of losing you."

"Can Maeve survive this?"

Kylen frowned and circled his arm around her waist, drawing her against him, the sun warm on his face. "I don't know. I've never known of an angel, fallen or not, possessing a human. We're in uncharted territory here."

"But you'll help her?"

"We all will."

EPILOGUE

It turned out that Meridian was a spiritually porous city. Camael's apparent ease in opening portal after portal was no accident—the town sat on a supernatural fault line, where the veil between the realms was at its thinnest. Now that the fallen angel had proven how effectively he could manipulate that weakness, the Authority was working feverishly to clean up the mess while Grim and Rashnu worked the problem from their own angles.

Camael was a busy, busy boy since inhabiting Maeve's body. Uninhibited by the limitations of a human host body, he was now able to come and go from Hell as he pleased. New portals kept popping up like Starbucks, spewing forth demon after demon. Mercifully, none of them stayed open for long. Camael's powers still weren't strong enough to hold one open permanently.

As Kylen stepped into the Maple Park cemetery

after yet another interminable night of hunting, he wondered how long it would be before the coming battle tore the city irreparably apart.

He flashed home.

The homestead was a respite from the chaos of the city. They had taken every precaution during the reconstruction, and with the newest wards and protections cast by Nate, the place was basically impenetrable. While before Ruth had originally been the main source of power for the circle of protection, now everyone who lived at the compound was part of the spell. With Temperance's help, Nate had even secured it against the four elements. Deacon dubbed it the fortress of safety, but Kylen knew that no place was truly safe.

It had been two months since the small rock-sided house had burned to the ground. Still, their ramshackle reaper trailer park had a homey feel to it.

Each pair of reapers had their own shiny, bullet-shaped trailer, with a makeshift common area in the middle. Only Nate lived alone.

Deacon and Nate poured over blueprints and plans for the construction of a new house on the few nights they took off from hunting and destroying demons. It was still the dead of winter in the Midwest, though, and they couldn't break ground until spring, a good four months away.

Despite their concentrated efforts, Maeve was as elusive as the wind. They'd tried to track her down as soon as they regrouped at home, but apparently Camael's plans included keeping her out of their sight. Nate spent every night tracking Maeve with Bo. He'd become obsessed with the search.

Camael valued his new ride too much to jeopardize losing her, but he would eventually grow bold and make a mistake. When he did, they would be ready.

Olivia opened the trailer door and carried in a

tray with orange juice, sliced fruit and a heaping plate of biscuits and gravy for them both. The trailers were too small to try to cook in on a regular basis, so the common area had been tricked out with a commercial grade kitchen among other things. It took a lot of food to keep nine reapers, Nate, Olivia and a pregnant Ruth fueled up, so they took turns with meal prep. So far, Kylen had only managed to produce take-out pizza on his shift.

No one had complained.

Every time he looked at Olivia, he was amazed anew at his blessings. He was working on believing that he deserved her.

"Oreo had breakfast detail." Olivia smiled and set down the tray on their small banquette table before reaching over to push back the red damask curtains. The curtains were the one interior-decorating concession he'd allowed when Olivia had given up her apartment to move to this crazy compound. He couldn't keep her safe anywhere else, although he agreed it would have been more comfortable for them to live in a real apartment. She was such a good sport about everything that he hadn't been able to say *no* when he'd come home to discover such atrocious curtains hanging on each of the trailer's tiny windows. Even now it made him smile.

Another small miracle.

"Can't go wrong with biscuits and gravy." Kylen pulled her into the booth beside him and nuzzled her neck. "How is Ruth?"

"She's good. Stir crazy, but good. Nate says her doctor demands bed rest for the rest of her pregnancy. One mess up, and she's going back to Oakland Hospital. Keeping her entertained is a full-time job. We've already watched all six seasons of *The Big Bang Theory*. It's going to be a long five and a half months!" She leaned back against him, and he spooned up a bite of biscuit to feed her.

"She's lucky to have you and Temperance around."

"Well, let me tell you, Temperance is not very entertaining. Who knew guardian angels were so serious and scary? She's very…committed in that terrifying-supernatural-entity sort of way."

"I'm glad that she so fiercely protects Ruth and the baby, especially since you spend so much time with her. That means Temperance's protection extends to you."

"You worry too much."

"You have no idea." Kylen fed her another bite of breakfast.

"Are you trying to fatten me up?" she asked.

"Yes." He wrapped his arms around her slightly rounded tummy and pulled her closer. He had managed to put some weight on her but not nearly enough. He wanted her fat and sassy. So far, the sassy part hadn't been a problem. He loved that about her. She didn't let anything slide. She complemented him in every way. The light to his darkness, the good to his evil, the mental clarity to his dysfunction. When he was with Olivia, he could almost believe he was a real man after all.

"What are you thinking about?" she asked, feeding him an orange slice.

"That I'm lucky."

"Yes, you are. We are both lucky."

Kylen brushed his lips against the back of her neck, just under her ponytail, and blue sparks sizzled across her skin.

"Mmm, that always feels good. Will you hunt tonight, or are you taking a night off?"

"We'll hunt."

"And Maeve? Any news?"

"No."

"I don't know who it's harder on, Maeve or

Nate."

"Maeve. Trust me. Being possessed tends to be all consuming. Nate and Bo's tracking may be the only way we manage to find her at this point. Apparently angels, good or fallen, have a way of staying off the radar when they want to."

"I hope it's soon. For everyone's sake."

"Yes."

Olivia turned to him in the booth and stroked her hand along the side of his face. "Now what?" she asked.

"Weapons?"

THE END

About the Author

Lisa adores beasties of all sorts, fictional as well as real, and has a farm full of them in her Southwest Missouri home, including: one child, one husband, two dogs, two cats, a dozen hens, thousands of Italian bees and a guinea pig.

She may or may not keep a complete zombie apocalypse bug-out bag in her trunk at all times, including a machete. Just. In. Case.

Keep in touch here:

Website: http://lisa-medley.com/books/
Facebook: /lisamedleyauthor
Twitter: @lisamedley
Google+: +lisamedley
Pinterest: medley3
Amazon: http://amzn.to/1axwex7

Don't miss a thing! Sign up for my New Release Newsletter http://eepurl.com/9Zhcz

Other Books by Lisa Medley

Haunt My Heart
A Civil War ghost gets a second chance at love in the 21st century. - Out now!

Reap & Repent
(Book I of The Reaper Series) – Available Now!

Reap & Redeem

(Book II of The Reaper Series) – Available Now!

Reap & Reveal
(Book III of The Reaper Series) - Spring 2015

Space Cowboys & Indians
A sci-fi romance Coming in 2015

Reap & Reckon
(Book IV of The Reaper Series) - Coming in 2016

THE REAPER SERIES:

The only thing worse than having nothing to live for...is having everything to live for.

A small group of reapers and supernatural beings in Meridian, Arkansas are all that stands between humanity and the apocalypse when a fallen angel stages a demonic invasion. In their battle to save the world, each will meet his or her match, discovering the power of love...and the importance of risking everything to protect it.

REAP & REVEAL

BOOK III OF THE REAPER SERIES

CHAPTER ONE

Nate Blackburn whistled for his hellhound, anxious to flash home after a less than fruitful night of demon hunting with the Authority. Of course, his quarry was an angel. The fallen kind.

Bocephus came bounding down the alley, drool dripping in stringy ropes from his floppy jowls. The great black beast heeled and sat at his side, resting his basketball-sized head on Nate's shoulder. Another long night and Nate was still no closer to finding Maeve.

It was near dawn and a chill shimmied up his spine. He told himself it was the December cold. Most of the demons would be looking for holes to crawl into to rest from their incessant debauchery and death mongering. Even they had to recharge.

A practicing witch, Nate had always known there were things that went bump in the night. But before taking up with the reapers, he'd never actually killed any of them. Now, of course, that had changed. Everything had changed.

Nate stroked the hound's head, twisting his fingers into his thick coat, reluctant to call it a night despite his lack of success. Bo had tracked Maeve's scent all through downtown Meridian, Arkansas, without managing to pin her down. She was always one step ahead...or several. What he found instead was her wake of destruction. The newly soulless wanderers and dead bodies were beginning to pile up. Even with eight active members of the Authority plus Nate, it was getting more and more difficult to collect the casualties and carry them to Purgatory. And now, because the disappearances had not gone unnoticed, the city was lousy with out-of-state manpower, too. Hell, the FBI had even made an appearance and implemented a citywide curfew. Not that it was doing any good. The media posted daily headlines urging people to stay inside, but even with the curfew and the added officers, it was impossible to keep businesses closed and people off the streets, especially at night.

It was a dangerous time for everyone in Meridian—supernatural and otherwise.

Few humans could survive a soul extraction, and if they did, they were left as nothing more than a primal shell. The reapers called them wanderers. To Nate's pop-culture mind, they were zombies minus the incessant drive to eat fresh brains. One thing was certain. Even the wanderers were as good as dead.

All the reapers, except for Kylen, who remained dubious, hoped that at some point the humans who had been soul raped might be restored. That would mean their untethered souls would have to be rescued from Hell before they became part of its machine. Then they would have to somehow be reinsouled. It had never been done before, and Nate was far from certain that it could be done. Still, they put in the effort. Hope was one of the few commodities they had left.

A cat's cry caused him to tighten his grip in Bo's scruff, and a growl vibrated through the beast. Sometimes a cat was just a cat. Sometimes it was something else entirely.

Sure enough, an imp rounded the corner of a long, brick building ahead as he continued down the alley. Clinging to the wall, the imp blinked its yellow eyes at him before shimmying up and onto the roof. More followed. The imps were scouts—minions for demons who walked the earth. And that meant one thing: a demon was close.

Looked like Nate was going to earn his pay tonight after all.

Bo whined beside him, but from anticipation rather than fear. The dog liked nothing better than to dispatch demons, a trait Nate admired.

The demon that entered the alley was riding a teenage boy's body. Thank God. Nate didn't think he could stand to take down any more women. If the demons discovered his weakness for that particular flavor of host, he'd be lost. The reapers who were part of the Authority weren't as sensitive as he was. They didn't care what sex the hosts were. Maybe, if he were very lucky, he'd live long enough to become so jaded.

The demon walked toward him with all the confidence of a demon in a fresh host. He twitched and jerked his new body down the alley toward Nate, not yet realizing he was walking toward certain death. Bo lived for this shit.

Nate gave the dog the attack signal and his skin crawled as he watched Bo take the young host down like a bear on a bunny. The act was complete in a matter of seconds. Bo looked back for reassurance of a job well done and further instructions.

"Good boy. Eat."

Bo ate. He could tear and crunch though a body in minutes. Good thing, too. The alternative was even messier. Imps watched, hovering overhead along the edge of the roof. When the black demon left the ruined host body in a stream of shapeless fog, it flew up and over the building and the imps followed it, disappearing from view. Nate watched and waited. No other souls streamed out. He was grateful for that at least. The demons were soul poachers, and these days they didn't even wait until a person was dead. Nate and the Authority reapers were in an all-out war for the souls of Meridian. If they lost Meridian, they lost the world.

The demon wasn't dead, but the host most assuredly was.

Lucky bastard.

Most of the folks in the bar tonight hadn't been so fortunate.

Nate had called in Samkiel and Raguel, the nearest reaper cleanup crew, to take care of the casualties after stumbling upon the scene. One body or even a couple, he and Bo could dispatch. Dozens were a different story.

When the biggest Hell release portal in decades opened in Meridian last May, several demons were freed to wreak havoc on the population. Just when the local reapers nearly had things under control, Camael, a fallen angel and the former Chief of the Order of Powers, had raised the stakes by opening another portal. The dozens became thousands and the whole situation became five billion times worse when Camael inhabited the body of Nate's newly assigned reaper partner, Maeve.

He hadn't seen her since.

And now? The full power of the Authority had been reactivated, after many years, and a new team of ten reapers had been recruited to put down the demon invasion and protect the realms from further infiltration. Hell on Earth was one thing. Hell in Heaven? Unthinkable.

Nate's long-time friend Deacon Walker was the leader of the Authority. He was sympathetic to Nate's cause, having lost a friend and fellow reaper, Kylen, to demonic possession for more than a century. The problem was that reapers were the perfect hosts for demons and, as it turned out, fallen angels. While demons burned through human hosts in a matter of days, sometimes hours, a reaper could be ridden indefinitely.

Maeve was a reaper.

Nate…was not.

The jury was still out about Nate's particular supernatural persuasion. While he possessed some of the more desirable traits and abilities of the reapers, his powers hadn't manifested enough for him to be fully invested as a reaper. There was no way of knowing if they ever would. The only word that still described him most days was *witch*.

The tattoos along his biceps itched and prickled as he prepared himself to head home. To most people, his markings looked tribal, but they weren't. They were very specific magic sigils. Magical protection. A guy couldn't protect himself from every spell, but it sure seemed like a good idea to try, particularly under the current circumstances.

He grabbed hold of the scruff of the hellhound's neck and felt the familiar pull from the invisible subway reapers used to travel from consecrated ground to consecrated ground—one perk he shared with the reapers. The alley before him shimmered and his vision faltered as he was dragged into the darkness that would bring him home.

***

Six silver-bullet travel trailers circled him end-to-end as he landed in the common area of Ruth Scott's family home. It was all that was left. Only the stone walls and fireplace had remained standing after Camael had burned the place to the ground despite Nate's circle of protection. Construction on the destroyed building wasn't supposed to begin until spring, but work was already under way. They'd salted the earth, reconsecrated the ground and enforced the circle of protection to include each and every member of the Authority as well as the auxiliary members.

Maeve wasn't among them.

Their combined reaper Reiki energy and Nate's spell made the place a fortress against all supernatural beings and the four elements when wielded with magic. Live and learn. Of course, his supernatural protections didn't do shit to keep humans away. That was what shotguns were for.

Deacon had a small arsenal stored in the communal area where they shared meals in the center of the compound. The first reconstruction had begun there—an octagonal domed structure had been erected in spite of the winter weather. They needed a place to regroup and strategize as well as eat and relax—and escape their roommates. There was only so long a guy, or in this case two, could hole up together in a thirty-foot trailer. That was way too much reaper testosterone in way too little space.

The only ones who didn't seem to mind the accommodations were the couples. Deacon and Ruth lived together in one trailer, and Kylen and Olivia shared another. The other reapers lived with their partners.

Nate lived alone.

Though Maeve was officially his partner, he couldn't imagine her agreeing to live with him even if she were here. Upon initiation, each member of the Authority had been partnered with a reaper who complemented their abilities if not their personalities. Maeve had clearly drawn the short straw when she was paired with Nate. Even now, he wondered why they had been partnered at all when they'd immediately been given separated mandates. Nate was to use Bo to track the demons for the Authority and Maeve was to protect the home front. That had been the plan, anyway.

Still, the compound had become his home. He'd given up his apartment months ago. It wouldn't do to have demons, imps or worse things following him back to endanger his neighbors after a night's work.

Before becoming a member of the Authority, he had been an EMT. Now he wasn't sure what he was other than a glorified babysitter when needed. Since Temperance, a guardian angel, had been sent to watch over Ruth and her unborn, he wasn't even needed for that job anymore. After Maeve's abduction, he'd switched from being lead demon tracker to fallen-angel tracker. Now he spent all of his time in the field with his hellhound doing just that—tracking Maeve.

What he thought he was going to do with his limited powers once he found her, he didn't know, but he was driven to find her. Obsessed, even.

Laughter and the smell of bacon wafted from the kitchen. His heart felt like a stone in his chest as he made his way to his trailer, bypassing the breakfast crowd. Bo had other thoughts and loped toward the sounds of food activity. It wasn't Nate's day to cook and he wasn't up for a debriefing. He needed rest, rejuvenation and…retribution.

Sooner would be better than later.

For them both.

Reap & Reveal Coming Soon! Sign up for the New Release Newsletter to be notified:
http://eepurl.com/9Zhcz.